Loving What's Left

D. K. Taylor

FinnLady Press

1

Published by: Janet Scott McDaniel
FinnLady Press

ISBN-10: 1721720839
ISBN-13: 978-1721720835

Library of Congress Control Number:
2018948932

Printed in the United States of America

This book is dedicated to all members
of the United States military,
both active duty and retired,
who give so much to ensure that we remain free.

To Joyce—
Thank you for all the times you read my drafts,
served as my sounding board,
and never wavered in your conviction
that I could finish this book.

Thanks also to Janet McDaniel of FinnLady Press,
for without her knowledge, advice,
and attention to detail,
this book would never have made it to publication.

Loving What's Left

D. K. Taylor

Chapter 1

Hawk rolled out of bed and planted his feet on the floor. He rubbed his hand over his short hair and down over the rough stubble of black beard. Another morning in Iraq. *He'd head for the shower and then get some coffee.* Halfway across the room, his cell phone rang and he changed direction. *Who in the hell would be calling him on his cell? Must be from the States—calls from his outfit, and other local calls, came in over the land phone.* He snatched up the phone and flipped it open.

"Hawkins."

"Hawk, old buddy."

He almost groaned. *Mark Vail was probably his best friend in the world. They'd known each other since both were learning to fly F-16's, but when Mark called him "Old Buddy," it always meant—get ready for a request—usually something he'd prefer not to do.*

"Mark!"

"Long time, no see."

"You still at Hill?"

"Yeah. What's up, Buddy? I hear you get a lot of flying time over there."

"Cut to the chase, Mark. I know you didn't call me in Iraq just to shoot the breeze. What do you want?"

"What do you mean, what do I want? Do I have to

want something?"

"Mark?"

When his buddy didn't answer, he repeated the question. "You still there, Mark?"

"Hawk, do you remember Kit?"

"I remember you <u>have</u> a sister named Kit, and I seem to recall you took great pains to make sure none of us ever met the girl."

"You don't have to be sarcastic . . . and, well, she's not a girl any more, and she's there."

"There where?"

Hawk struggled to remember anything Mark had ever said about his sister. *She'd been in college the last he'd heard. No, not college, West Point. Uh oh, he suddenly had a feeling he knew what was coming.*

"She's there in Iraq. I'm sure I told you she went to the Academy. She's a lieutenant—been in Iraq about six months. Naturally, when I heard you were in Iraq too, I thought—"

"Oh no you don't. Keep me out of this, Mark. I'm not looking up your little sister."

"Aren't you even curious to meet her?"

"I'm more curious to know why you're suddenly so anxious <u>for</u> me to meet her, especially after six years of making sure I didn't get anywhere near her."

"Hawk, I never did that. It just never worked out."

"Right. Well, I'm not interested."

"Come on Hawk. You have to help me out here."

Here it comes, Hawk thought. Mark is finally getting to the point. "Why?"

"Come on Hawk. She's my baby sister, and I <u>need</u> to know if she's all right. She's at Camp Taji, commander of a small transportation outfit there."

He couldn't picture Mark's little sister as CO of a company of soldiers. Not the way Mark had always given the impression that he and his brothers had to look after her, protect her. He scrubbed his hand over his hair and let out a breath. "So?"

"So, I'm worried about her. Every time I talk to her —or get an email from her— she says she's 'fine.'"

"Okay. So how come you're worried?"

"You don't know Kit."

"No, I don't," Hawk said dryly.

"This is serious, Hawk. Kit would say she was fine no matter what. I already checked—Taji and Balad are only about 90 miles apart. You could go and see her."

"No! No way. I'm not showing up and telling this girl her brother sent me to check up on her."

"Hawk, don't be ridiculous! Of course you wouldn't say that, but you're both in Iraq. She's my sister and you're my best friend, and it would be natural if you just dropped in to see her."

Hawk fumed. *This was not going well.* "Mark, I am not going. You know better than anyone, I'm bad news for any woman, let alone your <u>sister</u>. You never wanted me to meet her, and you were right. Don't insist I do this."

"Hawk! I'm not asking you to marry her. Just go and see her, and let me know if she's all right. That's all I'm asking."

"You're not going to give up on this, are you?"

"No, I'm . . . no . . . I can't."

"All right, all right. I'll go and see her, but that's all I'm agreeing to."

"That's all I'm asking. Just call me and let me know how she is."

11

Hawk flipped the cell phone closed and laid it down, shaking his head. He banged his hand on his forehead in frustration. *There was no upside to this. He was truly in the middle. Mark would not let him forget he had agreed to contact Kit, and she would not be happy to have her brother "checking" on her. That was a given.*

Again headed for the shower, he stopped dead. *Mark had always carefully guarded his sister, never letting any of them meet her, never even showing her picture. So why trust him to meet her now? Either he <u>was</u> truly desperate . . . or he knew his friend too well not to be suspicious.*

Kit brushed the film of sand off her desk and flipped the page on her calendar. *Today was an anniversary of sorts—she had been here in Iraq six months today. Only nine more months to go!* She looked around the office where she spent so much of her time. *It was stark in its simplicity—a battered desk, the U.S. and unit flags, the usual chain-of-command photos on the wall, and two beat-up arm chairs against the far wall. A small window behind her desk let in the harsh morning light. Her desk was bare except for a plaque proclaiming she was "1st Lt Vail," and two baskets—one marked "in," and the other "out."*

She smiled at the one personal item on her desk, a framed snapshot of her with her four brothers—Mark, Matt, Luke, and Jon, her twin. *Their names were a legacy from their minister father. It had been ten years since their parents were killed in an automobile accident, but she still missed them. She had been fourteen at the time, the youngest of the five children, by thirty minutes. Mark, nineteen and the oldest, had immediately taken responsibility for all of them. He still felt responsible; it was just who he was.*

God, she missed them. Growing up, she and Jon had been like two halves of one whole. When he'd left home to join the Navy, it had been like losing a part of herself. Now he was a SEAL. She never knew where he was, but she knew whenever he was in danger, could feel it in her heart.

She touched the faces in the picture. *It had been taken the day she graduated from West Point, the fourth one of the siblings to join the military, and their pride in her was evident in their wide grins.*

They might be proud of her, but they still worried about her being in a combat zone, even though all but Matt had been there themselves! Luke was headed to Afghanistan again, after less than a year in the States. Who knew where Jon was; he and his team were always in one danger zone or another.

Mark had been here in Iraq the year before she arrived. Now at Hill Air Force Base in Utah, he was the one who kept most closely in touch with her, calling about once a week, always asking if she was okay. She felt herself grinning. *Her standard answer was, "I'm fine." The last time he called he'd snapped back at her, "You'd say that even if you weren't."*

She was lucky, not too many women got the opportunity to be a company commander in a combat zone. Even though she'd been in the top quadrant of her class at the Academy, and despite the fact that she'd completed jump school, she probably wouldn't have ended up here if it hadn't been wartime, with the whole military, particularly the Army, scrambling to fill slots in Iraq and Afghanistan. *She'd been in the right place at the right time—CO of the Transportation Company in North Carolina when her whole battalion had been deployed here to Camp Taji in December.*

She sighed. *Thinking about her brothers made her homesick.* She punched up her laptop and keyed in her email code. *Maybe there would be a message from one of them. Sure enough, there was one from Mark.* She scanned it, shook her head, and let out a groan. *He was doing it again! "Hi Little Bit. Hawk Hawkins is there in Iraq, not too far from you, in Balad. Look for him to stop by one of these days. Mark."*

"Ugh!" *It wasn't what he <u>said</u> in the email. It was what she could read behind the words. Mark, obviously tired of her answers of "Fine," had decided to find out for himself. Darn his meddling anyway. Still . . . she'd always been curious about the elusive Hawk. This could be a good thing. She had never met the man, which was strange because Mark and Hawk had been friends since flight school. She'd heard plenty of stories about him— his wildness, his outrageous tricks, his courage in the air . . . and the trail he blazed through women—many women, never just one. Mark had talked a lot about Hawk. The reason they'd never met had to be because Mark hadn't wanted them to meet. Interesting.*

So, why was he orchestrating it now? It definitely raised a red flag. Tonight, as soon as she got off work, she'd place a call to that overprotective brother of hers and get some answers!

A *tap sounded on the doorframe of her office; her first sergeant had arrived. She smiled at the man filling the opening with his mammoth size and bulky body. Noncoms were the backbone of the Army, and Sergeant*

Karley definitely made her life easier.

"Mornin' LT. Coffee?"

"Good morning, Sergeant. I can't get it too soon this morning."

"Comin' right up, Ma'am."

She'd come in early, but still she'd beaten him to the office by only a few minutes. Days began early here, and soon the outer office would be bustling with the hubbub of a transportation company headquarters. She took a last look at the photograph and set it back on her desk. Mark hadn't said when Hawk would show up. Was it imminent, or down the road?

She reached for the stack of paperwork in her in-box and was scanning through it when Sergeant Karley returned with a mug of steaming coffee in each hand. He handed one cup to her and set the other on the corner of her desk.

"Thanks, Sarge. Have a seat, and tell me what's hot today?"

"Same-o, same-o. Units screaming for their vehicles, motor pool complaining about parts shortages. Jones put up his 'short-time' calendar today."

She smiled. "Counting off the days until he returns Stateside, hmmm?" *She would miss the red-headed chief clerk with the thick southern drawl.* "Have we heard anything from Personnel about his replacement?"

"Nothing yet. I'll have a memo for you to sign today, just to jog 'em up."

"Good." She took a sip of the strong coffee and glanced out the window. *The sun was already high enough to cause heat shimmers over the motor pool roof. The sun was good though. When she'd arrived in December, it was to a sea of mud. She hadn't expected*

15

the amount of rain they got here. No sooner did it dry out a bit than they'd get more rain. She'd take the stifling heat over gummy mud any day, although 110-degree days and 90-degree nights did take some getting used to.

'Ma'am?"

"Sorry. I was thinking that I prefer the heat to the mud when we first arrived."

"Some choice!" He hesitated a minute.

"What's up?"

"The pool is finished repairing those three Humvees from Balad."

"And we need to get them back to their unit. How soon can you set up a convoy? And who can we spare to drive?

"Well, there's the rub. The Motor Sergeant up there has already been on the horn this morning screaming for the vehicles, and I told him we'd get 'em out tomorrow."

"But?"

"But, we're really hurting. The motor pool can only send two drivers—they can't spare anyone else. Two of their mechanics had to go out yesterday to do on-site repair of two backhoes at Camp Dragoon. I've got to come up with drivers for the lead and following Humvees, plus 'shotgun', and a medic."

"It's getting more and more difficult, isn't it?"

"Yes Ma'am. I've got it set up to leave at dawn tomorrow, but we'll be without a chief clerk."

"Jones?"

"Yes Ma'am. He volunteered to go, and he's qualified to ride shotgun.

She was aware of the recent policy requiring everyone sent to a combat zone, including cooks and clerks, to be weapons qualified. "I know, it's just—"

"He's a short-timer. But it can't be helped. Most of "A" Company is up at Baghdad International Airport supporting a project. Their contact truck operator is up there with them. Corporal Keller, one of our young kids, lost his fingertip this morning. He was replacing the lift cylinder seals in one of the dump trucks and used his finger to check the alignment of the cylinder keepers. The bed shifted—took his finger off at the first knuckle. He seems to be taking it pretty well, but he was still a little groggy from the anesthetic when I saw him."

"I'll stop by and see him this afternoon."

"That would be good Ma'am. I'm afraid we'll have more of that type of thing if we don't keep a check on it. The men have been working six days a week since we got here."

"I'm aware of that, and we may soon have to go to seven. Tell the supervisors to monitor the men closely."

"I will."

"I know. Go with the plan; just keep me posted. When is the earliest you can expect them back?"

"If they push, and there are no unexpected delays, maybe day after tomorrow."

"Okay." *Unexpected delays' meant—if they didn't run into any IED's or insurgents.*

"Keep me informed."

"Will do, LT."

As he left the office, she returned to the paperwork, but Mark's email was still in the back of her mind.

She was already shedding her BDU top before she closed the door of her quarters that afternoon. Flipping it on her rack, she pulled the brown t-shirt free of her pants, and sat down to remove her boots. *Gees, it was 90 degrees in the room, and the A/C was out again.* She flopped on the bed and picked up her cell phone, punching in the number she knew by heart. *With the time difference to the States, Mark would probably just be getting up. Sure enough, when he answered, his voice was rough with sleep.*

"Captain Vail."

"Mark."

"Kit! What's the matter? Has something happened?"

"Not on my part, you rat."

"Uh oh. You got my email?"

"This morning! Mark, when are you all going to realize I've <u>grown up</u> and you can stop legislating and maneuvering my life?"

"Now, Kit. Don't be mad. You know we love you."

"I know that Mark. But you have to stop interfering in my life."

"I don't <u>interfere</u> in your life!"

"Just what do you call sending Hawk Hawkins over here to 'check' on me—and don't bother to deny it, I know that's why he's coming. I don't even know the man. And that's another thing! All this time the two of you have been friends, and I've never even met him. Now, suddenly, out of a clear blue sky, he's coming to visit me."

"My, my, Kit! So suspicious."

"And why do you suppose that is? If I had a nickel for every time you or Matt or Jon or Luke has sprung something on me . . ."

Mark's reply was quiet. "We just wanted to protect you, Kit."

She could hear the growl in her voice, and hoped he could tell that this was the last straw. "That's the point, Mark! I got through West Point. I'm a company commander in the United States Army. I don't want or need your protection any more. I'm my own person, and I need you to recognize that." He didn't immediately say anything, and she wondered if they had lost the connection. "Mark?"

"I'm here, Little Bit. I know you're grown up . . . and I didn't exactly send Hawk to check on you—at least that wasn't the only reason."

"It wasn't?" Her voice reflected her skepticism. "But you did send him, and he doesn't even know me, so what other reason is there?"

"Well . . . I sorta hoped, that is, I wanted you two—"

"Mark! Are you sure this is my big brother? The one who's never hesitated a day in his life, who always knows what's best for all the rest of us? Just what is going on, Mark?"

"Little Bit . . . I'm not sure this time, probably for the first time in my life." He laughed uneasily. "I'm not sure whether to tell you, or not. I wasn't going to, but, I will."

"Tell me what, Mark? I hope you know you're weirding me out."

"Yeah, well. It's just . . . I'm not certain telling you this is the right thing to do. I'm pretty much flying by the seat of my pants here. I hope I'm not doing more damage than good. And, I don't want to betray Hawk."

This had to be one of the strangest conversations she and Mark had ever had. What in the world was he trying to tell her?

The silence stretched out before Mark spoke again. "Hawk thinks I'm sending him to check on you, and I hope you won't tell him any different."

"Now I'm really confused. I don't understand anything you're telling me. You asked Hawk to check on me, but you don't really want him to, but you want me to pretend you do. Why?"

"This is harder to explain than I thought it would be. I can't tell you any more. I just thought it was time the two of you met."

"Um hmm, right! Did you think I was unaware that you went out of your way to make sure that I never met your best friend . . . or any of your Air Force buddies? I used to think you were ashamed of me."

"No, Kit!"

"Mark! What's wrong with you today? You don't sound like yourself at all. I—"

"Kit, first of all, I'm sorry you got the wrong idea. I never—none of us ever—were ashamed of you. Just the opposite. It was the fact that you were . . . are . . . so pretty and so special. We never wanted those guys messing around with you, not until you were old enough to take care of yourself. I guess our mistake was we couldn't see that you had grown up into a lovely woman; one entirely able to make your own decisions and live with them. I guess—"

Mark's words made her feel warm all over. "Thank you, Mark. That's the loveliest thing you've ever said to me. I'm so happy you finally admit I'm grown up—and that you like the way I turned out."

"How could you doubt it, Kit?"

"I guess because I had four brothers who were afraid I might get 'uppity,'" she said dryly.

Mark laughed. *Whew! He seemed to have gotten himself out of that mess okay.*

"However . . ."

Or maybe not. "What, Kit?"

"You still haven't answered my questions."

"Oh, I thought I just did."

"Not hardly, brother. You were saying you thought it was time Hawk and I met. Why? What caused you to change your mind?

"Kit . . . I . . . Hawk is my best friend. He's almost like a fourth brother to me."

"I know that. And?"

"And he's been a loner for a long time. Since . . . well, never mind that. He's been a loner, and he needs someone. I think you could be that someone."

She slammed her hand into her forehead. *Definitely weird. So far out in left field she couldn't even wrap her mind around it.* "Mark, I don't even know Hawk . . . he doesn't know me . . . we don't know each other." *Darn, she was sputtering. She couldn't help it, this was not the Mark Vail she was used to.*

"Well, now you will. You're about to meet each other."

"I'm about to meet him . . . because he needs me . . . because it's time we meet . . . do you realize how <u>dumb</u> this sounds? It makes no sense at all. It's not like you. In fact, it's so not like you that you're scaring me. Has something happened to you? Are you—?"

"Kit, stop it! It's nothing like that. I'm just asking you to get to know my best friend. I want two people who mean a lot to me to know each other."

"Mark—"

"Kit, I'm only asking you to get to know him. It won't be easy; he's a very private person. But I have confidence in you. You may be able to get under his

21

radar screen. In fact, I think you may be just what he needs."

"Me?! Right! The guy who can have any woman he wants—and those are your words, not mine."

Mark mumbled under his breath. "Damn, sometimes I talk too much."

"What?"

"Nothing."

"So, tell me—why is this woman magnet going to be interested in me? Perhaps you better explain it to me."

"Because you're different from his usual women."

"I don't think I want to ask <u>how</u> I'm 'different'."

"Probably better not to. Take care, Kit. I have to go now, or I'll be late for work."

"Wait a minute, Mark! You can't—"

"Gotta go. So long, Kit. I'll be in touch."

He'd hung up! Drat! Now she had more questions than she had before. She scrubbed her hand through her short hair. *Brothers! Who needed 'em? Still, he had admitted she was grown up, and he had said he thought she was pretty. That was something.*

Mark laid down the phone and ran his hand through his short hair. *He was truly shocked. Kit was right—he hadn't thought she knew about his efforts to keep his buddies away from her. But she was totally wrong about his reasons—had it exactly backwards in fact. He knew his buddies too well. Hell, they were just like him, and he couldn't bring himself to let her meet any of them— except Hawk. He'd had a different reason for keeping those two apart. But it had simply never occurred to him*

that Kit would think he was ashamed of her. He and his brothers had idolized her from the day she was born, although perhaps they hadn't always let her know it. That would have to change.

Chapter 2

She sat up the next morning and looked around in confusion. *Sheesh, it was already hot, and the sun was streaming in her window. What time was it? Why hadn't her alarm gone off? She'd stayed awake so long last night, thanks to Mark's crazy phone conversation, it's a wonder she woke up at all without the stupid alarm going off. Now she would have to really rush in order to get to work on time.* Grabbing a clean set of ACU's and her shower basket, she headed to the shower.

Twenty minutes later she was jogging up to the door of her office building. *She wouldn't have made it except that makeup and hairstyles were a total waste of time here on any day, so she never bothered.* She walked in the door and glanced around the room. *Even though she was on time, she was the last one to arrive.*

Nodding good morning to her troops, she went to the coffeepot, poured herself a mug of the lifesaving liquid and headed for her office. *She would not worry any more about Mark's confusing comments. She dove into the ever-present stack of paperwork in her in box, and was so absorbed in what she was reading, she almost didn't hear the tap on her door. When she finally looked up, one of her men was standing in the doorway.* "Corporal Bronson?"

"Ma'am, there's someone here to see you."

He didn't continue, and she couldn't see around him. "Well, who is it, Bronson?"

"Uh, Ma'am, he said he wanted to surprise you; didn't give his name."

Kit felt her shoulders slump, and a groan escaped her mouth.

"What do you want me to do Ma'am? Shall I get rid of him?"

She laughed. "No, no. I appreciate the offer, but this one I'd better see. Give me two minutes and then send him in."

"You got it, Ma'am."

It had to be Mark's friend. She had to laugh, despite her frustration. It was so typical of Mark—wait until it's a fait accompli before notifying her—when it was too late for her to do anything about it. Bad enough when she thought Mark was checking on her. Now, after their weird phone conversation, she didn't know how to react.

Waiting in the outer office, Hawk heard her laugh and smiled. Curiosity flowed through him. *He would finally meet Mark's sister. Who was this Kathryn Vail with the delightful laugh who stirred such protective attitudes in her brothers? The clerk returned, grinning, and Hawk realized her men liked and respected her.*

He entered her office a few minutes later, surprised to be facing her back. She was staring out the window behind her desk. He *took the opportunity to observe her. She was smaller than he'd expected, given Mark's 6' 4" height. She would barely come to his shoulders. No*

25

wonder her brothers called her "Little Bit." Despite the loose and shapeless ACU's she wore, he could see that she was perfectly formed. Her silvery blonde hair was a mop of tousled curls.

She didn't turn around immediately. Intrigued, he continued to study her. When she abruptly turned to face him, he was startled. *Not only was she not what he'd expected, she was adorable. Her eyes—the bright, clear blue of an October sky—immediately caught his and held them. Her tentative smile revealed a single dimple winking in one cheek.*

"Good morning," she said. "Captain Joshua Hawkins, I believe?"

"Call me Hawk." He was surprised. *She'd been expecting him. Somehow, he'd gotten the impression that Mark wasn't going to forewarn her that he was coming.*

Kit took a deep breath before speaking. *Wouldn't you know he'd be handsome as sin? No wonder he had women falling at his feet. Darn! And thanks to her beloved brother, she didn't know how to proceed here. Oh well, probably best to pretend that all she knew was what had been in Mark's email, and that they'd never spoken.* "I'm sorry you got stuck with checking on Mark's little sister." She hesitated, then made her decision. *She'd just go with what he* thought *Mark had asked him to do—and forget the weird part.*

Before he could reply, she continued. "I don't suppose you could very well refuse, being his friend and all."

She'd surprised him again. Why would she think he'd consider looking her up to be a chore? He felt a twinge of guilt that she'd come so close to the mark. What had her brothers done to her?

Kit rubbed her small hand over her face. "I want to

26

say, I can't believe Mark would do this to me, but I can. I really can. He never gives up."

"Why do you think that Mark sent me to check up on you?"

"Didn't he?"

How should he answer? It didn't seem to occur to her that anyone would find it a pleasure to meet her, although she was one of the loveliest women he had ever seen.

"Well . . .?" she prodded.

When he still didn't answer, she continued. "You don't have to lie. I know my brothers, especially Mark." She tossed her head, causing the riot of curls to become more jumbled as she studied him thoughtfully. "So, you're the infamous Hawk Hawkins I've heard so much about?"

"'Fraid so." *His gut tightened, and he wondered what she had heard about him. It had been a long time since he cared what people thought, but he realized he did care what this woman thought.*

"What did Mark tell you about me?"

It obviously pained her to ask the question, and he withheld the grin that was fighting to appear on his face. "Quite a lot—after he found out I was in Iraq."

"I just bet he did. He told me you were good friends. If you're such good friends, how come we've never met?"

A glint of humor showed in his black eyes. "I have a pretty good idea why."

"And why's that?" she said, obviously puzzled.

"Why do you think?"

"I haven't a clue. I used to embarrass my brothers pretty regularly when we were growing up; still can, if you want the truth. Maybe he was afraid of what I could

27

tell you."

A flush of color flooded her face at the last, and Hawk was amazed. A woman who could still blush! Unbelievable. "I don't think that's it," he said, grinning. "Mark knew if he told us anything about you, we'd all be demanding an introduction. No way was he letting any of his buddies close to his kid sister, at least that'd be my take on it." *Kit tilted her head as if puzzled, and he saw frustration in her blue eyes. Then she threw her head back and the words erupted from her mouth.*

"I'm twenty-four years old, a lieutenant in the United States Army, and he <u>still</u> thinks he has to protect me!"

Hawk laughed. "He loves you, very much, as I suspect you know very well."

"I do know. I love him too. But if you'd grown up with four brothers and had to fight for every scrap of independence . . . I finally thought I'd made it. Guess not."

She sighed, and Hawk felt an unaccustomed urge to protect this woman he didn't even know. He was beginning to see why her brothers felt that way. "Kit, he knows you're all grown up, and he's so proud of you and what you've accomplished."

"Did he say that?"

"He did." *He probably better keep quiet about the rest of what Mark had said.*

"So, if you're not here to spy on me, how come you're here? You're a jet jockey like Mark?"

"I'm an F-16 pilot!"

"I stand corrected." She grinned. *He really was incredibly good looking, with his dark eyes, raven black hair clipped militarily short—and his flight suit, despite its loose fit, still revealed his lean muscular frame.*

28

Darn, and double darn. "And you're here because . . .?"

He laughed. "You were pretty much right. Mark was faced with a hard choice when he found out I was in Iraq. He could ask me to look you up and get first-hand info on how you're really doing—"

"I knew that last 'Fine' was too much. Darn." *His grin told her he knew about her consistent answers to Mark's questions, and she blushed again.*

"As I said, he could forget his misgivings and ask me to look you up, or he could stick with his refusal to let me anywhere near you and pass up the only opportunity he was likely to have to check up on you."

"So, his curiosity won?"

"Not curiosity," he said softly. "Love. But I have to tell you, his request was accompanied by an admonition, couched in a promise that, knowing Mark, he'll carry out."

"What promise?"

He laughed again, his dark eyes sparkling with mischief, and she realized he wasn't the least bit intimidated by her big brother.

"Well, what promise?"

He waited a few seconds, anticipating her reaction. "That if I hurt his baby sister in any way at all, my ass was grass and he'd be the lawn mower."

Kit groaned. "Brothers! Now you know what I meant before."

No wonder Mark kept her a secret. Kathryn "Kit" Vail was adorable, and spelled danger with a capital D. To him anyway. He shook his head. *What was he thinking? This was Mark's sister, damn it. He was here to check on her welfare, not jump her bones.* He noticed the paratrooper wings on her BDU top. "You went through jump school?"

She shrugged. "I didn't ever want to have to tell my men to do something I hadn't done, or couldn't do."

Kit Vail was something else. He shook his head.

Kit noticed, and asked, "Is something wrong?"

"No, why?"

"You keep shaking your head. I thought maybe something had bitten you."

"No."

"Did you just get in?"

"A couple of hours ago. I checked into the Visiting Officers' Quarters and took a shower. It was too early to look you up."

"How did you get here?"

The regular helo run between here and Balad. I know the pilot, and I hitched a ride. They normally go back the same day, but he's going to RON this trip."

RON—that meant they'd be here overnight. The phone on her desk buzzed, and she picked it up. "All right, Sarge. Tell him I'll be right with him. Give me five minutes." She replaced the receiver, and looked at Hawk apologetically. "My appointment is here. Could we meet somewhere later? Maybe lunch? "

"Sure, but can we make it dinner? I've got a few things to do today."

She gave him a knowing look. "Like reporting to Mark."

He grinned. "No report, yet. I need to do more research."

Giving him a disgusted look, she replied, "'I don't believe you said that."

He laughed. "Fine. I'll see you at 1800. Where shall we meet?"

"Kit bit her lip as she thought. *It was difficult to come up with a place that would be private enough to talk. The Army no longer permitted alcohol in any combat areas, hence no clubs, either. She quickly ran the options over in her mind—bowling alley, dining hall, Popeye's. Then she had an idea.* "How about I pick you up at your quarters, since I've got the vehicle? Then we can go by Popeye's and get dinner to go and find somewhere to eat, even if it's sitting in the Hum-vee?"

"Why don't you just meet me there? I'm supposed to meet a guy there concerning something else, and I'll just wait for you."

"Sure, I'll meet you there."

"I'll see you at Popeye's at 1800."

He turned and left her office, passing a young sergeant on the way in. *Her appointment*, he supposed.

As he left the building, he stopped to pull his cap out of his flight suit pocket and adjust it on his head. Still thinking about Kit, he headed for his room in the Visiting Officers' Quarters, grinning as he remembered Kit's look when he mentioned "research." *She was definitely an interesting woman. This job had possibilities.*

Speaking of which, he'd better call Mark and let him know he'd looked her up. He'd always thought Mark was too protective of his little sister, like a mother hen with a chick. Now that he had met Kit, he understood. It wasn't that she wasn't capable of taking care of herself—she very evidently was—it was more that she inspired feelings of protectiveness, caring, love . . . Whoa! He stopped so abruptly, the sergeant behind him narrowly avoided plowing into him. He muttered an apology as the sergeant veered around him. Utterly shocked at his

31

thoughts, he let out a whistle.

He'd better get himself in control before he made that call to Mark, or his buddy would be all over him.

★ ★ ★

Back in his room, Hawk used his cell phone to place the call. Mark answered on the first ring, and Hawk tried to make it sound as if this was just a routine call. "Hey, buddy! "

"It's about time I heard from you."

"It's only been two weeks! Kit's been here six months. What's the rush?"

Mark ignored the question. "You've seen Kit?"

"Yes."

"And?"

Hawk hesitated. "And, she's fine."

Mark sputtered at the word. "That's it! She's 'fine.' Dammit to hell, Hawk. I didn't send you there to learn she's fine. I already knew she's fine; that's what she's been telling me since she got there."

"Well, now you know she's been telling you the truth. She's okay. And just to set the record straight—you didn't <u>send</u> me anywhere! As I recall, you <u>asked</u> me, <u>begged</u> me as a matter of fact, to go and see your sister."

"Okay, right. Whatever. Now, tell me how it went."

"How what went?"

"Hawk! Your meeting of course. When did you see her? What did she say? Was she mad?"

 Hawk rolled his eyes. *This was going well.* "Mark, I don't know what you want me to say. You asked me to go and see her. I did. You asked me to let you know how she was doing, and I have."

There was silence on the line, and then Mark groaned.

"You're falling for her!"

"I don't _fall_ for women. No women."

"Just what I thought. I knew you two would be like a match in a haystack. That's why I took such care you never met, why I never talked much about Kit to you . . . or about you to her."

"You're nuts."

"Right, Hawk! If you hurt my baby sister—"

"Kit is nobody's _baby_! She's a fully grown, beautiful woman, entirely capable of making her own decisions."

"Hellfire! It's worse than I thought. And I suppose she wants you too?"

"I don't know what she wants, and what do you mean, _too_?"

"Now you listen to me, _Buddy_. You run through women like a plow through snow. So help me, if you do _anything_ to hurt Kit, so help me—"

"Now just hold up a minute, Mark. In the first place, I don't plan to hurt Kit. I _know_ she's your sister. And in the second place . . . in the second place—"

"In the second place, what? How serious is this? How many times have you seen her?"

"That's it, Mark. I just met your sister today. I've called and 'reported' that she's all right. That's all I agreed to do. We're done here. Talk to you later."

"Hawk, don't hang up. Maybe I was a little—"

"A _little_? Bye, Mark."

After Hawk hung up, Mark slowly replaced the cell phone in his pocket, an ornery grin on his face. _The man is hooked. He may not know it yet, but he's caught in the net._

33

Chapter 3

Kit managed to leave her office a few minutes early that afternoon. She raced back to her quarters, grabbed fresh underclothes and headed for the shower, after which she donned a clean uniform. *Unable to "dress up" for her meeting with Hawk, she at least wanted to be fresh. It wasn't all that far, but in the heat and humidity of Iraq, one didn't have to go far to be a steamy mess. Thankful she had access to a vehicle, she climbed in and headed for Popeye's where she had promised to pick up Hawk. She had to smile at the idea of having dinner at a fast food restaurant here in Iraq, one of the newer innovations for the soldiers' comfort.*

She knew she was being ridiculous by worrying about her appearance. Given Hawk's reputation with women, there wasn't a chance he would see her as anything but a duty. She was neither glamorous nor sophisticated. She didn't know how to flirt, even if she wanted to. And whatever she said to Hawk would get back to her brother. After all, that was the reason he was here—at least the reason he thought he was here. What in Heaven's name had Mark meant by the statement, "He needs you."? And what was he up to? There has to be more to it than he told me. But what? The only thing to do is pretend he is here to check on me, and see what happens. So, why am I letting him affect me this way? At least he doesn't know how I'm feeling; that would be just too humiliating. There was a problem though—she had never been good at hiding the way she felt about anything. Not from her parents when she was growing up, and not from her brothers, especially Mark. She gave herself a mental shake. *It is odd that he had told Hawk to check on me and told me Hawk "needed" me. Mark was turning into a real Machiavelli. Wouldn't it be "interesting" if she and Hawk compared notes?* A shiver of apprehension skittered through her. *Mark seemed to be playing both ends against the middle . . . but why would he do that? She needed to remember he was the reason Hawk was here and keep that fact firmly in mind. Even so, she was looking forward to the evening ahead.*

Popeye's appeared in front of her, and she pulled up beside the building. She climbed out of the vehicle, took one last look at her less than glamorous ACU's, and shrugged. Inside, she was met by a blast of cold air. *Thank goodness the air conditioning was working; it usually wasn't, but what a luxury when it was.* She squinted in the bright lights, trying to locate Hawk. *There he was, in conversation with another Air Force Captain and an Army Lieutenant.* As he stepped away from the support post he had been leaning against, she grinned. *One thing you had to say about flight suits: they certainly showed off a handsome pair of buns—and Hawk had the handsomest pair she'd ever seen. She pushed that thought out of her mind just as he looked up and saw her.* Smiling, he said something to the other two men and started walking toward her.

Her stomach pitched nervously as she watched him striding confidently toward her. *Why did this man have such an effect on her? It wasn't like her; she'd never felt this way in her life.*

Hawk stopped in front of her. "You look lovely."

She looked down at the camouflage uniform she was wearing. "Right! Nobody looks great in these things."

He reached out and grasped her upper arm, and she felt a shock through her whole body. "Come on, I've got a table—if someone hasn't grabbed it already."

She glanced around; the place was packed, and there were no empty tables. She looked at Hawk questioningly. *She'd thought they were just going to order their food and take it with them, but Hawk headed straight for a table where a young Air Force Lieutenant sat eating a hamburger and watching them with interest. He was wearing a flight suit like Hawk, and his dark hair tried to curl despite being closely cropped.*

"Thanks for saving the table, Joe. I owe you," he said to the Lieutenant who had stood up at their approach.

"De nada. Any time Hawk. Do I get an intro to the lovely lady for my trouble?"

Hawk frowned, but complied. "Kit, this is Joe Sanchez, otherwise known as Romeo. Joe, Kit Vail."

A wide grin lit Joe's face. "Hi Kit. How have I missed seeing you before? You just arrive?"

Before she could reply, Hawk waved his hand dismissively and said "'Bye, Joe. See you later."

"Right, I was just leaving," Joe said dryly. "I hope I see you later," he grinned at Kit.

"Goodbye, Joe," Hawk said pointedly.

"I'm going, I'm going, Captain."

Once he was gone, Kit asked, "Is Joe at Balad with you?"

"Yeah, he's the helo pilot I came up with. So, how

36

was your day?" he asked, an obvious attempt to turn the conversation away from the departed lieutenant.

"It was okay, busy as usual. We had a request for a mechanic from LSA Anaconda downrange, and a demand for parts to repair another vehicle. I had to discipline a troop for getting into a fight, and met with headquarters re next week's inspection. Just an ordinary day in the life of a Transportation Unit at Taji. How was your day? Did you get your 'business' taken care of?"

"Sort of." *He didn't want to discuss his phone call with Mark. Even though he'd given Kit the impression that he wasn't going to report to Mark—and he hadn't, exactly—he did call him and tell him that he'd met her. He was afraid Mark had seen through his careful phrasing and knew that he liked Kit more than Mark might wish he did. He wouldn't be all that worried. They had been friends for a long time. Mark knew him well enough to realize that he wouldn't intentionally hurt his sister, but he probably thought she was vulnerable—and she might be. The real problem was—he was afraid he might be, too.*

"Hawk? Is something wrong?"

At her soft query, he realized he'd been staring off into space. "No. Just thinking." He stood up suddenly. "I think your idea of taking our food and going somewhere was a good one. You can't hear yourself think in here, let alone have any meaningful conversation."

A shiver went through her. *Meaningful conversation. What did that mean?*

"What would you like? I'll get our orders, and then we can leave. You mentioned you had a vehicle?"

"I have the company Humvee. I'll just have a burger with all the trimmings, except onions, and a large Coke

37

. . . and an order of fries."

He looked at her as if astounded.

"What?" Kit demanded.

"I'm used to women ordering salads; they all seem to be afraid they're going to gain weight."

He was grinning, but she still blushed, remembering how her brothers had always teased her about how much she ate. "I'm a runner—we need to keep our caloric intake up. I never have to worry about gaining weight."

Another surprise. This woman was full of them. He smiled at her. "One large burger and fries coming right up."

As he headed for the busy counter, Kit watched him, puzzled by the way this man affected her. She'd just met the man, and yet . . . and yet . . . she had a weird feeling that her life had changed forever. Mark's comments came back to her, and she frowned, trying to puzzle them out.

She was still deep in thought when Hawk returned, a bag and two drinks in his hands. "You ready?"

She nodded and stood up, glad to be able to put her confused thoughts on hold.

Only minutes later, she pulled into a parking area close to the motor pool where she worked. *She'd selected the area because no one would question her being here, and it had a lovely view of the nearby desert, over which the evening sun was now setting in a fiery ball. It was still very hot, but the temperature would dip with the sun.*

"Wow, what a view!" Hawk leaned back in his seat and watched her without saying anything more.

Kit accepted his perusal for a few minutes, then said, "What? Is my lipstick smeared? Why are you looking at me like that?"

"I was just wondering why you decided to join the U.S. Army. With your looks, you could have done any number of things. Why the military?"

His raised eyebrow told her he expected her to react to the remark, but her hackles went up anyway. "Don't tell me you're sexist?"

"No, I'd really like to know. The Army is a tough life. Why did you choose it?"

Kit studied him skeptically. *He seemed serious, but . . .* She gently bit her bottom lip as she considered the question.

While he waited for her answer, Hawk opened the bag of burgers and began pulling out food and napkins, dividing the items between them. Kit took the proffered burger, spread the napkin in her lap, and popped a fry in her mouth before answering.

"I guess I really never thought of doing anything else. Three of my brothers are in the military."

Hawk leaned forward to set his drink on the dash. "I wondered about that. Why would four children of a Baptist minister all join the armed forces?"

Kit reached over and took the remaining Coke. When she looked at him and motioned to the drink, he realized she was asking for the straw. He opened the bag in his lap and extracted two straws, handing one to her. She took the straw and inserted it in the top of the Coke. Her fingers played idly with the straw and he realized she was hesitant about answering his question.

"Kit?"

She looked up, a grin splitting her face, and he thought, *'what a charmer she is'.*

"Actually, you're asking the wrong question. My

father was the aberration. I come from a long line of military men, going all the way back to the Civil War. Up until my father, the eldest son always joined the military service, usually the Army. My grandfather—my dad's father—was a Major General in the Army. He almost had apoplexy, according to my dad, when Dad told him he was planning to attend seminary."

"What happened?"

"My dad did go to seminary, and my Uncle Bill joined the Army. He recently retired as a BG.

"Was Mark the first son to abandon the Army for another service?"

"Yep, but Granddad was sort of expecting it. Mark never wanted to do anything except fly, which he could have done in the Army. But he wanted to be a fighter pilot."

"What about the rest of your brothers?"

"After Mark broke the mold, I guess Granddad decided to just be happy if we joined any service. Matt chose to follow our dad's footsteps and is now a Baptist Youth Minister in Alabama. Luke joined the U.S. Marines, and flies Cobras. He's presently stationed at Camp Pendleton in California."

"And Jon?"

"Jon and I are twins, and he was usually my partner in crime growing up."

She smiled, and Hawk wondered what she was remembering.

"Jon was always the renegade. He refused to go to college; said he wanted to do things, not tell other people what to do. He went down to the Navy Recruiting Office on the day he graduated from high school and told them he wanted to be a SEAL."

"From what I hear, you don't just tell them you want to be a SEAL."

"No, you don't, but Jon was determined . . . and tough. He made it through Bud/S. I never doubted he would."

"Sounds like the two of you are a lot alike. You must have missed him."

"I still do, and we are a lot alike. I was just as much a renegade as Jon; I just managed to keep it hidden better than he did. I hated it when he left like that . . . and I was so lost."

"You never tried to change his mind?"

"No! Of course not! I knew it was what he always wanted. I just . . . didn't think he'd leave so suddenly."

"What happened?"

"It's not important. When Jon makes up his mind, nobody, but nobody changes it. He loves his job, but we never know where he is, and . . ."

She stopped talking; focusing inward on something only she could see. Hawk knew she was thinking of her brother and wondering where he was, and he knew there was more to the story than what she was telling him.

"You worry about him?"

"I wouldn't say worry. I know he's doing exactly what he wants to do, I just . . . Sometimes I wonder where he is and what he's doing. I can always feel when he's in danger. I guess it's the 'twin' thing."

"So, back to my original question. Did you feel obligated to join the military, or did you want to?

"I never felt obligated to. I don't think they really thought I would. I was a runner in high school. Pretty good, actually." She looked at him through her eyelashes; pink tinged her cheeks.

Curious, Hawk prompted her to go on, "And . . ."

41

"In my senior year, I got a call from the track coach at West Point asking me if I would be interested in attending there. I was dumbfounded, but the more I thought about it, the more I liked the idea. Grandfather knew the U.S. Senator, and he appointed me. Luckily, my grades were good enough. I easily passed the physical, and here I am. And this is enough talk about me. Let's talk about you."

Now it was Hawk's turn to delay. He popped the top on his can of Coke and took a long drink.

She waited a few minutes, then said, "Where's the ketchup?"

He laughed. "Don't tell me you're one of those?"

Her grimace of pretended shock made him laugh, as she answered. "You don't put ketchup on your fries?" Kit waited for him to assemble his own food and take the first bite of his burger before she picked up her previous conversational thread. "So, tell me about you. Where are you from, family, etc.? I know you were in flight school with Mark, and that's where you met."

He frowned, realizing she wasn't going to let him off the hook until he told her what she wanted to know. "Not much to tell. I don't have any family any more. I was an only child. My parents were divorced when I was too small to remember. My mother died when I was five, and my aunt, her sister, raised me in Boston. She died three years ago."

"And your father?"

"I don't know, never knew anything about him."

He had no family. She couldn't imagine it. "But weren't you ever curious? Didn't you ever to try to find out who he was or what happened to him?

"No."

Although she didn't understand, Kit could see it was not a subject Hawk wanted to discuss. But, no family?! She couldn't imagine life without her brothers. "But . . . but, how sad. What do you do on holidays?" *Appalled that she had spoken the question, she didn't know what to say.* "I'm sorry. I didn't mean . . . I shouldn't have said that."

"It's all right. I'm used to it. Actually, holidays were never that big in my life. There were just the two of us, and my aunt never made a big deal of the holidays."

"No wonder you're a loner," she said softly. *Then cursed herself for another goof. What was wrong with her? She couldn't seem to say anything right.*

Hawk frowned. "Why do you think I'm a loner?"

Kit winced. *Now she'd done it.* "Uh, I must have heard Mark say it sometime or other."

Hawk grinned. "Do you always say the first thing that pops into your head?"

Kit smiled ruefully. "Pretty much, I guess. I told you I used to embarrass my brothers all the time. I never seemed to know when to keep my mouth shut. I'm better than I used to be . . . but, obviously, I'm not cured. Please forgive me."

Hawk shook his head. "It's fine. Actually, I'm surprised that I told you about my family. I don't usually discuss it."

"Why is that?"

"No information—no explanations."

He spoke abruptly, and Kit realized the subject was closed. Searching for a safer topic, she took a deep breath. "So, did you always want to fly?"

"No. And I don't come from a long line of military men. The idea never entered my head until I had a buddy in college that thought it would be a lark to join the ROTC. I didn't care one way or the other, so I let him talk me into it. Surprisingly, I liked it. He said he was going to join the Air Force after we got out of college, but I had no plans to do that. Actually, I had no plans at all. Then a couple of members of the Thunderbirds came to the school one day as part of an Air Force recruiting drive. I had a chance to talk with them, and realized flying was something I could really get excited about. I signed up on graduation, passed the physical and the eye test for pilot school, and found out I was a natural at flying. I was at the top of my class and opted for F-16s, and I got it."

"Have you ever been sorry?"

"No. I love it. When you're up there, high above the earth with nothing but sky and clouds, it's like nothing else. I can't describe it."

"Have you ever been shot at?"

Hawk nodded. "I fly a war plane, Kit."

"I know, that was a really stupid question," she said, cringing inside at her inability to carry on a sensible conversation. *There was just something about this man that kept her on edge, rattled her brain until she didn't even know what she was saying.*

Hawk's thoughts were just as confused. *Why in God's name did I give her my whole life's history? I never do that—and I just met her. There's something different about her, something . . . special.* Desperate to change the direction of his thoughts, he blurted out the first words that came into his mind. "If you're finished, let's get out of here."

Kit pulled her attention back, disoriented and not sure what Hawk had said. "What? I . . . what did you say?"

She was confused, and no wonder. What in hell was wrong with him? Trying to mend his fences, he smiled at her and softened the gruff tone of his voice. "Where were you? Far from here, I think. I asked if you were finished and suggested that we leave."

"It didn't sound like a suggestion."

"I'm sorry. It came out wrong. Finish your sandwich."

Kit looked at her remaining fries and partially eaten burger, then up at him, and he knew she was puzzled at his sudden change of attitude.

"Actually, I'm not all that hungry." She began to gather up the remaining food. "We can leave now. Where did you want to go?"

He was stymied. Now what? He searched his mind for somewhere—then inspiration hit. "Would you like to go to the movies?" *He couldn't make any more conversational blunders in a dark movie theater.*

"Could we go for a walk instead?"

"A walk! You want to take a walk?" *He groaned inwardly. A walk would be even worse than the current situation.*

"I like walking," she said. "I thought that way we could talk and get to know each other better."

Just what I'm trying to avoid, he thought.

An impish grin lit her face. "After all, you still have to report to Mark. Have you found out enough for your 'report'?"

He laughed. *He might as well give up.* "No, now that you mention it, I haven't. Let's walk. Where do you suggest we do this walking?"

"Well, I like to walk on the track. I try to run once a day, but when I need to think, I go there and just walk laps around it. It's pretty safe, and at this time of night there won't be many people there."

"When do you find time to run?"

"Before work, mostly. I usually get up at 0500 and run for 45 minutes and then take a quick shower and head to the office."

They walked in silence, each concentrating on his own thoughts, as life on the post swirled around them. With 15,000 troops living and working here, it never truly quieted down. Vehicles moved slowly up and down the streets complying with the 10mph speed limit. Men and women went about their duties. The post was so big, with a huge PX, a Subway, Burger King, Pizza Hut and theater—sometimes it was hard to remember they were in a war zone—but there was always the danger of a random mortar coming in, even here. A study in contrasts, she thought.

"I thought you wanted to talk?"

Hawk's comment was laced with amusement, and she turned to face him.

"Do you ever find it hard to believe we're in the middle of a war, Hawk?"

"You mean because it's so . . . civilized?" he answered, sweeping his hand around to take in the buildings and traffic and people surrounding them.

"I guess that's sort of what I mean. I'm not sure. I know it's out there, the war I mean, even though we're not exactly on the front lines. I know when I send a convoy out, there's always the possibility that they won't come back, or not all of them at least . . . and I never forget that. It just—"

"Seems so surreal sometimes, yeah. I know what you

mean. It's even more pronounced at Balad. That's the largest base in country, and they have everything from movie theaters to a miniature golf course. Some of the people there serve their whole tour without ever seeing a real Iraqi—but then I take off in my F-16, and by the time I put my gear up I'm in a combat zone. I can be bombing targets within a couple of miles of the runway."

He understood. He really did, she thought.

"Like a parallel universe."

"Exactly."

"Hawk, do you think war was always like this—two separate realities that . . ." She frowned in concentration, trying to explain what she meant.

"Well, since this is my first war . . ."

Looking up, she saw a slight smile on his face, and felt immediate disappointment.

"Now you're laughing at me. I just meant . . ."

Hawk reached out and touched her face, his expression serious. "I wasn't, Kit. I know where you're coming from, and I think it is different—certainly from the trenches of World War II or the jungles of Vietnam. But every war has its unique characteristics, and its sameness."

Kit looked up. *Her eyes were sad, and he wanted to change things for her, even knowing he couldn't.* "Why are we discussing such a heavy topic? I thought we came out here so I could get to know you better."

"Uh uh, not me, us."

He raised an eyebrow, and she could hear laughter in his voice as he spoke. "But I'm the one doing research for a report."

"Oh, right." *She'd forgotten Mark! How could she*

have been so dumb? Of course, that's why he was here. She wouldn't forget again.

She bit her lip, then smiled. "I guess I forgot the reason you're here. I know you only came as a favor to my brother . . . but, I . . . I feel that I can tell you things I wouldn't discuss with anyone else. I'm sorry."

Hawk was pleased by her revelation. "Don't be sorry, Kit. I'm honored that you feel that way. And if it helps, you're the first one I've ever told about my family, or lack of one."

Now why had he said that? Damn, he was in trouble here. When she looked at him like that, like he was something special—when he knew he wasn't, was far from it in fact—but for her, he wanted to be, and that was a problem.

They were approaching a small soccer field. The field was empty, but glaringly lit for security reasons. Taking Kit's arm, Hawk gently steered her toward some small bleachers. "Let's sit for a while."

By this time, the sun had almost completely set, and the sky was dark. It felt as if they were enclosed in an intimate room as the surroundings blended into the dusk and disappeared from view, giving the feeling of being alone and private.

Privacy was rare since she had arrived in Iraq, and Kit felt almost uneasy. She looked around the area, trying to see into the dark shadows.

"What's wrong?" Hawk asked. "You seem nervous."

"No—it just feels so private and . . . alone."

"Unbelievable! When's the last time you could say that?"

"Probably not since I got here. It seems . . . odd."

"Feels great to me," Hawk said, as he sat down beside

her on the bottom row of the stands and looked out over the empty field.

"This is probably the only place here where you could be alone and reasonably safe—totally surrounded as it is by lighted buildings, tents, etc."

"I'm surprised we're the only ones taking advantage of it. Do you suppose nobody else has discovered it yet?"

"Maybe not." Kit propped her elbows on the row of seats behind her and leaned back against the seat, looking over at Hawk. "How long are you here for?"

"Our deployments are six months. You?"

"Army tours are fifteen months. I've been here six months—today in fact."

"Do you mind it?"

"No, not so much. Sometimes I get homesick." Kit looked at him through her lashes, trying to see how he took her admission. When he just nodded, she continued. "Actually, I feel pretty lucky."

"Lucky?! Why?"

"Well, I know that in the normal course of things, I probably would never have had the opportunity to be commander of a company in a combat zone. It just happened that when my outfit came up for rotation, they needed a CO for the transportation unit and that was my field. With the shortages of personnel all across the Army now, I got the job."

"How do you like it?"

"It's a challenge, that's for sure, but I like it. The troops in my company are great, and there is something different every day."

"No problems with the guys accepting a woman CO?"

"Not really. Growing up as I did, with four brothers, I know how guys are and I'm pretty careful about ruffling feathers, but mostly it's good. It's just . . . sometimes it's lonely."

"The loneliness of command, hmm?"

"Well, there are only a couple of women in the unit, and they're enlisted."

"And the Army says no fraternization."

"Right."

"Are you sorry you chose this career?"

Kit's head snapped up, and blue eyes flashed at him. "No! Definitely not. I wouldn't change with anyone."

Hawk was surprised. There was steel under that fragile looking exterior.

"How come I'm always the one doing all the talking? What about your job?"

He shrugged. "There's not much to say. For a fighter pilot, getting into combat is the dream. I couldn't have chosen a better place to be or a better time to be there."

The edge of the seat was digging into Kit's back, and she leaned forward to ease it.

Hawk turned until he was straddling the seat. He grabbed Kit's arms, twisted her around, and pulled her between his legs until her back rested against his chest, his arms clasped in front of her body.

Surprised, Kit stiffened.

Hawk's lips brushed her ear as he whispered, "Shhh, relax. Isn't that more comfortable?"

It definitely was. Kit didn't know when she had felt so safe, or so secure. The problem was . . . what was the problem?

"Kit?"

"Um . . . I . . . Yes."

"Yes, what?"

She could tell he was smiling. "Yes, it is more

comfortable. And stop teasing me. I told you, I'm not—"

"Not what?"

She hadn't meant to say that, but there was no way to avoid the truth now. At least, he couldn't see her face. "Not very experienced in this kind of thing." She spoke so softly that Hawk could barely hear her.

He smiled, knowing she couldn't see his face. His voice was soft when he spoke. "Kit, don't be sorry. You're not like anyone else I've ever met." *And that's going to be the problem he thought. She was already getting through his defenses.*

Kit heard Mark's words ringing in her ears loud and clear—"because you're not like those other women." She sat up so abruptly she almost fell off the seat in the process, banging her head against Hawk's chin.

"What the hell was that about, Kit?" Hawk grumbled as he quickly grabbed her, saving her from landing on the hard concrete. As he set her back on the bench, he ruefully rubbed his chin.

"I'm sorry," she said, softly touching the red mark where her head had hit his chin.

"Why'd you jump like that?"

Unwilling to let Hawk know the real reason, she blurted out the first thought that came to her. "When's the last time you talked to Mark?"

He was totally blindsided by the unexpected question. "This morning—why?"

"No reason. I, uh, thought you didn't have enough information to <u>report</u> to him?"

"I didn't <u>report</u> to him. I just told him I was here."

"You mean he didn't ask how I was?"

"Yeah, he did." *Hawk grimaced as he remembered*

51

the conversation.

"What else did you tell him?"

Hawk's grin was full of mischief. "I told him you were 'fine.'"

Kit giggled. "I'm sure he loved that."

Another grin flashed across his face and Hawk nodded.

"You're not going to tell me what else you talked about, are you?"

She had him there; he definitely didn't want her to know what he and Mark had discussed. She already knew more than he wanted her to know. Since his brief and traumatic marriage to Carol he'd sworn no woman would ever get a piece of him again. And they hadn't. He'd made sure of it. And it wasn't going to happen now. "Nope."

Resolutely, he stood, almost dumping Kit on the ground in his haste. He grabbed her arm to steady her, angry at himself. "Come on, Kit, we need to be getting back."

Kit's mouth opened, but no words came. She stood there looking at him.

She was biting her lip, a trait he was coming to realize meant she was unsure of herself. He knew he had confused her.

When she finally spoke, her words were hesitant. "Okay, Hawk. I didn't realize . . . you must have an early flight."

Jumping on the excuse, he nodded quickly. "Yeah, I do. I should have mentioned it before. Come on, let's get out of here."

He grasped her arm to help her down to the ground and felt a tremor go through her body. Refusing to let himself think, he immediately dropped her arm, and Kit jumped down. Without turning around, she headed for the field's exit gate, walking so quickly he had to lengthen his stride in order to catch her.

"Slow down, Kit, we're not in that big of a hurry."

"I'm sorry, I didn't realize it was so late."

She spoke stiffly, and Hawk felt a moment of regret, but he was unable to say anything that would change the situation.

Neither of them spoke as they retraced their steps and headed for the quarters area where both were billeted.

Kit strode blindly ahead, her steps rapidly eating up the distance until their destination was just in front of them.

He started to reach for her but she shook him off, refusing to look at him. Stopping in front of one of the modular trailers, she finally spoke. "This is where I live. I—I guess this is goodbye."

"Kit—" *He didn't want to leave her like this, but what could he say.* "Kit, I'm sorry."

"What did I do, Hawk?"

"Not you, Kit. You didn't do anything. I wish it could be different, but there are things in my past you don't know about, and—"

"Then tell me, Hawk. I thought we agreed earlier that we could tell each other anything."

At last she was looking at him, and now he wished she weren't. Her eyes were bright with tears, and it took all his considerable control to keep from pulling her into his arms. "I can't, Kit. I'm sorry, sorrier than you know that I'm not what you think I am. I need to go now before I do something we'll both be sorry for."

Kit's head dropped, and she turned swiftly. Her hand

on the door, she spoke softly without turning around, "Goodbye Hawk."

The door slammed behind her, and he scrubbed a hand through his short hair, anger and frustration eating at him. *Damn, damn, damn. He'd sworn after the incident with Carol—he laughed bitterly at the word—if you could call marriage an incident. After their short and disastrous marriage, he'd made a vow to himself that he would <u>never</u> let any woman get to him again, never let anyone make him care enough to be hurt. So what had happened? In one day, one bloomin' day, Kit Vail had stormed his defenses, wriggled her way under his armor, and broken down his protective wall.*

He clenched his fists, his thoughts painful. *He'd just hurt Kit immeasurably. She had no idea what had gotten into him—was probably still convinced it was something she had done that set him off. And the ironic thing was— it was too late, like shutting the barn door after the horse was gone. Kit had already— She was everything any man would want—cute, funny, and so adorable that he—* He brushed his hand through his hair again. *What the hell was he going to do? He knew the answer, the only possible answer. Stay the hell away from her, that's what. Far away from her . . . and don't call her either!* His conscience gave him a twinge of regret at the hurt he knew he was causing Kit, but better a quick cut now. He was no good for her and he knew it, if she didn't.

His decision made, he turned resolutely toward his VOQ room, knowing he would get no sleep after he got there. Good thing he actually did have an early flight tomorrow.

Chapter 4

It had been three weeks since she had last seen or heard from Hawk. Thankfully, the pressure and stress of her job had kept her extremely busy. One of her men had been killed when his vehicle ran over an IED on the road to Baqouba. That had been her first experience at writing the required letter to his family; it was the hardest thing she had ever had to do.

She was so tired. She didn't know how her troops continued day after day with the long hours, the Spartan comforts, and the unremitting heat. Thank heavens for GI humor.

Nights like this—when she fell into her bunk too tired to fall asleep—her mind drifted to Hawk and she went over every word, every nuance of their few conversations. At first, they had seemed to be kindred spirits— liking the same things and finding so much to talk and laugh about. Then—she still didn't know what had happened—it was as if he was furious with her, or himself—she couldn't decide which.

Sleep refused to come, and she rolled and tossed on her damp sleeping bag, damning the new nylon bags that just weren't suitable for this climate. Even if you slept on top of them, they stuck to your body every place they touched. Each morning when she woke up, her cot was soaked clear through with perspiration and stained white with salt.

She kept seeing Hawk's face when they'd said goodbye. What had happened? Was it her? Something she had done? Was it because she was Mark's sister? Surely that wasn't it? He was definitely not afraid of Mark. Mark! In desperation, she got up from her damp and tangled bedding, went to the window and stared out. Her thoughts centered on Mark's conversation. Somehow, there was a clue there, if she could just figure it out. So much for her "helping" Hawk Hawkins. She'd told Mark she wasn't the one to help him, whatever his problem was. One thing both Mark and Hawk agreed on—she was "different from his other women." Well, big whoop! What good did being different do a person?

Mark's latest email didn't help. He'd asked what she'd heard from Hawk, and when she had last seen him. Even though she had been angry at Mark's sending Hawk to check on her—and she still believed he had—it hurt to admit that Hawk hadn't liked her enough to contact her more than once. Obviously, he'd felt he had done his duty and that was it.

Even Mark had seemed surprised when she said she had only heard from him the one time.

Every time she thought about Hawk's abrupt departure she got mad. She hadn't done anything. It wasn't her fault—whatever had caused him to turn into an iceberg. And she didn't have to take it lying down— whoops, bad choice of words—they hadn't even come close to lying down. Darn that man!

It was a good thing Mark had emailed her, rather than making a phone call. On paper it was possible to pretend it didn't hurt. Over the telephone Mark was too *good at picking up on her emotions and feelings. He always had been.*

It was a long time before sleep came.

Hawk looked at the calendar tacked to the inside of his door. Three weeks had passed since he'd been in Taji—three long weeks since he had seen Kit Vail. And he had fought against calling her every single day. He'd thought he could just put her out of his mind, that it would get easier as the days went by. But he couldn't, and it hadn't.

He was really surprised he hadn't heard anything from Mark, and that was a blessing he supposed. Even as the thought went through his mind, his cell phone jangled. He flipped it open and groaned as he heard Mark's voice. *It was as if he had conjured him up just by thinking about him.*

"Hey, Man."

"Now what do you want, Mark?"

"Well, I haven't heard from you lately. And I got to wondering if you'd been to see Kit."

"I went to see her. And I called and told you she was <u>fine</u>."

"But that was three weeks ago."

"So?"

"You mean you haven't seen her or talked to her since?"

"No, I haven't."

"Why not?"

"Listen, Mark, I don't know what you're up to, but you can give it up right now. You asked me to go and see

Kit. I did. You asked me to let you know if she was all right. I did that too. Mission completed. Done. Finis. So drop it."

"You mean to tell me you're not going to see her again; when she's right there, only a couple of hours away? What happened when you saw her? Did you do something to hurt her? So help me Hawk Hawkins, if you—"

"Mark, you're making me crazy. What the hell is the matter with you? First you want me to stay away from your sister. Then you want me to go see her. Now you're worried I've done something to her. I didn't do <u>anything</u> to her."

"Did you hurt her?"

"Did she say I did?"

"No, no. She didn't say anything. Just that you had been there, and that she'd thank me not to send any more guys to check on her."

"Well, there are you are. That's what I told you she would say."

"Hawk! It's her birthday on July 4th. We've always made a big thing out of her being born on the Fourth. I know she's going to feel bad this year. Couldn't you—"

"Couldn't I what? Mark Vail, you're going to keep pushing on this until you don't like the result. I'm <u>not</u> seeing Kit anymore because I <u>don't</u> want to hurt her. Because I <u>always</u> end up hurting women—"

Mark mumbled under his breath, "That's because you always drop them, and they don't want to be dropped."

"What was that you mumbled? Speak up, Man."

"Nothing. I didn't say anything. But can't you do this for <u>me</u>, Hawk. I'm not asking that much. Didn't you like her at all? I thought—"

58

"You thought what?"

"Nothing. I didn't think anything at all. Just do me this one favor, Hawk. Help her have a nice birthday . . . and I'll never ask you for anything else."

"Right. Like I believe that."

"Please, Hawk."

"Fine. I'll do it. Just remember this—whatever happens, it's on your head. I tried."

"Thanks Hawk. Thanks a lot. I really appreciate this. You can call me after—"

"No! I'll do it, as a favor to you. But I'm done reporting. You want to find out anything about your sister, you call her. I gotta go now. Goodbye."

Hawk continued to sit on the bed long after he finished talking to Mark, his thoughts chaotic in his head. What had he done? Agreeing to see Kit Vail again had to be the dumbest thing ever. It had been almost impossible to refrain from calling her after he saw her the first time. The past three weeks had been more difficult than he could have imagined. If he saw her again, he would never be able to put her out of his mind. Mark had to be crazy, insisting he do this.

He stood, straightened his shoulders. *Fine! Mark wanted a celebration. He'd give her a celebration she'd never forget, and then he was done . . . and Mark would owe him . . . big time.*

Chapter 5

Hawk frowned at the face looking back at him from the mirror, as razor in hand, he swiped through the foam on his face. *A week had passed since his conversation with Mark, and the 4th of July was almost on top of him. He had taken no action on his promise to Mark. He hadn't called Kit because he would then be committed to seeing her, and he still had doubts about the wisdom of that, despite his promise. It might not work out anyway, with their heavy mission schedule right now. He was tempted to just do nothing, let the date pass, and tell Mark it just hadn't been possible.*

He ran his hand through his hair, scowling as he realized he wouldn't take that option. No, he had agreed to do this, and he had to try. He glanced at his watch and made one last swipe with the razor. He was due at Operations in twenty minutes. He dried his face and then stepped into a clean flight suit—his decision made. He'd call Kit this afternoon when he got back.

It was late afternoon when he returned to his room, after an uneventful flight and a long briefing. He had flown every day for the last week, and he was tired. He flopped on his bed and picked up his cell phone. He had gotten the number for Kit's office and hoped she would still be there this late in the day. The phone rang, and he smiled as he envisioned her face.

A gruff voice interrupted his thoughts.

"Company commander's office, Corporal Jones speaking."

"Corporal, this is Captain Hawkins at Balad. Is Lieutenant Vail in?"

"Yes Sir—hold one."

The line went dead, and he realized the corporal had put him on hold. *He wondered if Kit would be too busy to talk to him. A moment later he heard her breathless voice.*

"Hawk!"

"Hello, Kit. How've you been?"

"I . . . fine—I've been—<u>fine</u>."

Hawk smiled, knowing she had chosen the word on purpose. "I'm glad. I've missed you "

Kit didn't say anything for a minute, and he knew she was surprised.

"I didn't think I would hear from you again."

"I . . . didn't plan to call you again, Kit." *He <u>shouldn't</u> be calling her.* "What are you doing for the 4th of July?"

"Tomorrow?! I'm working in the morning. Why?"

"I thought I might come down tomorrow on the Catfish Air flight. Maybe we could have dinner?"

"That would be great. When—"

"I'll call you in your office when I get in. How long are you working?"

"Until 1300."

"Okay. I'll see you tomorrow."

Hawk put the phone down and scrubbed his hand across his face, feeling the sandy grit mixed with sweat.

God, he needed a shower. But first he'd better swing by Catfish Air and make sure he could catch a hop to Taji tomorrow. He'd spoken to Joe last night, and it was okay, but who knew what might have come up since then? Then he'd head over to the BX and see what he could come up with to make Kit's birthday really special.

Kit slowly hung up the phone, a look of amazement on her face. *She had given up all hope of hearing from Hawk . . . and he hadn't planned to call her! He had said as much. So why had he? But he was coming tomorrow!* She grinned and hugged herself with excitement.

Sergeant Karley came into the office and dropped a pile of correspondence in her in-box.

"Good news, Lieutenant?"

She knew she was blushing, and she bit her lip before answering. "Good news. A friend from Balad is coming in on the helo tomorrow."

"It wouldn't be the good-looking Captain who was here a couple of weeks ago, would it?"

He remembered, and his eyes were twinkling. "It would." She grinned as she said it. *The Sergeant was old enough to be her father and she knew his teasing was well meant.*

"Well Lieutenant, then you better take the day off, don't you think. We can do without you for a day. You've been working seven days a week lately, and you need some time off."

"Thanks Sarge, but I'm okay. I'm scheduled for half-a-day tomorrow. I'll be in the office until 1300."

"Yes, Ma'am."

He left the office, and she reached for the papers in her in-box, smiling at the thought of tomorrow and Hawk's arrival. *He couldn't know it was her birthday, but just his coming was a wonderful gift.*

Hawk was at the flight line over an hour early the next morning and he had to laugh at his eagerness to get to Taji and Kit. *He hadn't felt like this since he was sixteen years old and taking out his first date after getting his license. That was so many years ago, and in the years since he'd become jaded and cynical, refusing to set himself up for another hurt after the failure of his brief marriage. Now he was going against every single one of his rules and letting a woman get to him. How had Kit managed to do it so quickly? And what was Mark's angle? There was something about their conversation that raised a red flag—he just couldn't put his finger on it.*

"Hey Hawk, you're early! You must be in a hurry to get to Taji. It wouldn't be that little blond lieutenant, would it?"

Shrugging off his concerns about Mark, he presented a bland face to his friend. "Mornin', Joe. What little blond lieutenant?"

"Right! I saw the woman, remember? And you had that 'She's my property' look all over you. That's all that kept me from making a move on her myself."

A sudden shot of anger surged through Hawk, surprising him with its violence, and he frowned at Joe. "You better not have called her."

Joe grinned. "No, but I thought about it. After all, I

63

am there every other day—" He saw the black look on Hawk's face and didn't finish the sentence. "I knew you'd react just the way you are now, so don't even try to deny that's why you're so anxious to get to Taji, my friend."

Hawk cringed, knowing he'd been had. *Joe was a good friend, but payback would come sooner or later.*

"I won't be ready to leave for thirty minutes yet if you want to get coffee or something. I'm on my way to check the helo."

Hawk knew that no matter how many guarantees he received from the maintenance people that the plane was good to go, no pilot would board his plane without doing his own personal walk-around check, so he nodded and headed toward the small terminal.

"I'll be inside."

The flight had been blessedly uneventful. Hawk patted his pocket to make sure the small package was still there, grinning with anticipation as the helicopter approached the Taji airstrip. It was not quite eleven and Kit had said she had to work this morning. He wondered if she would be at the flight line, but knew he couldn't expect that, especially since he hadn't really told her when he would get in. He'd call her as soon as they landed.

Joe set the craft down in a perfect three-point landing and Hawk congratulated his buddy as he undid the straps holding him in the seat.

"Thanks, we aim to please. You better hurry up, your lady is waiting."

Ignoring Joe's speculative look, Hawk jumped up

64

from the seat and looked out. *Kit was standing at the entrance to the terminal, the wind molding her ACU's against her and blowing her curls around her face. He felt a shiver of excitement. She had apparently called Ops for his ETA.* "Thanks, Joe. I'll see you tomorrow. Okay?" Already striding toward Kit, he spoke over his shoulder, not even looking at his friend.

"Right. I'll call if there's a change. You're a lucky man, Hawk Hawkins."

Hawk didn't reply. *Kit was coming toward him, and Joe probably expected him to kiss her, his reputation with women being what it was. He'd definitely like to, but it wouldn't be appropriate—and it would embarrass Kit.*

"Hey Kit, long-time no see."

"Hello. Joe isn't it? I haven't seen you in a while. Do you get here often?"

Hawk didn't give Joe time to reply. "Hello, Kit." *Her smile told him she was glad to see him.*

Several seconds elapsed as they stood there, neither speaking. Joe shook his head and grinned, his farewell unnoticed by either of them. When they finally spoke, it was at the same time.

"Hawk!"

"Kit."

Laughing, Kit reached out and touched his arm, and he put his hand over hers, realizing how glad he was to be there. "I've—I've got to head back early tomorrow morning," he said quickly re-phrasing what he had started to say. *Damn, I almost told her how much I missed her! Get a grip, man.*

"Have you had lunch yet?" Kit asked. She looked at her watch, and then shrugged. "Oh, I didn't realize it was

65

only 1100. Of course you're not hungry."

"Actually, I am. I skipped chow this morning." *This is going to work out great, he thought to himself. Part of his surprise for Kit was in the dining hall, and at this time of day it shouldn't be all that busy there.* "Let's head over to the dining hall now."

"Actually, it's a dining tent." Kit smiled.

They had taken only a few steps when she stopped him by reaching out and touching his arm hesitantly. "I was surprised to hear from you—I didn't think you would call again."

And he hadn't intended to. "Well, as it happens, I had a special reason to call you."

"Why?"

"You'll see."

He started walking again and she realized he wasn't going to tell her why he had waited so long to call. Mystified, she made no comment until they were standing in front of the huge tent which served as one of several all-ranks dining halls on the post. "Here we are; it shouldn't be too crowded at this time of day."

They had no sooner entered the tent than Hawk excused himself. "Kit, wait right here for a few minutes. I need to see someone."

Her eyes snapped at the phrase, "wait right here," but he didn't give her a chance to object.

"I'll just be a few minutes."

She nodded as he walked off. *He could be the most aggravating man!* A few minutes later he returned, trailed by a tall mess sergeant with a huge grin.

"This is Sergeant O'Herlihy."

"Sergeant." Kit nodded to the man, her confusion visible on her face. *What was the man up to now? They were headed to a small table off to one side of the dining tent. The place was busy, but not full; and no one seemed to be paying any attention to them. She didn't see any of the personnel from her unit, although this was the usual place for them to eat.*

At the table, the Sergeant pointed to a "reserved" card in the center and said, "This is your table. Go ahead and go through the chow line. I'll take care of everything else." He winked at Hawk and moved off.

"Thanks, Sergeant. I appreciate it."

"What do you appreciate, Hawk? What's he talking about?"

Instead of answering, he lightly put his hand on her back, steering her toward the chow line. Forced to concentrate on her choices, she let the matter drop for the moment.

When they came back to their table, Hawk removed the "reserved" card and pocketed it. She repeated her earlier question, "What's going on, Hawk? How come you know that Sergeant? And what is he going to 'handle' for you?"

Hawk's eyes held a glint of humor as he smiled at her. "Don't be so impatient, Kit. All will be revealed, in good time."

She felt like hitting the man, but he obviously wasn't about to tell her anything until he was ready. She picked up her fork and started eating. After a few minutes, she looked up thoughtfully. "Have you heard from Mark lately?" *That seemed to surprise him.*

"Um, not . . . lately."

"I haven't heard from him either, and it's strange because—" She tilted her head and studied him.

"Strange? Why strange?"

67

"Because he never forgets my—"

She stopped in mid-sentence, her attention drawn to a commotion at the other end of the tent. A private was coming their way carrying a birthday cake alight with candles. He was followed by two other men in kitchen attire and the sergeant, all of them singing happy birthday.

'Saved by the bell . . . or the birthday cake,' he thought. *A grin broke out on his face as he watched Kit's astonishment. Her face turned a rosy shade of red. She was definitely surprised.*

"How did you know it was my birthday?!"

The mess sergeant spoke before Hawk could answer. "Ma'am, if you'll blow out the candles, we'll cut the cake for you."

Kit turned and smiled at the man. "I will—and thank you for this gorgeous cake. Please thank your staff for me."

"I'll do that ma'am, and you're quite welcome."

Kit leaned forward and blew out all the candles with one breath.

"Guess you'll get your wish," Hawk said softly. "Care to tell me what it was?"

"How do you know I made a wish?" *She had, but she wasn't about to tell him.*

Hawk only smiled.

The sergeant produced a knife and proceeded to cut the cake, setting slices in front of both of them.

"Thank you, Sergeant. It tastes wonderful," Kit said as she tasted the first forkful. "Now, please give the rest to the men and women in the kitchen."

"They'll appreciate it, ma'am. Thank you." With another wink at Hawk, he left them.

Kit laid her fork down. "Mark told you to do this, didn't he?"

"I told you I hadn't talked to him in several—"

"That doesn't matter, I know he told you. How else did you know it was my birthday? Because Mark told you to see that I got a cake, that's why."

Hawk's expression was serious. "No Kit, he didn't. Mark did tell me it was your birthday. He also told me that your family had always made a big celebration of it because you were born on the Fourth of July."

"And you expect me to believe that he didn't tell you to come here and do this?"

He had probably earned her doubt. "I wish I could say it was all my idea, but you're right, it wasn't."

"I knew it!"

"Wait, let me finish. Mark did call me—but not in the last several days. He did tell me your birthday was coming up, and made the suggestion—"

"Right! Suggested! Sure."

"As I was saying, he might have suggested that I do something for your birthday, since I was here, and none of them was. But that's all he said, Kit. Everything else is my idea. I wanted to come, and I thought you might get a kick out of a cake."

Suddenly happy, Kit laughed. "I did. I do! Thank you, Hawk. I love the idea of a cake, and I certainly never expected anything like it. I didn't mean to sound so—"

"I know, Kit."

She suddenly remembered his earlier words. "You said 'everything' else. What did you mean? What else have you done?"

"Well, I came here."

"Oh, okay—and I am glad you came."

69

"But . . ."

"There's a but. What but?"

Hawk broke out in laughter. *In addition to everything else she was, Kit was fun.* "Finish your cake, and we'll get out of here."

Pushing her plate away, Kit laughed again. "I'm finished, let's go." Outside, she headed for the vehicle that was one of her perks as unit CO. "When do I get my surprise, and where is it?"

"Get in the vehicle, Kit."

She climbed in and looked at him expectantly. He settled back in the seat and turned toward her with a teasing grin. "Are you sure you want it now? I could let your anticipation build."

Kit raised her arm as if to strike him. "Stop teasing me, Hawk. You said 'in the vehicle,' and I'm in the vehicle."

"Okay, okay, I guess I've teased you enough." He reached inside the pocket of his flight suit and removed a small, wrapped box. After looking at it thoughtfully, he handed it to her, smiling as he did so. "Happy birthday, Kit." She tore off the wrapping, and then hesitated.

"Well, open it."

She carefully removed the lid and opened her mouth. The box held a round, silver, coin-like disk, similar to the unit coins exchanged by many of the military. It was engraved, and she picked it up to examine it more closely. After reading the words, she burst out laughing. "Hawk! You're a 'Pogo' fan!"

"My aunt was, and she introduced me to the little fellow when I was barely old enough to read. I was lying in bed one night, thinking about how Mark was so aggravated at you always telling him you were 'just fine.' I remembered the little bug in 'Pogo'."

"Fremont."

"That's him! When he ran for President—"

"The only thing he ever said was ''jes' fine.'" This time when she looked at him, her eyes were shining. "I love it, Hawk. My Dad had every Pogo book Walt Kelly ever wrote, and he was always quoting someone from the strip. I think his favorite was Pogo's, 'We have met the enemy, and they is us.'"

"That was one of my aunt's favorites too. I was afraid you might not be familiar with it, since the strip was popular in our parents' time and—"

"I can't believe that we both were introduced to the comic strip when we were kids. It's such a coincidence . . . maybe an omen." She peeped up at him through lowered lashes.

"Maybe. Did you look at the back?"

The print on the front read, "'Jes fine sez bug . . .' and Kit." When she turned it over, she saw the date—her birthday. She squeezed her eyes shut and bit her lip, overcome with emotion. Then, slowly and carefully, she replaced the medallion in its cotton bed and closed the box. Holding it in one hand, she reached out and grabbed one of Hawk's hands with the other. "It's the most special gift I've ever received Hawk."

"I wanted to give you something you could keep with you, like a talisman."

"I will, Hawk. I thought this was going to be just another day, but you've made it really special. Thank you."

"You're very welcome, Kitten. You deserve to have a special day." *He reached for her hand and squeezed it tightly before reluctantly letting it go. He'd like to do more than squeeze her hand, but that was impossible, given they were in such a public place . . . and there was really nowhere else to go.* "Before we do anything else, I better get over to the transient quarters and get a room, and then check and make sure Joe hasn't been trying to find me. I told him to call me there if he had a change in flight plans."

When they pulled up in front of the quarters for transient officers, Kit parked the vehicle. "I'll just wait here for you."

"Don't be silly, Kit. It's hot as all get out here. Come in with me. I'll get a room and check for messages. Then we can go to my room, maybe have a cold drink—"

Kit hesitated. *With any other guy she'd know exactly what was on his mind, but she never understood Hawk at all, and was afraid to make any assumptions. When she looked up, he was laughing at her, one eyebrow raised. Darn it! He knew what she was thinking.*

"What's the matter, Kit? You believe all those stories you've heard? Afraid?"

"I don't—I'm not. I'm coming."

"Okay, let's go."

He was waiting by her door when she got out.

Inside, the building was deserted except for a bored clerk reading a battered magazine at the desk. He looked up when he heard them come in.

"Private, I'm Captain Joshua Hawkins. I need a room for tonight."

The private looked at Kit and then back at him. "Single or double?"

Kit unconsciously raised her chin, even as she felt warmth color her face at the knowing look in the clerk's eyes.

Hawk's voice was reprimanding when he answered. "A <u>single</u> room, Private."

"Yes Sir." The man was red-faced as he handed over the key, avoiding Hawk's eyes as he did so.

Hawk picked up his bag and turned to go, then looked back and asked, "By the way, have there been any calls for me?"

"No Sir, no messages."

"I'm expecting a message from a Lieutenant Sanchez. If he calls, let me know right away. I'll be in my room."

"Yes Sir."

Damn! He should have expected that. What people thought or didn't think had never bothered him, but he realized, too late, that to Kit it did. This was obviously not a good idea. At the door, he mumbled under his breath, then inserted the key card in the lock. The room was typical—small and square, a tiny window with a grid of bars and limp drapes. It contained a standard cot, a small, metal desk and accompanying chair, one club chair that had seen better days, and an extra straight chair. He shut the door, flipped his bag on the cot, and turned to face Kit. Her smile was uncertain. "I'm sorry about bringing you in here, Kit. It was a bad idea. Chalk it up to what you've heard about me."

"No, no, it's fine, Hawk. After all, where else could we go? I share a room, and my roommate sleeps during the day. It's okay."

Motioning toward the room, he said, "Shall we flip for the chair?" She looked worriedly at the bed, and he laughed. Fine, Kit. You take the chair, and I'll take the bed. Would you like a soda? There's probably a machine down the hall."

73

"No, I'm . . . fine." *Brilliant! Couldn't she think of any other word?*

Hawk threw his keys on the desk and moved his flight bag. He flopped down on the bed, leaning back against the wall, hands behind his head. "At least it's air conditioned in here. Thank the gods for that."

Kit laughed. "My quarters weren't until just recently . . . and it's not very reliable. It always seems to shut off during the worst heat spells."

"Tell me, Kit, what surprised you most about being here? You're much closer to things than I am. I'm 'in country,' but I get a bird's eye view of things. There's a sense of disassociation about everything I do."

"Well, I don't know if surprised is the right word. I'm doing what I was trained to do. I get up every morning and come to work in an office. I supervise the men and women under my command. I do know that when I send out a convoy, I'm sending them into harm's way, but I don't think it really hit me about where we are until I had to write my first letter to the parents of one of my men."

"That had to be difficult."

"It was so hard—at first, I didn't know what to say . . . or how to say it. In the end, I realized that I could be receiving such a letter someday, and I just wrote from my heart. I know it was only words, but I hope it helped to comfort them."

Hawk looked at Kit for several minutes, and when he spoke, his voice was speculative. "Mark's wrong about you. You're not his little sister any more. You're all grown up, and you're a very special woman. I wonder when he's going to realize it."

"You don't know how glad I am to hear you say that. I just knew Mark had convinced you that I was in dire

74

need of looking after."

Hawk smiled. It wasn't so much that her brothers thought she <u>needed</u> looking after as that they wanted to protect her and keep her from harm—and he felt the same way. That was a surprise. He almost laughed out loud thinking of her reaction if she knew what he was thinking.

"What's funny?"

"You are, Kit Vail. You're such a bundle of contradictions."

"How so?"

"You just are." *He refused to answer that. Maybe someday he'd tell her, but now was not the time. Better to change the subject.* "Tell me about Jon. You said he's the family renegade. Why's that?"

She had to smile as she thought about her twin brother. "Jon is smart, brilliant almost. He could do anything he wanted. He just never wanted to do what he thought people expected him to do. I remember when we were six, he decided we should stop doing things together, said just because we were twins we didn't have to be alike. I said, 'But Jon, we like doing things together.' His answer was, "Yeah, well, we'll pretend we don't."

Hawk laughed, and Kit did too. "He sounds like a character."

"He is that."

"You mean, he still is?"

"Yep."

"So did you stop doing things together?"

"Not hardly—Jon just made sure people didn't always know it. We'd leave the house on our separate ways, and then meet up later. I'm sure our parents knew about it

75

and had a good laugh, but Jon kept right on doing it. When it came time for our junior prom, Jon said he wasn't going. I told him if he didn't go, I wasn't going either. Mark stepped in and decreed that we'd both go, or else. Jon said fine, he'd be my date—we'd go as a couple."

"What did you think of that?"

"Well, I was okay with that part of it. It was the rest I wasn't too sure of, but Jon convinced me it was the right thing to do, that it would be fun . . . and I went along with him, as I always did." She began to giggle, and broke into laughter. "You should have seen Mark's face when we came down the stairs to leave for the dance. It was a priceless moment—one of the few times in my life I've ever seen Mark speechless."

"Why? What were you wearing?"

"You should have seen us! Jon was wearing a white dinner jacket with all the trimmings, and I had a beautiful, feminine, white ballerina-length dress . . . with red and white striped stockings and black ballet slippers, white mittens, a red shaggy wig, and my face made up to look like Raggedy Ann. Jon had red and white striped socks, black shoes, white mittens, the shaggy red wig, and his face made up as Raggedy Andy. We were out of there before Mark could come out of his shock and stop us. We ran all the way to Jon's car, and Jon got us out of there. All the way to the dance he couldn't stop laughing. I thought it was funny too, until I realized we were going to our <u>prom</u>—where all our friends would see us—looking like rag dolls. But, Jon thought it was great, and I wasn't about to chicken out."

He could see Kit as she must have been back then, growing up as the beloved little sister, but often the butt of their jokes, always the willing servant, never letting them see her fears or worries, always trying to please them—and yet she had grown up into this lovely, funny, caring woman. "Don't keep me in suspense. What happened? Was it awful?"

She giggled again. "Let me tell you, it was something. They announced the promenade, and everyone formed up to parade across the gymnasium stage and be introduced."

"You mean you kept up the charade."

"Of course. The emcee was our principal, Mr. Jonkowski, and the expression on his face when he first saw us told me we were in big trouble. But as usual, Jon charmed his way out of it. Somehow he always managed to do it. In the end, Mr. Jonkowski introduced us: 'And our next couple, Miss Raggedy Ann Vail and her escort Mr. Raggedy Andy Vail.' We skipped and bumbled across the stage in an entrance Jon had had us rehearse, bowing and curtsying in the center. The applause was thunderous. And the rest of the evening was fun. We had a ball."

"What about the romantic evening most girls expect their proms to be?"

Hawk's voice was soft. Was he feeling sorry for her? Pity was definitely not what she wanted from him. "I didn't care about romantic evenings as long as I had Jon. He made everything fun. He was my other half."

"Until graduation."

She looked up to find him watching her, his eyes filled with compassion—he understood. "You're right. Until graduation. I knew it was coming. I already had my appointment to the Academy. I had tried to get Jon to apply. He was as good an athlete as I was, and his grades were as good as mine. Where I loved running, he was a star wrestler. He was as fast as I was at running—he just wouldn't do it because I did." Memories clouded her vision, and she brushed her hand through her hair.

Curls flew in all directions, and he wanted to pick her up and hold her on his lap, but he didn't. He wanted to ask her to come sit with him. Instead he waited for her to go on. When she didn't, he spoke, "What happened, Kit?" She shook her head, and her voice was sad when she finally continued.

"Mark kept insisting that Jon had to go to college, that it was criminal to waste a good brain like his, and Jon kept saying it was his brain to waste if he wanted to, and he was not going to college."

"I'm surprised that Mark didn't—"

"No, don't. It wasn't like that. Mark simply wanted the best for Jon, for all of us. And Jon loved Mark. He just had to be who he was. I knew that, but I couldn't make Mark understand. I tried, I really tried, but, I—"

The tears in her eyes were too much for him. He rose suddenly, and before she could realize what he was doing he had scooped her up and returned to the cot with her on his lap. He leaned back into the wall and brushed her tears away with his thumb. "Don't, Kit, it wasn't your fault. You couldn't have changed either of their minds, no one could. You understood about Jon, but you also need to understand about Mark—he has always felt responsible for all of you, and he always will."

"Did he tell you about Jon and him?"

"Not this story, but I know from other things he's said in the past. I know how much he loves all of you. You don't know how I've always envied him his family."

"Hawk, I'm so sorry you're all alone."

78

"Don't worry about it; I'm used to it. Now, finish the story. What happened after graduation?"

"The night before graduation Mark and Jon got into another argument about his going to college, and how it was too late for him to get in anywhere but the local community college. Jon didn't say anything, just went storming out. I was afraid he wouldn't come back for graduation, but he did. Later, I realized it was because he wanted that piece of paper."

Kit relaxed and leaned back against Hawk, and he let out a long sigh. *It felt so good to hold her.* "Go on with the story."

"That night, Jon told me he was leaving the next day. He swore me to secrecy and said he was joining the Navy. He had already talked to the Navy recruiter, told him he wanted to be a SEAL."

"I've been told it's not that easy."

"Oh, it's not. But, Jon eventually made it."

There was pride in her voice as she said it, but he knew what it must have cost her. "And what happened to you, without your other half?"

"It felt like part of me was missing, Hawk. It really did. It was the hardest summer of my life. Mark was great. I hadn't thought he would understand, but he did. They all kept telling me that Jon would be fine, and of course, I knew that. It was me—I was afraid I would fail. Matt graduated from college that same time, headed for seminary. Luke still had two more years of college. Mark had graduated from MSU the year before, having put his dreams on hold to stay home and take care of all of us after my parents were killed. With everyone leaving, he told us he was joining the Air Force as soon as I left for West Point. I thought it was the end of my home."

Hawk turned her to face him.

"And was it?"

"Of course not, but I thought it was. We're still close. You know Mark keeps in touch with me—more than I might wish sometimes." She looked up at him and grinned.

"And the others?"

"We keep in contact. Matt's married now, and his wife Elaine is usually the one who writes—Matt always adds a postscript. Luke seldom writes letters, but he's pretty good about email, and he calls about once a month. I hardly ever catch him when I call, but I email him a lot."

"And what about Jon? Does he call you?"

Kit smiled. "I always hear from Jon . . . except sometimes, like now. When he's in the States, he calls me a couple of times a week, but then he'll be gone for months at a time. I haven't heard from him in two months this time, but he's all right. I'd know if he weren't."

"Does it work that way for him too?"

"I don't know, maybe." Kit suddenly squirmed around until she was facing him. "Now, Hawk Hawkins, it's your turn. I've told you practically my whole life history. Tell me, don't you have any family at all?"

"That really hangs you up, doesn't it?"

"I just don't believe that it doesn't bother you at all. I can't . . . imagine it." *What would it be like not to have anyone care about you? It was inconceivable to her*

"There isn't a whole lot I can do about it." He shrugged as if he didn't care.

"But, what about cousins, or . . . or . . . something?"

"My father was an only child, according to my aunt.

My aunt was my Mom's only sibling, and she never married. So, no cousins. Not a one."

"God, Hawk! I feel as if we should adopt you."

Hawk raised his eyebrows. "I don't <u>think</u> so." *He might not know how he felt about her, but he knew he definitely didn't want to be her brother.*

"Don't get so upset. I didn't mean it literally. I just—"

"Will you forget about it, Kit? I've survived this long without any family, and I expect to continue just fine." Kit huffed out a breath, then moved off his lap to sit cross-legged on the cot, facing him.

"Okay! So, what's the mystery about your father? How come nobody knows anything about him? How come you don't want to know if he's still alive?"

"You're not going to let this alone, are you?"

She grinned back at him. "Nope, so you might as well tell me."

"What if I told you I don't know anything?"

"Are you saying you don't?"

Instead of answering immediately, he raised one eyebrow and tipped his head. "How come you've moved off my lap?"

"Because I want to see your face when you answer my questions." *Only partially true, but she wasn't about to tell him that sitting so close to him gave her ideas she wasn't ready to recognize yet, about things she wasn't ready to do yet—even if he might be—and she wasn't sure about that, either.*

"Suppose I said I'll tell you what you want to know, but only if you come back here and sit on my lap." *He watched as she considered it, and her cheeks reddened. She mesmerized him. God, he didn't realize women still blushed like this. No wonder her brothers tried to keep*

81

her under wraps. "Well? What's your answer?"

"I don't think so. I think I'll stay where I am."

She looked down at her lap and mumbled something he couldn't catch. "What's that?"

"Nothing. I'll just stay here."

She lifted her chin in another movement he was becoming familiar with, and as if daring him, reiterated her request.

"Stop putting me off, Hawk. Talk. What about your father?"

He leaned back against the wall, placed his arms behind his head, and looked up at the ceiling, then drew in a deep breath and let it out. "Fine. But remember, this is all hearsay as far as I am concerned. I never knew my father at all, and my mother died when I was five. Once, I asked her how come other kids had dads and I didn't have one. She said that, of course, I had a Dad. I asked her where he was, and she started to cry and just shook her head. Young as I was, I knew it was something she couldn't talk about, and I never asked her again."

"But, didn't you ever ask your aunt, after you were older?"

"Of course. She said it was a sad story and better I didn't know. Of course, I insisted. She said they had met in college, and for my mother it was love at first sight. The expression of hatred on my aunt's face told me it wasn't going to be a pretty tale. Apparently, my mom got pregnant with me. She told my aunt, and Aunt Jean said she was all excited and happy and said, 'of course, they would get married right away.'"

He stopped there, and Kit leaned in closer. *She wanted to touch him, comfort him, but his face was so forbidding, his body so stiff, she sat back.* Her voice was soft as she said, "Go on, Hawk."

"There was no 'of course' about it. My aunt said he refused. Later, he transferred to another school and she never heard from him again."

"What happened to your mother?"

"She quit school and went to live with my aunt, who was her older sister. She had me, and then went to work at the same company where Aunt Jean did."

"Did she love you?"

"Yes, I think she did, but she never seemed happy. My aunt said she was never the same person after it happened."

"How did she die?"

"She was hit by a car while crossing a downtown Boston street. She was killed instantly."

"Oh, Hawk, how awful!"

"I really don't think she wanted to live."

"But that's awful, that you grew up knowing that."

He shrugged. "Stop feeling sorry for me. I don't. I had a good childhood. Aunt Jean loved me, and she had been there from the time I was born. She had a really good job, and I never wanted for anything."

"Still—"

"Enough. I've never told anyone my life story, not even Mark. I can't believe I've told you, but we're done talking about it."

He reached over and grabbed her, and she let him, her mind still on how alone he was.

"Kit, I'm really glad Mark asked me to look you up."

His face was serious as his black eyes bored into hers. He grasped her chin in his warm hand and moved his mouth closer to hers. Kit closed her eyes, afraid to breathe. "I'm glad too, Hawk." His lips brushed hers softly, and she let out a sigh. His mouth moved over hers, and his tongue probed gently until she opened her mouth. She could feel the rapid beat of his heart and knew he must be able to feel hers as well. She wound her arms around his neck and eased closer, loving the feel of his hard, muscled body against hers. When his arms enclosed her more tightly, nothing had ever felt so wonderful.

Hawk groaned and pulled back, reaching up to release her arms from his neck. "I shouldn't be doing this."

She felt as if he had thrown cold water on her. "Why not? It wasn't just you. It was us. Why shouldn't we? I thought . . . it felt wonderful to me."

"It felt wonderful to me too, Kit." He leaned his forehead against hers, his breathing rapid.

"Then why not, Hawk? Tell me, because I don't understand."

"I know you don't, Kit. I don't know if I can explain. I'll try—but you better sit over there." He motioned her to the chair where she had formerly sat. He stood, wiped his hand over his hair and gripped the back of his neck, then walked over to the little window. He stood there, staring out, his back to her. Before he said anything, there was a loud banging on the door.

"Sir. Captain Hawkins."

Hawk spun around from the window and headed for the door as he spoke. "Yeah, I'm coming." He swung the door open to face the desk clerk. "What is it?"

"Your call, Sir. Lieutenant Sanchez is on the phone."

Already halfway out the door, Hawk turned. "Wait here, Kit. I'll be right back."

She nodded. He'd seemed to welcome the interruption. Would he explain? And if he did, would she like the explanation? Probably not. He returned a few minutes later and immediately grabbed his flight bag off the floor from where they had knocked it a little while before.

"Can you give me a ride down to the flight line?"

"You have to leave <u>now</u>?"

"I'm sorry, Kit. Joe's got a high-priority package that has to get to Balad immediately. He said I could wait until his return trip day after tomorrow, but I can't do that. I have to be back by tomorrow, so I have to go now."

"I understand Hawk. I just—"

"I know, Kit." He put his finger under her chin and tipped her face up until she was looking into his eyes. "Don't ever change, Kit." He leaned forward and kissed her briefly. "You're one very special lady." Pushing her ahead of him, he exited the room, and pulled the door shut behind them. He had already checked out and as he laid his key card on the desk, the room clerk eyed them curiously. This time, Kit never even noticed. She didn't realize she had left the building until she found herself standing beside the Humvee, but she climbed in and watched as Hawk did too. Then, she started the vehicle, looked behind her and moved into traffic.

Five minutes later, they were at the flight line where Joe was already circling his helicopter in the routine inspection. He looked up and waved. "Hi, Kit. Come on, Hawk, get the lead out. I gotta get going."

Hawk turned to her. He started to say something, then changed his mind and touched her cheek instead.

"Hawk."

"'Bye, Kit."

"Goodbye, Hawk."

He started toward the waiting helicopter, and she called after him, "Thank you for my birthday."

He didn't turn, just waved. She stood on the hot pavement, watching long after the helo was airborne, until it had disappeared from sight.

Chapter 6

Darn it all. Another night lying here twisting and turning, unable to get thoughts of Hawk out of her mind. Luckily, Jaci worked nights at the hospital and slept days. Otherwise, her secret wouldn't be much of a secret. Jaci already suspected something, and if she heard my rolling and tossing every night, she'd have it out of me in the blink of an eye. A tired groan escaped her, and she sat up in bed. Without turning on the light, she reached out until she felt the small medal laying on her nightstand and closed her fingers around it. *The day Hawk had given it to her had been one of the most wonderful days of her life, until the knock on the door and Hawk's sudden departure. She'd figured he was saying goodbye for good—he didn't plan to come back. And, she'd been right. After three weeks, it was obvious he wouldn't be calling her.*

Anger coursed through her. *Darn, darn, darn! Twice now the man had pulled back and taken off like a scalded dog just when things were getting interesting. Once might have been her fault, but twice—no way. The thing was, she could see Mark was right—Hawk needed her. No one should be as alone as he was. It bothered her to think about what a loner he was.* She opened her hand and studied the small medal in the dim moonlight from the window. "Jes' fine." *Well, things weren't just fine, but they would be if she could do anything about it—and she could, at least she could try. She wasn't going to let him walk away from her—not once but twice—with no explanation. The man <u>owed</u> her an explanation, and she intended to see that he gave her one. The question was—how to go about it.* She chewed her lip as she pondered her options.

She could call him—if he would take her call. And besides, she needed to see his face when he explained. She could go to him. Come to think of it, the unit was sending a convoy up there on Friday. She needed to meet with the Transportation Officer at Camp Anaconda. Now was the perfect time, and Anaconda was adjacent to Balad. She'd call in the morning and make an appointment to see Colonel Hildebrand on Friday.

If she and Hawk were face-to-face, he'd have to tell her what had happened . . . and she would know from his expression if he were lying.

She took a deep breath and let it out, feeling a sense of peace. *The sun would soon be coming up, and her day would begin, but she could catch at least an hour of sleep first.* She squeezed the metal disc in her hand before putting it back on the night stand. Then she lay back down on her damp cot and immediately fell asleep.

Kit began having second thoughts as they bounced over Suicide Road on their way to Balad. *Two days ago, the idea of accompanying the convoy had seemed like a good one. It was an emergency convoy hauling parts and a diesel mechanic to the Army camp to repair a*

downed cat dozer. The dozer, essentially an Army vehicle, had become one of the workhorses of both services and, as a consequence, was one of the most frequently damaged. She really needed to see the TO at Anaconda, so what more natural than to go up with her men?

Now that she'd had time to think about it . . . what if Hawk was flying? Of course, the convoy wouldn't be returning until tomorrow, and his flights never lasted more than several hours. But, maybe he wouldn't want to see her . . . maybe he would be busy with other duties . . . maybe he would be out of the area . . . maybe . . . Enough with the maybes! She'd better keep her eyes on the road. She was in the lead vehicle and needed to help keep a lookout for anything suspicious in front of them. Besides, even if she didn't see Hawk, she still needed to see Colonel Hildebrand.

The heat was oppressive, and the dust and sand blown by the ever-present desert wind made it difficult to breathe. She tied her olive drab handkerchief over her nose and mouth, as had most of the men. It helped some, although the fine sand managed to sift through everything—tents, uniforms, and even the motors, keeping the mechanics busy cleaning and servicing their vehicles. It had been dawn when they left Taji, barely light—it wasn't safe to travel except in daylight hours. Even though the posts were only about ninety miles apart, with maximum convoy speed about 30mph, it would be mid-morning before they arrived.

Suddenly, they were hit by one of the frequent dust storms that blocked out the sun, forcing them to creep along to keep from losing their way. Usually, the storms were at higher altitudes with only a little dust at ground *level. This one, however, was low, and visibility was near zero. By the time the line of vehicles approached the heavily guarded gates of Anaconda, she was ready for a shower and change of clothes, but it wouldn't be happening. She barely had time to get to the Colonel's office without being late. Even though he was undoubtedly used to people coming in covered with dust and sand, she hated to appear in front of a superior officer looking less than her best. Oh well, it couldn't be helped.*

"Thanks for the ride, Sergeant. Drop me off at the TO's office before you head for the motor pool, please."

"Yes, Ma'am. Where do you want us to pick you up?"

"What time will you be heading out?"

"Mid-afternoon—if we can get the engine running by then. If not, we'll work as late as it takes, and hit the road at dawn tomorrow."

"Fine. Call me on my cell when you're ready to go."

"Yes, Ma'am. We'll head on down to the motor pool now."

Kit was entering the small metal building that housed the TO's office before the Humvee was out of sight. *It was just 1000, so she was on time.* She carefully latched the wooden door behind her in an attempt to keep out the blowing sand.

"You look like you got blown in by a dust storm, Lieutenant."

She spun around to face a round-faced, rosy-cheeked Lt. Colonel, and threw her hand up in a salute. "Lieutenant Vail from Taji, Sir, and we did come through a dust storm on the way here."

"Dicey things, those sand storms. Never know who else is out there in them. How bad was it?"

90

"This one was at ground level, Sir, so it was difficult to see through, and it lasted about an hour."

"Coffee, or something cold to wet your whistle?"

"A Coke would be wonderful, if you have it."

"Coming right up. Come in my office and take a load off. I'm Colonel Hildebrand, by the way. It's good to meet you after all the times we've talked."

"Yes Sir."

An hour later, her conference finished, Kit stood in front of the Transportation Company clerk. "Could I borrow your telephone and a directory?"

"Sure thing, Lieutenant. You can use that desk if you'd like. Jiminez is out this morning."

Thanking the clerk, she took the directory, but didn't sit down at the desk. Paging through the list of organizations, she again wondered about the wisdom of her actions and then chastised herself for second-guessing. *She'd made the decision   now she would go with it.*

She found the listing for Hawk's unit and ran her finger down the column of numbers—Operations. *That's what she wanted.* She quickly dialed the number.

"Operations. Captain Danielson here."

"Captain Danielson, this is Lieutenant Vail from Taji. Would Captain Hawkins be around today?"

"You're in luck, Lieutenant. He just walked in."

The man obviously covered the telephone receiver, but not very well. She could still hear his yell. "Yo Hawk! Some woman from Taji—" Before he finished the sentence, someone grabbed the phone.

"Kit?"

"Hawk?"

"Yeah. Sorry about that. Danielson thinks he's a

comedian."

She heard laughter in the background.

"Kit, where are you?"

"I'm here, Hawk. I thought—"

"Here? Here where? What are you doing here?"

Kit shut her eyes and grimaced. *This was going well.* "I'm at the TO's Office here at Anaconda. I thought, that is, I came up with a convoy bringing vehicle parts and a mechanic to repair one of the dozers. I had a meeting with the Anaconda TO." *She knew she sounded defensive, and it angered her.*

"I can't believe you're <u>here</u>. For how long?"

"Until they can get the vehicle repaired. Maybe this afternoon, maybe tomorrow at dawn."

"I had an early flight this morning and just got out of briefing. I'd ask you to meet me for lunch, but I'm a mess."

"<u>You're</u> a mess! You should see <u>me</u>! We drove through a sand storm to get here."

Hawk cursed under his breath, running his hand through his dark hair as he thought about the danger she had been in. *No wonder Mark worried about her.* "Where are you?"

"I'm still at Transportation. My men dropped me off. I don't have wheels. I was hoping you would be here, but—"

"Stay right there. I'll pick you up."

"Have you got wheels?"

"I'll get some. Don't move. Stay there, okay?"

"All right."

"I'll be there in ten minutes. Stay right where you are."

"Hawk! I said I'd wait. I don't have transportation, I'm

not going anywhere. Okay?" The phone clicked as he hung up. She put the receiver down, irked by his attitude. Where did he expect her to go, for Pete's sake? In the space of one minute, he'd told her three times not to move. So much for her hopes that he might be glad to see her. This was beginning to look like an incredibly bad idea. As she stood replaying their conversation in her head, she unconsciously slipped her hand into the pocket of her camos, curling her fingers about the silver medal that proclaimed "Jes' fine." She squeezed it tightly, and then straightened her shoulders and walked over to the clerk. She handed the phone directory back to him. "Thanks, Corporal."

He nodded toward the coffee pot in the corner. "Cup of coffee while you <u>wait</u>, Lieutenant?"

She smiled. *Obviously, he'd heard the irritation in her voice.* "Thanks. Guess you noticed I'm not long on patience."

He laughed with her, and she filled a cup with coffee, and then ambled toward the back of the building. A screened door opened out onto an area of hard-packed ground where two GI's in camouflage ACU's were playing with a small black and white dog. She watched idly as she drank her coffee, still angry that Hawk had spoken to her as if she were a child.

Ten minutes later, Hawk pulled up in front of the TO Building in a Hum-vee he'd borrowed from the Ops Officer. He looked around the area for Kit. When he didn't immediately see her, he felt a quiver of panic that she might already have left. *He'd heard the resentment*

93

in her voice at the way he had spoken to her.

It couldn't have sounded like much of a welcome, but he'd been so shocked to hear her voice, and then to know she was here on base. And that she had been on the dangerous Suicide Road. More accidents happened there than on any other road in the country. Logic told him he was being unreasonable. Kit was a company commander in charge of 200 men and women. She'd been in country for six months and was obviously good at her job. Still . . . He wiped his hand over his face. *He had to get a handle on this. Even a hint of protective attitude, and Kit would assume he was just like her brothers.* He didn't stop to wonder why that mattered to him. He scanned the area again; then turned off the motor and hopped out of the vehicle. *Where in hell was she?* He removed his sunglasses as he entered the building and looked around.

"Could I help you, Sir?" The voice came from the back of the room where a clerk looked up from shuffling papers. Before Hawk could answer, the clerk continued, "Would you be looking for a lieutenant who doesn't like to wait?"

So he wasn't the only one who had noticed her resentment.

"I am. Did she leave?"

"I don't think so, Sir. Try out back." He nodded down the hall, toward a screened door.

Hawk let out a deep breath. "Thanks." He strode down the hall and started to push the door open. He saw her, and his heart rose up in his throat. She was drinking a cup of coffee, staring at a spot on the wall. "Kit! I <u>am</u> glad you're here!" When she looked up, her blue eyes were flashing.

94

"All you said was 'Wait!' Three times you said it! Why would I leave?! I came to see you, but you didn't even say hello! I didn't expect you to drop everything. I was just telling you I was here, but—" *Uh oh, now she'd done it. When would she ever learn to think before she spoke?*

He felt the muscles in his arms tighten as frustration coursed through him. He wanted to pull her into his arms and hug her tightly. He wanted to kiss her—but he couldn't do either of those things. With both of them in uniform, military protocol forbid any public show of affection. In addition to which, he'd already decided . . . He stared at her helplessly, tension tight between them. He needed to explain his abruptness with her on the phone. He needed to mend some fences. He started to reach out to her, and then snatched his arm back. Clenching his jaw, he gritted out, "Kit, let's get out of here. I can't explain here. Hell, I need to hold you. I need—"

Kit's head flew up, shock and surprise in her eyes.

Had he really said that? This woman had him so off balance he didn't know which end was up. He laughed in his mind at what his buddies would think—'how the mighty are fallen.' He was the one who never let a woman get to him—at least not since Carol. Love 'em and leave 'em, that was his motto—a girl at every base. Right!

"Hawk?" Her voice was soft and tentative.

"Come on, Kit. We need to go." She hesitated and he forced himself to smile and say, "Please."

She worried her bottom lip with her teeth, and a wave of tenderness flowed through him at the gesture that he could already recognize as so her. Finally, a tiny smile crossed her face, although he could still feel her confusion.

"All right, Hawk. But look, I don't want to take up your time. I should have called. Surprises aren't good; it was stupid. I would have called, but . . . I didn't think you would talk to me after—" She lowered her head so he almost didn't hear the rest of the sentence. "—after last time."

He rubbed a hand across his forehead, dislodging his flight cap and resetting it before he spoke. "Kit, look. I—I know I've confused the hell out of you. I've confused myself."

Kit couldn't hear the last part of the remark, but what she heard was enough that she frowned, as she tried to figure out what he was saying.

Hawk shrugged his shoulders, then grinned at her, and took her arm. "Stop wondering. I promise I'll try to explain, even though I'm not sure I understand it. Anyway, let's get out of here." Touching her elbow, he steered her around the corner of the building. *He wasn't about to go back through the office and give the clerk another chance to grin at him.* "The vehicle's out front. Let's find somewhere to talk."

Kit turned, and a tremor of excitement rushed through her at the feel of Hawk's hand on her back. When he almost immediately dropped it, she was sorry. *She had never felt this way about any man before, as if she were not in control of her own emotions, that they were swinging wildly from high to low. She wasn't sure she liked the feeling.* She stopped in front of the vehicle and looked up, her eyes wide as Hawk opened the door for her.

He groaned. "Stop looking at me like that Kit, and get

in the damned vehicle or I'm going to kiss you right here in front of everybody. God, I've missed you."

Kit climbed in, her thoughts in a turmoil. *He was the one who had left so abruptly . . . and if he'd missed her so much, why hadn't he called? How come she was the one to look him up?* A frisson of pleasurable anticipation skittered through her, however, at the idea that Hawk was glad to see her. *Maybe, coming here hadn't been a mistake after all.*

As he climbed in and settled into the seat, Hawk turned to face her, and she could see a blaze of strong emotion in his eyes. Almost before she could take it in, he grabbed the pair of dark glasses hanging in the open neck of his flight suit and put them on.

"Where can we go, Hawk?"

"I know where I'd like to go," he said softly as he fitted the key into the ignition.

Kit leaned toward him and asked, "What did you say?"

Hawk started the vehicle before he answered.

"What, Hawk?"

"Nothing." *Damn, he had to get a grip.* His glance left the road for a second and he looked over at her. "You mess with my mind, Kit Vail. I look at you, and I see all the things I know I can't have."

Puzzled, Kit continued to look at him, although his gaze was now totally focused on the road in front of him.

"I don't understand, Hawk. What do you want?"

Stopped for a traffic light, he glanced over and his dark eyes bored into hers. She was stunned by the hunger in them, and then he spoke.

"I want you, Kit. I've wanted you from the first

minute I saw you. What do you think of that?"

Bubbles of happiness floated through her. *He wanted her as much as she wanted him.* Her elation disappeared at his next words.

"But I'm no good for you, Kit."

"You don't know that."

"Yeah, I do. You don't know anything about me or my past."

"Then tell me."

He stared through the window without answering her. Kit leaned over and touched his arm. He jumped as if burned, but still he didn't look at her.

"Perhaps I know more than you think," she said, recalling her telephone conversation with Mark.

Then he looked at her. "Oh?"

She grinned impishly. "Mark did mention you, on occasion."

Hawk raised an eyebrow.

"I know you've had lots of women, but you never settle down with just one. Why is that, Hawk? Someone really hurt you somewhere in your past, didn't they?"

Hawk's head swiveled and he glared at her. *He did not want to discuss this. But she didn't look away.* "Back off, Kit. You don't want to go there."

Swift anger coursed through her. "I'm not afraid of that glare. Remember, I grew up with four brothers—you can't just stare me down."

He didn't look away from the road, and she continued, "So stop telling me what's good for me. It's not your decision. I'm perfectly capable of making my own decisions, thank you very much. Maybe I have wants, too. And, contrary to the opinions of some people, I'm old enough to know what I want."

98

She was quivering with anger, and he could barely keep from smiling. *She was cute when she was angry . . . and she was definitely mad right now.*

"All right, Kit," he said softly. "What do you want?" He watched as she stared back at him, biting her bottom lip. His lips turned up in a faint smile. *Once again she had said more than she meant to, and now she was trying to figure a way to extricate herself. He could see the instant her decision was made as she looked up defiantly.*

"Maybe—maybe I want you. Just because I don't have a lot of experience doesn't mean—" She hesitated again, and her face flamed. Then, raising her chin, she floundered on. "I don't have much experience. Guys never asked me out—my brothers always put the fear of God in them. I knew lots of guys, but they all treated me like a sister . . . and . . . and I don't know why I'm telling you all of this. I'm sure you couldn't care less." She stopped and put her hands over her face.

Hawk slowed the vehicle and pulled off the road. *It was all he could do not to draw her into his arms. She was such a delightful mix of child-woman, and he shouldn't go anywhere near her, but he was very afraid he wasn't going to listen to his own conscience.* He reached out and pulled her hands gently away from her face. "Kit, listen to me. I envy the man who will give you the experience you say you don't have. But it won't be me . . . even though I wish like hell it could be." The last was uttered under his breath. Then he put one finger under her chin and raised her head until their eyes met.

"Hawk."

His name came out on a long breath, as Kit stared at him, her heart in her eyes. *Good thing they were out of sight of people and he had pulled over because, despite his fine words, his resistance was shot. This woman did things to his soul.* "Kit." He reached out and pulled her into his arms. "I know this is wrong. You're too innocent for a rogue like me, but when you look at me like that … I'm only human…"

Kit's eyes sparkled with mischief as she looked up at him. "But think of the fun you can have 'educating' me." Then, suddenly embarrassed at what she had said, she buried her face in his neck.

Hawk laughed out loud and pulled her face up to his. "You little imp!"

He lowered his head and Kit knew he was finally going to kiss her. Her whole body quivered in anticipation as Hawk's mouth came down on hers. What started out as a gentle touch rapidly became a torch that set them both on fire. She reached her arms up, wanting to be closer, but he pulled away.

"Kitten, you're killing me. We've got to get out of here." *She was totally lost, her eyes full of questions.* "We really need to talk, Kit." She nodded, looking around nervously. Her face flushed a lovely pink, and then she turned away from him. *Damn!* He touched her arm gently. "Kit, look at me." She didn't immediately turn and he touched her cheek.

"Don't be embarrassed, Kit. I love your responsiveness. You're everything a man dreams of. Too bad this is the wrong time and the wrong place—and I'm the wrong man." Without giving her an opportunity to comment, he straightened in the seat, restarted the engine, and pulled out on the road.

He drove for several minutes, and she saw the sign "Balad AB," and knew they had left the Army portion of the installation. She stared out the window as Hawk continued to drive. He eventually stopped in front of a dining hall. He leaned back in the seat, his arms draped over the wheel, his face a study in seriousness.

He turned and looked at her without speaking. *Her face was the picture of confusion. He'd probably scared the hell out of her back there, but he had to put some space between them—now.*

"I thought—"

"I know, Kit. You have to be confused, and it's my fault. I said we needed to talk, and we do. But, I need to get my head on straight first, so we're going to have lunch."

"O-kay."

He jumped out of the vehicle, and this time Kit got out without waiting for him. She looked around curiously. Hawk strode ahead of her, and once inside the dining hall, headed straight for a table in the back of the hall. The room was crowded and several people hailed him, but he just waved and continued toward the table.

He was hoping not to see anyone from his squadron. Most of them knew Mark, and if he had to introduce Kit, they would realize that she was Mark's sister. He definitely didn't want that to happen. He probably shouldn't even have come here, but where else was there? Certainly not Popeye's or Burger King.

Hawk was walking so fast that Kit could hardly keep up with him. *What was wrong with him? What was the rush? He finally stopped at a table nearly hidden in a dark corner. He pulled a chair out for her so her back would be to the wall and facing the dining room. Most men chose to sit with their backs to the wall, facing the action. She would have bet that Hawk was one of them.*

101

So why wasn't he doing it now? The only explanation was—he didn't want anyone to speak to him, or see her with him! He'd also bypassed the chow line.

"I wanted to get this table before it was taken. I'll go through the line for both of us. What would you like?" She hesitated, and he continued, "The food's not bad here."

"Just a salad and coffee."

"What kind of dressing?"

"Italian is fine."

"I'll be right back."

He left the table, and she was alone with her thoughts. *Why had he pulled away from her so abruptly on the way here? And why the abrupt change of attitude now? She could understand the "wrong time and wrong place." After all, they were in a war zone, in the middle of a war . . . but the "wrong man." Why did he keep insisting that? It didn't compute with Mark's, "He needs you." Mark would never let Hawk near her if he really wasn't good enough for her—heck, that had always been her objection, his "vetting" all her boyfriends. So, what was going on? She just couldn't think about it now.*

She looked out across the crowded space. Several women had just come in. They were wearing flight suits with pilot wings, and one of them had stopped to talk with Hawk. The woman turned and glanced at her, then smiled before turning back to Hawk.

A wave of jealousy shot through her. The woman was gorgeous. Who was she? It made no sense for her to feel jealous—but she was. She couldn't stop watching. Hawk reached the cashier's desk and paid for their meals. As he headed toward her, he turned around and laughed in response to something the woman called after him.

What had she said?

Hawk set their food on the table, put the tray on a nearby rack, and pulled out his chair.

"She's very beautiful." *Had she really said that out loud?* She looked away from Hawk and turned her attention to the food in front of her.

"Isabelle? Yes, she is."

If he thought her comment out of place, he didn't indicate it, but he didn't elaborate either. And I'll be damned if I'll pursue it, even though I want to. She focused on the salad in front of her, struggling for something to say as the silence between them lengthened uncomfortably. "Hawk—"

"Kit—"

They broke into laughter as they both spoke at the same time. The tension between them eased somewhat, but Kit still wouldn't look at him.

"What's wrong, Kit?"

She looked up, startled. "Nothing."

"Then why are you staring at that salad as if you expect to find bugs crawling in it?" She snapped her head up, wrinkling her nose at his description.

"Yuk! And, I'm not!" *She felt the heat rise to her face. Thank goodness he couldn't read her mind. He was still watching her, and then he spoke softly.*

"Kit, Isabelle is just a friend." Her eyes flashed back at him.

"Did I ask? I just said she was beautiful."

"That she is. She's also a good pilot, and we've flown together a long time. We're <u>friends</u>."

"I'm sorry Hawk; it's really none of my business. I just . . . every time I'm with you, I . . . it's like I'm a different person. I say things I don't want to say, blurt outrageous

103

questions, like—" She looked down at her plate and shook her head in disbelief. *She'd done it again.*

"And why do you think that is, Kit? You know, you're not the only one. I've already told you things I've never told anyone before."

Hawk's voice was soft, and she looked up, studying him. "I don't know. You didn't call, Hawk. Why didn't you call?" She bit her lip, and squinched her eyes. *She hadn't meant to say that either . . . but she needed to know.*

Hawk brushed his hand across his face. *He knew he'd hurt her, and he didn't want to answer the question, but she deserved an explanation—he just wasn't sure he could give it.* "I'm sorry I left Taji in such a rush Kit, but it was necessary—if I hadn't left right <u>then</u>, we would have been in bed together that night." He watched her eyes widen in surprise. Her mouth dropped open. Then her face reddened. His eyes speared hers. "I see you know I'm telling the truth." He watched the turmoil in her eyes suddenly change to anger.

"It's Mark, isn't it? If I had been any other woman, you wouldn't have hesitated. I hate you, Hawk Hawkins."

Her answer surprised him, and he laughed. "No, you don't, Kit. You're angry, but you don't hate me. And yes, you're partially right—but you're also partially wrong. Right, if it had been another woman . . . but it wasn't, it was you. And, it has nothing to do with Mark; I'm not afraid of your brother." He smiled, remembering Mark's ". . . ass is grass" remark. "He knows I wouldn't purposely hurt you."

Kit leaned forward, but before she could say anything, Hawk continued.

"I said I wouldn't hurt you <u>purposely</u>. I know I did hurt you, and I'm sorry. But Kit, I'm not the right man for you." His voice was gruff with determination. *That was definitely the wrong thing to say—he knew it the minute the words were out of his mouth. It was like setting a match to tinder.*

"Damn it all, Hawk. You make me so mad I could—I could . . . spit," she sputtered.

"I wouldn't advise it here," he said dryly, unable to contain a grin. *She was delightful, a combination of irrepressible gamine and outrageous hoyden, definitely one of a kind.*

"Don't you dare laugh at me."

He scrubbed the grin from his face, but his eyes still sparkled with mirth when he spoke. "I wouldn't think of it." Kit glared back at him, but as he watched, the anger seemed to flow out of her, and her eyes filled with sadness.

"Why any other woman Hawk, but not me? What's wrong with me? If it's not my brothers, it must be me . . ."

Her voice trailed off, and he knew he'd really hurt her. There probably wasn't any way he could make it right, but he had to try. "Kit, look at me. It's <u>because</u> you're not like any other woman." Her head flew up, anger again brightening her eyes. He reached out and touched her hand where it lay on the table between them. "Don't Kit. With any other woman, it wouldn't have meant anything more than an enjoyable evening spent with a pleasant companion—and despite what you have heard, it doesn't happen all that often—and certainly not with the lovely Isabelle." At this last, he cocked one eyebrow and grinned, before continuing.

105

"With you, Kit, it wouldn't have been that. It would have been much more. You're too special. Men, including me, always know that. Kit, you need a good man—one worthy of you, a man who will love you."

"You keep saying you're no good for me, that you're not the man for me. Well—"

He watched her draw herself up and look him squarely in the eyes. Then she tipped her chin defiantly. Oh Lord, he was in trouble here.

"Did it ever occur to you that I might be—that I might be the woman for you?"

He almost spit his coffee across the table. *Her slight hesitation and the rosy blush told him she wasn't as confident as she was trying to appear and his heart warmed. He wanted to scoop her up in his arms and protect her forever. Of course, he couldn't. But, how could he keep from hurting her anymore?* "Ah, Kit, don't—"

"Hawk Hawkins, if you tell me again that I don't know you, that I don't know your shadowed past, so help me, I won't be responsible—"

She was looking at her water glass, and he wondered if she was thinking about throwing it at him. He could believe it of her. Anyone taking on this woman would be guaranteed an interesting life. She thought she wanted him, but he was no good for her. Somehow, he had to convince her to back off. If she knew the true story about his past, she probably wouldn't want him. Hell, Carol hadn't, he thought bitterly. Maybe he should just tell her . . . but he wasn't ready to go that far, not yet anyway. He almost flinched when she picked up her glass of water—he thought she was going to throw it at him—but she raised it to her lips, took a long drink, and then carefully set it back down. She studied him. She was waiting for him to continue, and he truly didn't know what to say. "Kit, we really <u>don't</u> know each other." *That spark was back in her eyes, and he put up his hand.* "Now wait a minute, Kit. Just listen to me."

She sat back, but the storm clouds were still in her eyes. She definitely didn't want to listen. He frowned. "Kit, what I said before—you deserve a man who loves you with all his heart . . . but . . . don't expect to hear those words from me. I swore a long time ago I'd never say them again. I can't. I don't believe in love. It doesn't exist, not for me anyway."

Kit went still. *It felt as if her heart had stopped beating. She knew in that instant that it was too late for her—she already loved him. Now what? Could she love enough for both of them? Was loving him enough? It would have to be, for she knew with deep certainty that she couldn't walk away from him. He needed her, even if he couldn't see it, and wouldn't admit it if he did.*

Shocked by her stillness and the sheen of tears in her eyes, Hawk leaned across the table toward her. "Kit, I'm sorry, but that's the way it is." At first, she didn't respond, then she blinked and bit her lip so hard he was afraid it would bleed. It was all he could do to keep from touching her.

"But, Hawk, why? Surely you know people who have been in love."

"Maybe, but not for me." *He felt as if a knife were cutting into his heart. This was the hardest thing he'd ever had to do.*

His frozen expression told her there was nothing more to say. If there was a way to change his mind, she didn't know what it was—and he wouldn't listen anyway, at least not now.

The intercom suddenly blared out in a burst of static, "Lieutenant Vail you have a telephone call. Lieutenant Vail, phone call."

Kit's heart dropped. "Oh no, not now."

"What is it, Kit?"

"I don't know, but I can guess. They got the dozer repaired and they're ready to head back. I thought, at least I hoped . . . I'll be right back." She rose from her chair and headed for the office.

Hawk watched her go with mixed feelings. *On the one hand he was relieved—she would have pressed for more details. He wasn't ready to give those details, but the hell of it was, he didn't want her to go either.* He gritted his teeth. *Get a grip, Hawkins—you can't have it both ways.* When he looked up, Kit was coming toward him, and her expression said her guess had been right— they were heading back.

"It's repaired?"

She nodded. "They're leaving ASAP. Have to get started before the weather turns." She sighed. "Well . . ."

Hawk rose from his chair and took her elbow. "Come on Kit, I'll walk you out. Are they going to pick you up here?"

She nodded again, unable to speak through her disappointment.

He wanted to make her feel better, but what was left to say that would not make matters worse? He'd already said it all. As they neared the exit, he could see the convoy approaching. He couldn't just let her go, not like this. "Stop worrying, Kit. It'll be all right." He glanced around and pushed her behind a large menu sign. Without thinking, he grabbed her shoulders and gave her the kiss he'd been aching to give her since she had arrived that morning. The feel of her body against his, drove every thought but her from his mind. She murmured his name, and he tightened the embrace, and deepened the kiss. Suddenly, the sound of a horn impinged on his consciousness, and he broke the kiss and pushed her away. "Your ride is here, Kit," he rasped." As he motioned toward the street, he spoke softly, "Stay safe, Kitten."

Kit nodded mutely before turning abruptly toward the door.

As she pushed it open, he called after her, "Goodbye Kit, I'll be in touch." She didn't turn around, and he wondered if she had heard him.

Chapter 7

An hour later, Kit was watching the road ahead, her eyes moving from one side to the other. Nothing was visible except the constantly swirling sand, a few random palms, and the rolling dunes. She wasn't in the lead vehicle this trip, but they all knew better than to relax their vigilance. While her eyes searched for signs of danger, her thoughts spun in circles trying to make sense out of Hawk's changeable actions. His kiss had been totally unexpected. She could still feel the imprint of his lips on hers, but then—like always—he had pushed her away, his face set and his mouth clamped. As she'd walked away from him and out of the building, he'd called something after her, she wasn't sure what, and it had been beyond her to answer. She'd had to escape before she broke down, and it had taken sheer willpower and all the strength she possessed to face her troops with a smile.

When the attack came, there was nothing they could do. One minute the road was clear—the next the bomb went off, rocking the lead vehicle. Shots came from somewhere over the hill. Kit drew her sidearm as her driver, Bones, took a hit in the arm. He continued to steer the vehicle, but it veered crazily. Smitty, the gunner, was most exposed. He was hit and immediately slumped over his gun. She was still trying to determine where the shots were coming from when a mortar round flipped the Humvee and she found herself under a pile of mangled metal, her right leg pinned. She could hear the men in the vehicles around her returning fire and herself screaming, "Don't you <u>dare</u> let them take my leg!" Then everything went black.

Hawk woke instantly at the ringing of the telephone beside his bed. He automatically noted the time— 0300—as he reached for it with an uneasy feeling. "Captain Hawkins here."

The caller didn't immediately speak, and when he did, he seemed hesitant. "Captain Hawkins, this is Sergeant Bonesworth—they call me Bones. You may not remember me—"

"You're one of Lieutenant Vail's men, aren't you?"

"Yes Sir."

Hawk couldn't think of any reason the man would be calling him at this time of night.

"I'm sorry about the time, Sir. They took me to surgery, and I guess I was out of it for a while. When I came to, I had to convince the nurse to get me a phone."

It suddenly hit Hawk. The man had said 'surgery'. "What the hell happened, Sergeant? Why did you need surgery? Where's the Lieutenant?"

"Well, Sir, that's why I'm calling. I thought maybe you wouldn't have heard, and I—"

"Go on. What happened? Is Lieutenant Vail all right?"

111

He was gripping the telephone so tightly his fingers had turned white.

"Sir, we were attacked yesterday, just about an hour out of Balad."

"Attacked?!"

"Yes Sir. The vehicle in front of ours ran over an IED. Then our vehicle got hit. The insurgents were just over the hill and we didn't see them until they started firing. Smitty, our gunner, bought it. They got me in the arm, but—"

Hawk's voice was raw as visions of the scene painted his mind. "Stop hesitating, man. Was the Lieutenant hurt? Where is she?"

"Yes Sir. The convoy started firing back, but we still couldn't see much. The lieutenant saw them first and got one guy as he started over the top of the hill. But we took a mortar round and it flipped our Humvee over."

"Was the Lieutenant hurt?" He emphasized each word as he tried to get the man to hurry up and get to the point.

"Yes Sir. Pretty bad, I think. Her leg got pinned under the vehicle and she kept screaming, 'Don't you guys let them take my leg off! Don't you dare!' Then, I think she passed out. We managed to chase them off. That's their style," he muttered bitterly, "hit and run."

Hawk couldn't breathe. *He was losing it, could barely hear the sergeant. By a supreme exercise of will, he pulled himself back from the edge. The man couldn't be talking about Kit, not his Kit.* He squeezed his eyes shut, holding the phone in a death grip, realizing he'd thought of her as 'his.' *He was afraid to ask the next question, but he had to.* "Bones, answer me. Where is the Lieutenant? Did they take her leg off?"

112

"I . . . yes Sir, I . . . she was pinned in the twisted . . . it's the only way they could get her out. There wasn't any other way. She's here now, we all are."

"Where's here?"

"The Anaconda Field Hospital at Balad, Sir—it was the closest. They helo'd us here by Blackhawk."

Hawk groaned.

"Sir. You still there, Sir?"

"I'm here." He spoke gruffly, barely able to get the words around the lump in his throat. "Is she all right?"

"They told me Smitty was the only one who didn't make it, but that's all I could find out. I thought you might not get the word . . . and Lieutenant Vail . . . I know—"

"I'm really grateful for the call, Sergeant. Thank you. If there's ever <u>anything</u> I can do for you, you call me. I mean it."

"Yes Sir. I have to go now."

"Right, and thanks, man. Take care of yourself."

"Yes Sir."

Hawk heard the phone being disconnected, but he continued to sit on the edge of the bed, holding the phone in numb fingers, trying to accept what he had just heard. *Kit was hurt! Did Mark know? He'd have gotten a call—he was Kit's next of kin.* Then he noticed the blinking light on his phone. He'd been so tired when he came in, he flopped on the bed and dozed off without checking for messages. He punched the button, and heard Mark's frantic voice, "Hawk, call me, no matter what time it is. Use my cell phone or you won't get me. I'm leaving as soon as I can get things lined up." *His voice sounded choked as if he were close to tears. He understood—he felt like crying himself.*

113

Mark knew. He slowly picked up his cell phone and punched in Mark's number. As he listened to the ringing and waited for Mark to pick up, his mind projected an image of Kit as they had said good-by only hours ago. He rubbed his hand over his eyes, trying to keep his mind from imagining the worst.

"Hawk—you got my message?"

"Just now. I know about Kit—I just got off the phone with one of her men, but all he knew was that they had taken her leg off, and that she's here at Balad. Mark, how is she? Is she going to be all right?"

"Hawk, slow down. I can't understand you. I don't know any more than what you just said. Her outfit called a few hours ago. Their medic had to take her leg off to get her out. I haven't been able to talk to her yet. She was still in surgery when they called. I already got emergency leave—that's what I've been doing. I'm on my way there now. They'll probably keep her until they get her stabilized. That's why I called; I wanted to ask you to check on her 'til I get there. You <u>will</u> go see her, right?"

"That's a dumb question! Of course I'm going to see her—as soon as I can get dressed."

"They might not let you see her, since you're not related—"

"They'll let me see her."

Mark could hear the "or else" Hawk didn't voice. "Call me as soon as you've seen her—and see if you can find out when they expect to take her to Landstuhl. Damn it, Hawk. Why Kit? Why not me?"

"Mark, stop it; she <u>will</u> be all right." *He knew just how his friend felt, but Kit had to be all right, she had to be.* "I'm going now, Mark. I need to call the hospital."

"Okay. I'll see you tomorrow."

"Tomorrow." Hawk put his cell phone down, picked up the base telephone, and asked the operator for the hospital registrar. Minutes later he'd verified that Kit was at the hospital. At first, they had refused to give him any information, but he'd finally convinced them he was calling for her brother. He'd been able to get her room number and learn that she was out of surgery.

He hung up and grabbed a clean flight suit, donning it without conscious thought. A glance in the mirror convinced him he'd better shave. Fifteen minutes later, he was out in front of the BOQ with the keys to the desk clerk's vehicle, having promised to have it back by daylight. In the car, he looked in the mirror and rubbed one hand over his face. *It's a wonder I didn't cut my face all to hell. He cussed impatiently at the 25mph speed limit, drawing a breath of relief when he finally pulled up in front of the hospital. He hesitated just inside the door of the building and looked around. He hadn't asked on the phone if they would let him see Kit— he could make a better case in person. Luckily, the registrar remembered his call and directed him to the surgical ward, where the nurse on duty looked up as he approached her desk.* "I understand you have Lieutenant Kit Vail here?"

The nurse was tall and angular; her hair pulled tight and clipped on top of her head. She looked harried, and she eyed him suspiciously. "And you are?"

He swallowed and then blurted out, "Her fiancé." *He spoke the lie without remorse—he had to see Kit, and they might not let him unless they thought he was someone close to her.* His ruse was successful, and she nodded and pointed him down the hall.

115

"She's in room 3."

When he reached the room, another nurse was just leaving. She accepted his presence without question.

"She's been very restless since they brought her in, Captain. The sedative we gave her will be wearing off soon and she may wake up. We pretty much keep her sedated. I'll be back to check her IV bag. You may stay with her, if you wish."

He nodded. "I do."

She left, and he sat down in the only seat in the room, a straight chair beside the bed. His eyes were drawn to the tent holding the sheet off what was now only a stump. He felt a sharp tug in the area of his heart as he looked at the woman lying so still in the narrow bed. *She was beautiful, even with her hair all mussed and damp.* He reached out and softly brushed it off her forehead. She turned her head slightly, as if looking for something, but her eyes remained closed, lashes fanned across her pale cheeks. *There was a neat row of stitches across her forehead. Otherwise her face was unmarked, but it was as pale as the moonlight sifting in through the room's only window.*

She looked so vulnerable, lying there asleep. There was no sign now of the feisty, determined, and independent woman he knew her to be. Their time together had been so short. He knew now he'd only been fooling himself when he thought he could let her go. Now they would be separated by circumstances and distance—but he'd do whatever it took to make sure she stayed in his life. He still had three months left here in Iraq, and she had a long, hard period of recovery. If only he could be there to help her through it. He curled his hands into fists, and his mouth firmed in a determined line. Maybe he couldn't be there physically, but he would help her get through it.

He had been sitting there almost an hour when Kit became restless, turning her head from side to side, frowning and groaning. "No, no! Don't let them take my leg! Not my leg!" She became increasingly upset, and Hawk reached out and laid his hand on her shoulder. "Kit. Kit. Don't—you'll hurt yourself. It's all right."

She stilled instantly, and another frown flitted across her face. Her arms were at her sides, on top of the sheet, and he reached down and took one of her hands. So small. He folded it into his own large one and gently squeezed. She was so tiny. How did she grow up to become a soldier? He felt her hand move and looked up to find her startling blue eyes regarding him with a mixture of confusion and curiosity. "Hello," he said softly.

"Hawk?"

"It's me. How are you feeling, Kitten?"

She grimaced, and a tremor went through her body. "I've been better."

She squeezed her eyes shut and he could tell she was trying to hold back tears. He wanted to comfort her but didn't know what to do. Obviously, the sedative was still affecting her because she blinked slowly.

"I'm so tired, so . . . tired. Hawk . . . don't leave me. I'm afraid."

"I won't, Kit, I promise. I'm going to stay right here." No sooner had he said the last word than her eyes drifted closed. When he tried to pull his hand free, she held on tightly. When the nurse came back in a little while later, Kit was still asleep and still holding his hand.

"She seems much calmer than the last time I came in.

117

Has she been awake at all?"

"Just for a few minutes. She said she was tired and went back to sleep."

"I won't give her any more medicine so long as she's calm. If you'll move, I need to check her vitals."

The minute Hawk removed his hand from Kit's, she started twisting and turning and mumbling. When he took her hand back, she calmed immediately.

"That's amazing! You seem to reassure her. What's your relationship? Are you close?"

"Yes." *He didn't elaborate on the brief answer. Afraid to repeat his earlier lie, and unable to think how to explain his relationship to Kit, he was relieved the nurse simply accepted what he had said.*

"Well, you seem to be doing a better job of calming her than the medicine. I'll leave her for now. If there's any change, just push the button on her headboard."

Kit slept quietly, her hand continuing to rest in his. He must have dozed off too, for he was jarred awake by the entrance of the nurse he had spoken with earlier.

"She's still sleeping quietly?"

"As long as I hold her hand."

The nurse smiled at him, then seemed to recall why she was there. "There's a call at the desk from a man who says he's her brother. He wanted to speak with her, but I told him she was sleeping. Will you talk to him, or do you want me to have him call back?"

Hawk figured it must be Mark and was surprised he hadn't called his cell phone. He looked down at his hand, clasping Kit's. Would she wake up if he removed it?

The nurse seemed to understand. "I'll stay here with her if you want to take the call."

118

"Okay. I won't be long." He carefully and slowly let go of her hand, then stood a few minutes waiting to see what would happen. Kit didn't seem to realize he was no longer holding her hand, so he nodded and left the room. At the desk, he picked up the phone and said, "Mark?"

A gruff voice answered. "No! This is Jon. Who the hell are you? And why are you with Kit?"

"I'm Captain Hawk Hawkins. You're Kit's twin! I'm glad you called. I was afraid no one would be able to reach you."

"No one did. Now tell me, why are you answering when I asked for my sister? Where's Kit?"

Hawk could understand Jon's frustration, and knew Kit would be really glad to hear from him. "I'll tell you anything you want to know, but wouldn't you rather hear about Kit first?"

"Yes Sir. I shouldn't have said—"

"Forget it. I would have done the same. They brought Kit here yesterday afternoon. She had been at Anaconda for a meeting with the TO here—came up with a convoy from her outfit. We had lunch together. Her mechanics finished their job early and she left before we finished lunch, about 1330. They were an hour from here when they ran over an IED, and then mortar fire flipped the vehicle Kit was in."

Jon's indrawn breath told Hawk he was picturing exactly what had happened. "Go on, Sir."

"Kit was pinned in the wreckage of the vehicle, and . . . and the only way they could free her was to amputate her leg."

"No!"

The silence told Hawk that Jon was probably fighting back tears. He waited.

When Jon finally spoke, his voice was quiet. "Is—is she all right? Is she conscious yet? Does she know?"

"The answer to all three of your questions is 'yes.' She was pretty much doped up last night, but she woke up for a few minutes a little while ago. She recognized me, and she knows her leg is gone."

"How's she taking it?"

"Knowing Kit, what do you think? That woman has more courage—"

"I'd still like answers to my first questions if you don't mind, Sir."

Hawk smiled, "You mean, who the hell am I, and what the hell am I doing here?"

"Umm, basically, yeah."

"Well, first of all, I'm Mark's best friend. We went through flight school together—"

"So you're that Hawk Hawkins! I remember now, Mark's mentioned you."

"I'm sure he has."

"That doesn't explain—"

"I'm getting there. I'm assigned here at Balad. When Mark found out I was only about three hours from Taji, he asked me to look Kit up. Kit was not happy when she found out he was checking on her again."

Jon laughed. "No, she wouldn't be. I take it she got over that, you being there and all."

"You might say that. We've become . . . friends."

"Kit usually tells me about her "friends," but I've never heard her mention you.

"Yeah, well that brings me to a question. How did you find out about Kit? She said you were on some secret assignment, 'incommunicado' in her words."

"I was, but I knew the instant it happened, I knew

120

something bad had happened to her. I always know when something happens to Kit. I suppose you don't believe that, but—"

"I do believe it, I do. Kit is the same about you."

"You must know her pretty well . . . if you know that."

Hawk swallowed, memories getting in the way of his words. "I guess I do know her pretty well, and I think she's a pretty special woman."

"She is, and you better not do anything to hurt her . . . or it won't make a bit of difference to me that you're a captain and I'm enlisted."

He spoke so fiercely that Hawk didn't doubt him for a minute. "Believe me, Jon, hurting Kit is the farthest thing from my mind. Can you say where you are? Are you able to get here? She misses you so much, seeing you would really help her."

"I don't know, man. I moved heaven and earth just to get to a telephone. I couldn't reach Mark—he must know."

"He does. I talked to him yesterday. He's already got emergency leave and is on his way. He'll be here tomorrow . . . today. But, if you didn't talk to Mark, how did you know to call here?"

"I finally reached Matt, and he told me where she was, but he didn't mention her leg. Said Mark just told him she'd been in an accident and he'd get back to him as soon as he saw her. Is she staying there long?"

"I don't know. I know that once she's stabilized, they'll move her to Landstuhl in Germany. She'll get an evac flight from there." Jon's voice became muffled, and Hawk realized he had covered the receiver and was talking to someone in the background.

When he spoke into the phone again, he said, "Tell her that, that . . . tell her I'll be there. I'm gonna try and get to where you are now. In three days, I won't be able to leave here. If I come, it's gotta be now. I've already talked to my CO, and he's working on it for me."

Hawk was amazed. "You were that sure she was badly hurt that you did all this before you even knew anything?"

"I told you—we always know . . . since we were kids."

"Look Jon. I'm gonna give you my cell number. Keep in touch so I can update you on anything new. You sure you want me to tell her you're coming—you don't want to surprise her?"

"She'll know. Hey, I gotta go. I'll be in touch." He didn't say anything for a minute, then spoke again. "Captain, you take good care of my sister, you hear?"

"Jon, I swear I won't let anybody or anything hurt her, and that's a promise."

"Thanks. I . . . sorry, I was rude."

"Forget it. I'm looking forward to meeting you. Kit says you're her other half."

"Yeah . . . bye, Captain."

Hawk was pretty sure he heard tears in the tough SEAL's voice. He and his sister were obviously an amazing pair. He replaced the telephone and hurried back to Kit's room, hoping she hadn't become restless in his absence.

The nurse looked up as he entered the room. She had a puzzled look on her face. "I'm glad you're back Captain. It's the most amazing thing. You hadn't been out of the room but a few minutes when she started tossing around in the bed, moving her hand around as if searching for yours. Then she started mumbling. I was just coming to look for you."

Hawk moved to Kit's bedside. As soon as he took Kit's hand in his, she stilled, and the mumbling stopped. She appeared to be in relaxed sleep once again. *He was surprised at the feeling of joy he felt knowing she needed his presence, that she reacted in this way to his touch . . . even if she didn't know it. He knew it, and he'd never forget it.*

The nurse, reassured that Kit was again sleeping, quietly turned to go. "I'll have a more comfortable chair brought in for you, Captain. Then, if you go to sleep you won't break your neck."

"Only if it's not too much trouble. I'll be fine."

Kit slowly opened her eyes and looked around. *It was obviously very early; barely light judging by the patch of sky visible through the window. Security lights were still burning. She was in a hospital somewhere, but how long had she been here? Her leg! Memory returned, and she forced herself to look down. As soon as she saw the tent, she knew—they had taken her leg! A scream rose in her throat. She bit down hard, grinding her teeth to keep the scream inside, a technique she had learned during years spent growing up as the little sister of four older brothers whose delight it was to make her scream. And what about her men—did they survive? She forced her mind backwards in time. The convoy had been returning from Balad to Taji when they had been attacked. Bones and Smitty had been hit before the mortar round had tipped the vehicle over, pinning her leg. She remem-*

bered screaming at her guys, "Don't you dare let them take my leg!" She groaned, and another tear slid its way down her cheek. As if they could do anything to stop it.

She gripped the sheet in both fists; then noticed the IV coming out of one hand. It pulled, and she relaxed that fist. Another tear forced its way out of one eye and rolled slowly down her cheek. *Hawk! She had dreamed he was here in her room. Would anyone tell him what had happened? Probably better he didn't know.* Turning her face to the wall, she let the tears come.

They had probably contacted Mark, but she hoped he wouldn't come. She wasn't ready to face anyone yet, not Mark or her other brothers, and certainly not Hawk. What would he think when he found out? Mark would tell him for sure. She sighed, wishing he was beside her—needing his strength. *God, she was in bad shape. They had no future—but she still wished he were here.*

Suddenly she knew she wasn't alone in the room. She slowly turned her head, and in the dim light, she could see someone sitting beside her bed. *Hawk! He was asleep in the chair, his head at an awkward angle. The shadow of beard on his lean cheeks gave him a dangerous look. How long had he been here? She remembered the dream—it must have been real. Hawk's hand lay on her bed, palm up, and she struggled to grab the fleeting memory of him holding her hand during the night.* Carefully, she slid her hand over on top of his, their palms together. Instantly his strong fingers closed around hers.

She watched him sleep, and a feeling of tenderness swept through her. *He pretended to be so tough, but his face was relaxed in sleep, and she could see the little boy he once had been. Had anyone ever truly loved him before her? Before her! No! She couldn't love him—not —not now.* Tears filled her eyes, and she snatched her hand away from his.

Hawk woke immediately and leaned toward her, his eyes filled with tenderness and compassion. "Aw, Kit." His head lowered, and his lips brushed hers softly. The kiss was gentle, meant to comfort, and it did.

"Hawk, have you been here all night?

"Since 0330."

"I was afraid it was a dream."

What was?"

"You being here. You held my hand, didn't you?"

"All night. It's the only way you would sleep quietly. Every time I took my hand away you started to struggle and cry out, so the nurse let me stay. She said I was better than a sedative. I'm not sure that helps my image." He smiled and reached for her hand. "Why did you pull away just now?"

"How did you know? You were asleep."

"I knew. Why, Kit?"

She turned away from him, unable to answer. *She couldn't tell him yet.*

He reached out, and one strong finger pulled her face around until she was looking at him. She stared wordlessly into his dark eyes, tears filling hers. "Oh Hawk—" She closed her eyes, then opened them, and swallowed.

He couldn't take his eyes off her. She was forcing herself to be strong, as if she reached deep down inside and pulled herself up. This was one amazing woman.

"How did you find out—that I was here?"

"Bones called me."

"Bones?"

125

"You know, your driver."

"I know . . . he was with me . . . he got shot. Is he all right?"

"I'm not sure. I think he said he'd had surgery. I was—I didn't ask. He said he was afraid no one would have told me, and he knew you would want me to know."

She smiled slightly, remembering how Bones had teased her about "her flyboy from Balad."

"I'll be eternally grateful to that man. I told him if he ever needed anything, all he had to do was call me."

"You don't even know him."

"I know enough. He obviously cares about you and knew I would want to know what happened to you."

"What about the rest of them Hawk? I think—I'm afraid Smitty was killed. I saw him take a hit, and it looked bad. He's dead, isn't he?"

Hawk slowly nodded. "Bones said Smitty was the only one who didn't make it."

She reached out, and her fingers closed around his as a sob threatened to overwhelm her.

Hawk couldn't take it any longer. He slid his chair closer to the edge of her bed, and leaned over, careful to avoid jarring her. Putting a hand on either side of her face, he lowered his head and kissed her softly, then leaned his forehead on hers.

"I wish you could hold me, Hawk."

"Me too, Kit, me too. But I'm afraid I would hurt you."

The tears Kit had been holding in broke loose and she cried softly.

"Go ahead and cry, Kit. Let it all out. You've earned the right." He leaned his chin on her head. *She was so strong and so brave. He felt honored she'd let him see*

126

her tears. Somehow, he knew she never let most people see any sign of weakness. A surge of protectiveness flowed through him as he carefully ran his fingers through her curls. *He swore to himself he would do whatever it took to keep this woman safe. It didn't occur to him to wonder how or when or even why. He just knew he would.*

It was amazing how just Hawk's presence helped, Kit thought, as she enjoyed the feel of his hand in her hair and the comfort of his warm body next to her. A sudden, sharp pain caused her to take a deep breath, and she bit back a groan.

Hawk sat up and gave her a sharp look, instantly aware of her discomfort. "Are you in pain, Kit? The nurse told me to buzz her if you needed anything."

"I, no, not as long as I don't move." She shut her eyes and clenched her hands on the blanket. "I wonder if Mark knows yet."

"He does. I talked to him just before I came over here. He's already on his way."

"I don't want him to come."

Hawk smiled. "I don't think you can stop him, I don't think anyone could stop him. You know that, Kit." *She sighed, and the look of vulnerability in her eyes nearly undid him.*

"I don't want him—I don't want anyone to see me like this."

"Like what, Kit? You're beautiful."

She looked at him, and the hopelessness in her eyes worried him.

"You lie. Like when you told me I looked 'lovely' in my ACU's."

He reached out and grasped her shoulders, lowering

127

his face until he was right over hers.

"I don't lie, Kit Vail. You did, and you do—look lovely, I mean. Remember this, if you don't remember anything else—I won't lie to you, not ever." As he said it, he felt a twinge remembering he'd told the nurse she was his fiancée.

She blinked. *Why was he telling her this so emphatically now? She couldn't get her mind around it, so she pushed it away to study later, and just nodded.* "When is Mark coming?"

"I told you, he's already on his way." Then he grinned. "I have a surprise for you. Someone else is coming too."

"Hawk, I told you I don't want people to see me."

"I thought we already went through that. Besides, I think you'll really want to see . . . Jon."

Her eyes widened. "Jon is coming here? But he's—we don't know where he is."

"He knew Kit. He knew, and <u>he</u> called. I talked to him last night while you were sleeping. I don't know where he was, but he said he'd be here before you leave Iraq."

Kit put her hands up to her face. "Jon is coming. I should have realized he'd know."

"You two are amazing. I don't think I could have believed it if I hadn't seen it with my own eyes—the way you seem to be attached by an invisible line." He shook his head, and then looked at his watch. "I'm going to have to leave soon, Kit. I've been waiting for you to wake up so I could tell you about Jon. The medics will be chasing me out when the doctor starts making rounds. I'll check with them to see what they have scheduled for you, and then I need to go back to my quarters and clean up. I'll check in with the squadron, and if I can get the day off, I'll be back this afternoon. If not, I'll see you this evening. I think you can expect Mark by tomorrow for sure."

Kit looked up at him, and squeezed his hand tightly. "Thank you, Hawk."

"For what?"

"For coming, for staying with me last night." She hesitated, then continued. "When we said goodbye yesterday, I didn't think I would ever see you again."

He leaned down and kissed her gently. "I told you I'd call you. Didn't you hear me?"

"I heard, but I didn't believe you."

Remorse shook him. *She had every reason to think that.* "Kitten, I'm so sorry—sorry that we fought, sorry I couldn't explain, sorry for what I said. But I would have called. I knew I shouldn't, but there was no way I could stop myself from calling you." He saw the doubt in her eyes, and leaned over her again. "Believe it."

She shook her head sadly and looked down at the tent on the bed—covering where her leg should have been.

"Aw, Kit."

The softness of his voice surprised her, and she looked up in time to see the compassion in his dark eyes. Instantly, she pulled her hand free of his, eyes flashing anger. "Hawk Hawkins, don't you dare feel sorry for me. I don't want your pity."

"And that's not what you're getting." Immediately aware of his mistake, Hawk back-pedaled quickly. "Why on earth would anyone pity you, you prickly, hard-headed, stubborn woman? You won't be as good as you were—"

Shocked at his words, Kit gasped, but Hawk wasn't finished.

"You won't be as good as you were—you'll be

better—just to prove to the world you can do it." He inclined his head slightly, one eyebrow raised, and the curve of his mouth turned up as he waited for her reaction.

Still in shock, Kit studied him carefully before answering. Then a frail grin broke through, and despite the sheen of unshed tears, she answered him. "You're damn right I will be! We Vails never give up, and don't you forget it!"

Glad that his intuition had been correct, Hawk squeezed her hand gently. and kissed the top of her head. "That sounds more like the Kit Vail I know and love."

Kit looked at him in disbelief. *'Love!' Had she heard right? Did he realize what he had said? Her eyes darted to him, but there was nothing in them to indicate that it had been any more than the repetition of a well-used phrase. Afraid to question him lest she hadn't heard correctly, Kit let it go, for now. She'd think about it later.*

"You said Mark will be here tomorrow?" She sounded resigned. "I suppose the rest of them are coming, too. Just what I need, the four of them telling me what I should have done and what I need to do now—and telling me that I look like a wet cat and—"

She blinked quickly, and Hawk struggled to keep the sympathy out of his voice, knowing that not only would she not want it, but that it would be the last straw as far as she was concerned. "Kit Vail! Don't tell me you're looking for sympathy. When have you ever let anyone, your brothers most of all, beat you down? And anyway, they're not all coming. Mark convinced them to wait until you get to D.C. He's the only one coming, or that's what he thinks. He doesn't know about Jon. I predict that within five minutes of Mark's hitting the door, you'll have him standing back cowering and shaking in his boots."

The image of Mark cowering before anything, let alone her, was too much. Kit felt laughter bubble up in her chest. Her laughter brought tears to Hawk's eyes, and he lowered his face to her hair so she couldn't see.

"Okay," Kit said, trying to sound resigned, although she really did want to see her brother. She just dreaded all his questions. Suddenly she grinned up at him. "Aren't you worried?"

Puzzled, he answered, "Worried?"

"About his threat. You remember—the lawn-mower?"

To his delight, she giggled. He'd been afraid his bubbly Kit would be gone forever.

"Have I hurt you, Kit?"

"Hurt me?" She hesitated before answering.

He had hurt her, and he knew it, but her answer, when it came, surprised and pleased him.

"No, no you didn't."

"Then I guess we don't have anything to worry about, do we?"

He smiled down at her, and Kit blushed and hid her chin in the sheets as she mumbled, "Guess not."

A nurse breezed in and announced briskly, "You'll have to leave now, Captain. The doctor's on his way—he'll be here any minute."

"When can I come back?"

"In a couple of hours, I should think." She looked at the military watch on her wrist. "Say, 1030 hours."

Hawk leaned over and lightly brushed his lips across Kit's forehead. "See you later, Kit." He walked out, his thoughts on the woman in the room. *He barely knew Kit, but her injury had nearly wiped him out. And, more than his horror at the fact that she'd lost her leg, was the sense of loss he felt at not having the opportunity to get to know her better. He'd damn sure keep in contact with her—if he had to move heaven and hell to do it. That decided, he felt a huge load drop from his shoulders. He took a deep breath—it was all a matter of logistics—and he was a master of logistics. If a whisper of worry as to why this woman had become so important to him flickered across his mind, he dismissed it immediately.*

After Hawk left, Kit lay in her bed awaiting the doctor's visit and wondering about her future. *She couldn't let Hawk remain in her life, no matter how much she wanted him—needed him. But . . . she didn't have to do anything right now. They'd be shipping her to the States . . . and Hawk still had the rest of his tour here to fulfill. She could wait until she got to Walter Reed to make plans.*

Sometime later her thoughts were interrupted by the doctor's entry into her room. He was an Air Force LC, and she remembered the Air Force manned this hospital, even though it was on the Army part of the installation.

"Good morning, Lieutenant. I'm Doc Brown. How are we feeling this morning?"

"How should <u>we</u> be feeling, Doc? <u>I</u> just lost my leg."

"And you're alive, and still beautiful," he said sternly.

She knew he was telling her that a lot of the men and women he saw were disfigured, maybe for life, and by that standard she supposed she was lucky, but it was still . . . hard.

When she didn't answer immediately, he continued, "You're also very fortunate that your amputation—"

At her grimace, he reached out and squeezed her hand. "Your amputation is below the knee. That's very good news." Anticipating her reply, he interjected, "Although I realize you can't see that, yet. However, with the amazing strides technology has permitted today, prostheses are miraculous compared to what was available in, say World War II. Once you're properly fitted, you'll be able to do almost everything you've been accustomed to doing."

"Except run."

"You were a runner?" the doctor said softly.

"Since high school," she said sadly.

"Well, it's not impossible, you know. You can still run. It just depends on how badly you want to."

"Right! We just don't get everything we want—no matter how badly we want it."

"Well, why don't you wait and see. I know a number of amputees who run—and do it competitively." When she didn't respond, he was silent for a minute, then continued. "I'm sorry for your loss, Lieutenant, and no one knows better than I do what a loss it is. But your life <u>will</u> go on, and it can be a good life. You might have to do some re-thinking, make a few adjustments, but you will. Believe me, I know you will."

"You sound like a chaplain, Doc."

"Yeah. Well, sometimes you need to be around here." He stood up and made some notes on his clipboard. "I'll be back this afternoon to take a look at your dressing. If everything is normal, you'll be leaving day after tomorrow for the Landstuhl Regional Medical Center, in

Germany, and then back to the States. You'll go to Walter Reed where you'll have the surgery necessary to prepare your leg for the prosthesis. You'll also get your rehab there."

Kit bit her lip and nodded, too near tears to do more than that.

He turned to leave but stopped at the door. "Don't look back, Lieutenant. Keep your eyes forward, and you'll be okay. You really will, even though you can't imagine it right now."

With that parting remark, he left, and she heard his footsteps go down the hall and turn into the room next door.

After his departure, Kit glanced at the large clock on the wall facing her bed. *The nurse said Hawk could return after 1030—it was now 1330. She wondered where he was, and if he would return soon. Would he insist on continuing their relationship, if one could call it that? She was afraid he'd feel responsible for her. She couldn't let that happen. She wasn't going to be anyone's responsibility. She couldn't tie him down to a one-legged cripple—and that's what she was. She had to face it. No use sugar-coating it. Hawk loved everything active and outdoors—and so had she, before. Now she had to let him go—and it was going to be the hardest thing she had ever done—but she could do it. She would do it. She had to.*

Tears flooded her eyes, but she refused to let them fall, blinking rapidly. *She had to come up with a plan, and it had to be perfect. Because if it wasn't perfect, Hawk would know, and then it wouldn't work. Mark was another complication she had to work out—but she would. Her leg felt as if it was still there—it ached, such*

134

a weird feeling.

She dozed off and woke to the feel of Hawk's lips caressing hers. She opened her eyes and smiled, forgetting for a minute where she was—and why. "Hi," she said sleepily.

"Hi yourself. I didn't know whether to wake you or not. What did the doc say?" He reached out and pushed a silvery curl off her cheek.

"He said my stump looks healthy, and that it will be ready for the final surgery to prepare it for my prosthesis when I get to Walter Reed."

Hawk knew by the emphasis she placed on the words "stump" and "prosthesis" that she was forcing herself to say them, and he suspected she was reminding him. It would be like her to try to scare him off, thinking she was "saving" him. If that was her intent, she'd find he wasn't the scaring kind. Something had changed for him since she was hurt. He wasn't ready to admit yet what it was, but he was aware of it. "When do you go to Walter Reed?"

"I'm not sure. Day after tomorrow I go to Germany, according to the doc. After that, I don't know—couple of days, I think."

"I wish I could go with you, Kitten, but thank goodness for cell phones and e-mail; we can keep in touch. And I'll be due for thirty days of leave when I finish my tour here, in three months."

"I'll be fine, Hawk. Don't worry."

"Who says I'm worrying—you're tough. Isn't that what you always tell your brothers . . . when you're not telling them you're "'Jes' fine'?"

Kit smiled as he had intended, but then a look of panic covered her face.

135

"Hawk! My Pogo medallion! I had it in my pocket. I can't bear it if it got lost."

He just grinned at her and reached into his pocket, producing the small medal and placing it in her hand. Her fingers immediately curled around it, and she held it to her heart and then looked up, a question in her eyes.

"The nurse just gave it to me. They found it when they cut your uniform off of you." At her deep sigh, he continued, "Don't worry. If it had been lost, I would have gotten you another one."

She smiled. *She didn't want another one. This one held wonderful memories.* "Did you talk to Mark?" As she spoke, the door of the room opened.

"Speak of the Devil," Hawk said, rising to grip Mark's hand in a warm handshake.

Mark walked to the side of Kit's bed and, leaning down, kissed her forehead. "Hi, Little Bit," he said, using her brothers' nickname for her when she was small.

"You look terrible, Mark."

"Yeah, well, I haven't had much sleep since I got the call about you, and military hops aren't exactly luxurious. But then again, I was lucky to catch one so quickly." Dismissing his condition with a shrug, he asked, "The question is—how are you, Kit?"

Kit noticed he looked at Hawk when he said it, and something passed between them—something she couldn't identify but felt intuitively was there. Pulling on Mark's sleeve, she spoke forcefully. "I'm down here, Mark; and I'm perfectly capable of speaking for myself. You don't have to ask Hawk—any more than you had to send him to check up on me."

"Well, seeing as how he's still here, I'm guessing you

forgive me for that," he said dryly.

Kit rolled her eyes and shook her head as a soft blush suffused her face. "Ummm."

Dragging up the only chair in the room, Mark sat down at her bedside. Hawk had already taken a seat on the opposite edge of the bed.

"Okay Kit, talk. And don't edit for what you think I want to hear. I can still tell when you're doing that."

"I'm not a child any more, Mark."

"I know that, Kit. But you still hold everything inside. And for our part in causing that, I'm sorry. Now, talk to me!"

Kit knew she could no longer avoid thinking about what had happened. When she closed her eyes, it all came flooding back, and she steeled herself to talk about what had happened.

Mark and Hawk exchanged a look of compassion and worry.

"It was three . . . no two days ago . . . I think. My men and I were returning to Taji from Balad after repairing a downed dozer. I was in a Humvee in the middle of the convoy, and Bones—Sergeant Bonesworth—was driving. There were four trucks and the Humvee in the convoy."

Mark interrupted. "What were *you* doing there? It's not usual for a company commander to go on a repair run, is it?"

"It's not all that unusual. I often accompany my men. I don't ask them to do things I don't do. Anyway, I had a meeting with the Transportation Officer at Camp Anaconda." She glanced over at Hawk before continuing.

A shudder ran across Mark's face, and he too looked

at Hawk. "Okay," he said. "Continue."

"The road ahead was clear, and then . . . it wasn't. They came over a hill—two vehicles— and we came under mortar fire. My gunner was firing as soon as they came in sight, but he got hit, as did my driver. I had my sidearm out—and I hit one of them just as he came over the sand dune. Bones was able to keep the vehicle on the road—although he was swerving a bit—until we got hit with the mortar . . . and the Humvee flipped over."

"What about the rest of the convoy? Couldn't they help?"

"They were there. They did. They continued firing until the insurgents turned tail and ran. But the damage was done. My gunner was dead—" She shivered, remembering, but forced herself to continue. "Bones had a shoulder wound, and I was caught in the mangled wreckage of the Humvee. I passed out before they finally got me out. I remember screaming that they better not let anybody take my leg off. But they did—"

Hawk squeezed her shoulder gently. "It was the only way they could save your life, Kit."

"I know that, but . . ." Her eyes filled with tears which she refused to let fall.

Mark looked as if he wanted to cry himself.

Kit straightened, gulped in a deep breath, and then asked, "Have you talked to the others?"

"I talked to Matt and Luke. They'll be at Walter Reed when we get there. Luke's already put in for emergency leave so he can stay a while, and so have I. Haven't been able to reach Jon, yet."

Kit flashed a look at Hawk. "Jon already knows—he's on his way. Hawk talked to him on the phone yesterday, or—"

Hawk interrupted. "This morning, early. He called this morning."

Mark looked thoughtful. "So he knows. I thought he might."

So Mark wasn't surprised. He was obviously used to the twins' eerie connection. He continued with his explanation. "Jon tried to call you, but you had already left. He called Matt, and Matt told him Kit was here, and you were already on your way."

"Matt's always comm central—he never goes anywhere, so we all check in with him when we're trying to locate each other."

Hawk felt a sense of envy for this close-knit family that managed to stay connected, no matter where in the world they happened to be. He realized how alone he was.

Mark asked another question. "Can he get leave?"

"He said he'd already spoken to someone about it, said he'd be here tonight or tomorrow."

Mark raised an eyebrow. "So soon? Where is he?"

"Didn't say, but I got the impression—" Hawk frowned, trying to recall Jon's exact words. "Oh yeah. He said he only had a 'three-day window of opportunity.' He'd be here within hours, or he couldn't be here at all. Said he'd moved heaven and earth to get to a telephone."

Kit had been listening while Hawk and Mark talked. Now she interrupted with a question of her own. "What did they say—Luke and Matt—when you called them?"

"They were shocked, but then they both said the same thing: you're tough, that you'll cope, that after all—"

"The Vails never give up." She finished the old family maxim for him, smiling slightly as she recalled all the times she and her siblings had heard it when they were

139

growing up.

"That's right. When do you get out of here?"

"The doc says day after tomorrow I go to Germany. Then Walter Reed in D.C., but I don't have that time frame."

Hawk stood up and pulled the cap out of the pocket of his flight suit. "Look, I'll leave you two to catch up." He leaned over and brushed a brief kiss across her forehead, noting Mark's raised eyebrows, although he said nothing.

Kit grabbed his hand. "You're not leaving."

"I'll be back—I'm going to get some coffee and something to eat, and I have to check in with the squadron."

Mark stood up too. "I'll be down in a bit. Wait for me, Hawk. We need to talk."

"Oh no," Kit interrupted. "Don't you dare talk about me behind my back. I know what you're doing. I can make my own life plans. And don't you forget it."

Fire flashed in her blue eyes, and both Mark and Hawk grinned, although neither attempted a denial.

Saying he'd see them later, Hawk left the room, and Mark returned to Kit's bedside.

Still angry, she refused to look at him.

"Don't be like that, Kit. We can't help being concerned. I'm your brother—I've looked out for you all my life. And Hawk is . . . just what is Hawk to you, Kit?"

When she didn't immediately reply, Mark gripped her chin and forced her to look up at him. "I already know more than you probably think. When I talked to Hawk after your accident, he was so upset, he was almost incoherent. And I've seen the light in your eyes every time you look at each other. I also noticed he kissed you before he left. I'm not surprised—I always knew the two of you would strike sparks if you ever got together, but I wanted you to have a chance to grow up first, to be on your own for a while before you settled down with one man. That's why I made sure you two never met."

Kit frowned. *So that was why . . .* "It's not like that, Mark. You've got it all wrong. We're just—friends. Hawk—Hawk doesn't want . . ." She stopped, not sure of what to say.

But Mark seemed to know. "Hawk's afraid. He has his reasons, which it is not my place to tell you, but give him time. Your accident really shook him, forced him to look at feelings he didn't want to admit he has. Just give him time, Kit."

She didn't want to hear this—not now. "We're just friends, Mark. That's all." At Mark's skeptical look, she blushed. "<u>Good</u> friends, okay? But <u>just</u> friends." *She couldn't let him know it was more than that, at least for her, or her plan would never work. She was <u>not</u> going to ruin Hawk's life. No way.*

Mark merely smiled. "Umm hmm. We'll see. I wonder what Hawk will say?"

Her head snapped up. "Don't you dare ask him about us. I told you not to discuss my life behind my back."

"Hawk and I have been friends for a long time, Kit. He'll tell me what he wants me to know. I promise, I won't pry anything out of him. But that's all I'm willing to promise." He crossed his fingers behind his back as he said it.

Kit knew that was his final word. She hoped Hawk would keep his thoughts to himself, whatever they were. She surely didn't know. She was pretty sure <u>she</u> loved

141

him, although she trembled at the word—couldn't even let herself think about it now. But in the short time she and Hawk had known each other he had kept his emotions on such a tight rein she was in a total state of confusion about how he felt or what he thought.

"Kit, I'm still here."

She looked blankly at Mark. "I'm sorry. I was just—"

"It's okay. I can see you're tired; I'll let you get some rest. I have ten days of leave. As I said before, I'm going to make arrangements to accompany you to Germany and back to the States. Matt and Luke will meet us at Walter Reed. I'll call them both tonight. Anything you want me to tell them?"

"Just . . . I . . ." She bit her lip, struggling with her emotions. "Tell them I'm okay and that I'm looking forward to seeing them. That's all."

"All right, Kit. And just so you know—I'm proud of you. I think you're doing okay, and I know you don't <u>need</u> my help, or protection, or advice. Just please remember, I'm always here for you—if you <u>want</u> any of the above."

Kit's face lit with a grin. "Just so <u>you</u> know, I think you're a wonderful brother; I'm proud of you, and I love you too—when I'm not mad at you!"

He burst out laughing. "Same old Kit, thank goodness!" He hugged her, kissed her on her nose, and then stood up. "I think I'll hunt up Hawk and have some of that coffee and chow. Get some rest; I'll see you this evening."

"Okay—but you remember what I said. Remember your promise."

He sketched a two-fingered salute. "I promise. See you later, Little Bit."

142

"Bye, Mark."

He left her room and walked down the hall to the nurses' station to ask directions to the hospital mess. A few minutes later he was headed that way, his thoughts still on Kit. *It was fine to tell her to hang tough and that the Vails never gave up—but he knew what a difficult time she faced in the days ahead. And he didn't know any way at all that he could help her. She was going to be on her own. She had denied any relationship with Hawk, but there was definitely more there than either of them admitted— he'd get the truth out of Hawk.*

He stepped into the dining room, scanning the tables until he saw Hawk sitting alone at a table in the far rear of the room—just sitting there, staring into space. *Whatever relationship he and Kit had, it was obvious her accident had knocked Hawk for a loop.*

Hawk snapped out of his daze and looked up as Mark pulled out a chair and sat down across from him.

"Have you already eaten?"

"No. Thought I'd wait for you. I'm not really hungry. How'd you think she looked, Mark?"

"Hard to tell. She doesn't seem to be too banged up— except for her leg."

Hawk looked up, anger in his dark eyes. "That isn't enough?"

"You know what I meant—so don't take my head off. I'm just as upset as you are. I talked to her doctor before I went to her room."

"And?"

"He said she was fortunate that they could amputate her leg below the knee—"

"That's what he told her! But it's hard to—"

"Okay, Hawk—I'm done beating around the bush."

143

Mark's voice was gruff, his tone serious, and his narrowed eyes held Hawk's.

"What are you talking about, Mark?"

"I want to know what kind of relationship you and Kit have."

Hawk straightened, and then looked at Mark consideringly. "I could tell you that's between me and Kit."

"<u>Is</u> that what you're telling me?"

"I'm telling you, if you want to know, you'd better ask her."

"I did."

"And what did she say?"

Mark hesitated for a second. "That you were friends." *He didn't miss the quick flash of . . . something, possibly regret, in Hawk's eyes, but it was gone almost immediately.*

"I guess that's your answer then."

"I don't believe it."

"Why not?"

"Come off it, Hawk. This is me you're talking to. I knew you were being cagey when you called me right after the two of you met at Taji. And I'm not blind—I can see the way you look at each other. So start talking. There is definitely <u>something</u> between you and Kit."

"You're reading too much into this. Kit and I barely know each other. What could be between us? I know I'm not good enough for her."

Mark snorted. "Don't give me that. I know why you've gone from woman to woman to woman for the last five years."

"Now see here, buddy."

Mark silenced him with a look. "No! You listen to

144

me, Hawk. Five years is long enough to torture yourself over something that wasn't your fault and never should have happened in the first place."

Hawk frowned, not sure where this was going, and undecided as to whether he was more angry or curious.

"Go ahead and get angry! I'm tired of keeping quiet about something I should have told you a long time ago —and I would have if I had thought I could make you listen. I never wanted you to marry Carol—you didn't know anything about her. But everybody else did! If you hadn't refused to listen, you wouldn't have married her, let alone the day after we graduated and three months before we were deploying."

Hawk's voice was as hard as iron when he spoke. "Suppose you tell me now just what 'everyone else knew.'"

Mark sighed. "I'm sorry, Hawk, but Carol Malloy was nothing but a gold-digger. She'd made it known she was getting out of that little town, and she intended to marry the first officer that asked her." He watched the confusion and anger spread across his friend's face before he spoke.

"And you know this, how?"

"Mac's girlfriend was also from there—they worked together."

Hawk's mouth dropped open, and Mark could see the minute he realized the truth. "Mac!"

"Yeah, Mac. The guy you almost killed that night in the bar when he tried to tell you about her."

"I thought . . . oh man! I . . . don't know what I thought." He scrubbed a hand through his dark hair before slowly shaking his head. "All these years . . . I thought. What an idiot—" He looked at Mark, his eyes

145

snapping with rage. "And you let me think it—all these years. Some best friend you turned out to be—the least you could have done is tell me I was no more than a meal ticket until she met someone better."

"Which it sure didn't take her long to do! She dumped you for a major she met two days after we left for the Gulf—three months after you were married!"

"Mac's girlfriend again?" he said dryly.

"Right." *Hawk was no longer seeing him, but was back in the past.*

"No wonder she was in such a hurry for a divorce. She couldn't even wait until I got back."

"Anyone could have told you, Hawk," Mark said softly. "But you didn't want to know."

"No, I guess not. I just—"

"Blocked the whole thing out."

Hawk shrugged and sat there shaking his head back and forth, eyes closed.

Mark leaned closer to emphasize what he was saying. "For five years, I've watched you refuse to date any woman long enough to get close to her—or let her get close to you. That's why I made damned sure you and Kit never met—until now."

Hawk's look was challenging when he spoke. "And what changed?"

Mark hesitated.

"You owe me, Mark. What changed?"

Mark spoke slowly. "I could see you getting as tired as I am of this woman-at-every-base merry-go-round, and . . . "

Hawk folded his arms across his chest and looked back at Mark. "Does this mean you're finally over Kit's friend Jane?"

146

"Don't go there, Hawk. This is about you and Kit, not me."

A thread of anger pulsed through Hawk's voice as he looked straight at his friend. "About me and Kit? I thought it was just about me," Hawk said dryly.

"It's about both of you."

"Are you telling me to stay away from Kit, Mark—because it won't work. I won't stay away from her."

Mark smiled slightly. "I thought you didn't think you were good enough for her?"

A mulish look appeared on Hawk's face. "I'm not—I wasn't, but . . . maybe I've changed my mind."

Mark was almost laughing as he spoke. "I don't want you to stay away from her—just the opposite in fact. Kit needs you—now more than ever. I can tell she cares about you, even if she won't admit it. But damn it all—I don't want you to hurt her. You could . . . and I just don't think she could take it if you broke her heart on top of this."

A shadow darkened Hawk's eyes, and he spoke sadly. "It's too late to tell me not to hurt her. I already did." Seeing the thunderous look on Mark's face, he hurried to continue his explanation. "Hang on a minute, Mark. I was trying to save her. I know I'm not good enough for her, and I tried, I really tried to stay away from her. Part of this is your fault anyway. You had to insist . . ." He hesitated for a minute, thinking, then announced quietly. "We had lunch together the day her convoy was attacked."

"What!"

"Yeah. I tried to be all noble and tell her she needed somebody better than me, but when I saw her leaving, I knew I couldn't do it. I called out to her, but she didn't

147

turn around. I was going to call her the next day, make sure she got back all right. I'll never forgive myself for hurting her . . . but I will make it up to her. Believe me, I will. The irony of all this is—now I'm afraid she won't have anything to do with me—because of her leg."

"I'm afraid you might be right, but—"

"But she doesn't know me by half if she thinks I'll let her get away with that. I wish I didn't have another three months here. Somehow I have to manage to . . . she's not going to get away from me—not now that I have found her."

Mark burst into laughter—he couldn't help it.

Hawk looked at him suspiciously. "What's so funny?"

"You are. I always knew the two of you were made for each other, but you're going to have one rough ride trying to tame her, Hawk."

Hawk's eyes were twinkling as he answered, "Maybe so, but she's worth it."

Suddenly serious, Mark leaned over and clapped Hawk on the shoulder. "Listen Bro, I'm glad you feel that way. There's nobody I'd rather have for a brother-in-law, but you gotta be persistent. Kit's got a tough row to hoe—she won't want to ruin your life—and she'll think she would."

"I'll convince her, Mark. I don't know how, yet, but I will. I'm going to take care of her from here on out; no matter how hard she fights me; no matter what it takes.

Mark smiled. "Glad to hear it. You're definitely going to need that determination; she's not going to make it easy for you."

"No." Hawk spoke softly, but he smiled as he said it. "Let's eat. I've got to get moving."

"Yeah, me too. I still have to check into the VOQ, and

then I have to call Matt and Luke.

Hawk had been sitting in the bare and antiseptic room for several hours watching Kit sleep when the door of her room slowly opened. He jumped up at the sight of the tall man in camouflage uniform.

"You have to be Jon," he said, immediately reaching out to shake the man's hand.

"And you're Captain Hawkins."

The two of them stood, taking each other's measure for several seconds, each liking what they saw in the other. Jon broke the silence first. "How is she?"

Hawk tipped his head, hesitating for a second, before answering. "Holding her own."

"She's sleeping?"

Hawk nodded. "Go ahead and wake her. She's been asleep for a while. She's anxious to see you. It'll be good for her."

He surrendered his place beside Kit's bed, and Jon slid in front of him, and leaned over the sleeping Kit.

Hawk watched him. He could tell from the way Jon's mouth was moving that he was having trouble staying in control as he looked at his injured sister sleeping peacefully. Jon slowly brought his hand up, swiped it across his eyes, then reached out and barely touched Kit's cheek.

She immediately turned into his hand, and her eyes fluttered open. A startled look appeared in them before a smile lit her face.

"Kit." Jon took a deep breath, and then continued speaking. "I can't let you out of my sight without you

149

getting in trouble, hmmm?"

She reached out to touch him as if to ensure he was really there. "That's my line, remember? You're the one who was always in hot water."

Jon acknowledged her comment with a smile as the two of them looked at each other. Then Jon leaned over and brushed his lips across her forehead. "I'm so sorry, Kit."

She moved her head back and forth on her pillow, shutting her eyes. When she spoke, Hawk could hear the tears in her voice. "Jon, I can't believe you're here. How? We didn't even know where you were. Who called you?"

"I knew, Kit—just like always. You should have known I'd come."

She nodded. "I told Hawk." She jerked her head around, looking for him. "Hawk. I was afraid you'd gone. Did you two meet?"

"Just a few minutes ago. Look, now that Jon's here, I'm going to take off and let the two of you visit."

"You don't have to leave."

"I know, but you two have lots to catch up on. I'll be back."

Kit watched until he was out of sight.

Jon had been following her actions. "He means a lot to you doesn't he?" he said softly.

Kit looked away from him before she spoke.

"We're . . . friends."

"We've never lied to each other, Kit—even though we maybe misrepresented the truth a little bit to other people." He grinned mischievously before continuing. "But never, never to each other." He reached out and pulled her head around until she was facing him.

150

As he continued to look at her, Kit reached for his arm where it lay on her bed and hugged it to her chest. "You're right, Jon. I'm sorry. He does mean more to me than a friend, but he doesn't know it. Promise me you won't tell anyone, especially not him, and especially not now."

Jon's face clouded, and he frowned. "In the first place, I think you're wrong about him knowing. He seems pretty smart to me. And secondly, run that phrase by me again."

"What phrase?"

"You know what phrase—'especially not now'—what the heck does that mean?"

"Now who's being dense?"

He opened his mouth, but she shook her head. "No! Don't argue with me, Jon. I don't want to talk about it. Tell me, how long can you stay? Can you tell me where you were? Do you have to go back there?"

She wouldn't say any more on the subject, at least not now. He'd drop it, but it worried him, and he wasn't giving up. He'd get it out of her later, and he'd definitely talk to Mark . . . and maybe even this Hawk. She hadn't noticed he never gave his promise.

Chapter 8

Mark was as good as his word and made all the arrangements to accompany her to Landstuhl Army Medical Center in Germany, where doctors would check her wound and make sure she was stable for the trip to Walter Reed. They'd be leaving today.

Hawk had called her last night, and they had talked for an hour. After he hung up, she had lain awake for hours more, fighting the pain rather than ask for pain meds. She needed her mind clear enough to make her plans.

The fact that Hawk still had three months left in Iraq would help. She'd never be able to push him out of her life otherwise. She simply didn't have the strength. So, she'd take the coward's way out—and simply disappear—she thought bitterly. She hated making that choice—her brothers would be ashamed of her if they knew. She'd always been able to face whatever came her way and fight her way through it . . . the loss of her parents, those first <u>lonely</u> years at the Point . . . even losing her leg—yes, even that she would overcome, although she'd be the first to admit it would take time, and she wasn't there, yet. Everything, but Hawk. She <u>would not</u> let him sacrifice his life to pity . . . or duty . . . or whatever. Even if it was more than that, she still *couldn't let him ruin his life.*

Awake most of the night, she'd finally come to a decision, worked out her plan. Now, although wiped out from the pain and worry and lack of sleep, she felt somewhat at peace. The sky outside her window reflected the pale light between the passage of night and full day. Someone was coming, most likely the nurse who would replenish her IV bag with the numbing pain meds. It was okay now—now she'd welcome the chance to stop thinking and let her problems and pain disappear into sleep.

The nurse left after checking her over and refilling the IV bag. *As she lay there awaiting the blessed relief of sleep, she silently railed at a fate that would let her finally meet the one man she could care about—and then force her to give him up.*

She awoke several hours later to the sound of footsteps in the hall and knew it must be Mark. He had managed everything about her transfer, refusing to let her worry about anything. Anything that he could control, that is. She continued to fret over what she planned to do. Disappearing without letting her family know would have been difficult enough—they loved her, and she loved them. But disappearing from Hawk . . . although he might <u>let</u> her disappear . . . maybe he'd be relieved . . . at least she was giving him a choice. If she never heard from him again, then she'd know her decision had been the right one. And if he looked for her . . . if he found her despite everything she could do— well, then she'd know he truly loved and wanted her,

that he wouldn't find her a burden or someone to be pitied.

Mark came into her room, approached the bed, and leaned down to press a kiss on her forehead. "Hi, Little Bit—ready to go?"

"Are we leaving now?" *She panicked at the thought of leaving without seeing Hawk again. He'd said he would try to get here before she left, but that he might not make it. His unit had been flying a lot of surveillance missions of late—he might not be able to get away. Knowing all that, she had still counted on seeing him one more time. Mark's look told her he knew.*

"Not right this minute. Our flight leaves at 2000 hours.

She exhaled a sigh of relief. *Hawk had all day to get here.* "Do you think Hawk will be able to—?"

"That seems awfully important to you for someone who's nothing but a 'friend'." A grin flitted across Mark's face as he used air quotes.

She could feel her face warm. "I said, he's a <u>good</u> friend. Forget I asked." She turned her head to hide the quick tears.

Mark reached out and turned her face gently toward him. "I'm sorry, Kit. I didn't mean to tease, but old habits die hard." He leaned down and gave her a quick hug.

"It's okay. It's better if I don't see him again."

Mark stiffened in surprise. "What do you mean by that? Of course you'll see him again. Why wouldn't you?" She wasn't looking at him, and his eyes narrowed as he rubbed a hand thoughtfully over his chin. *Kit was up to something—and he had a feeling he knew what— but he'd wait and see. Maybe she would tell him.* "Hawk called this morning to see how you were."

"We talked last night."

"You did, hmm? Then you should already know he'll be here today—this morning."

"Last night he didn't know for sure."

"He called me early this morning. He was scheduled to fly, but the flight was cancelled due to weather."

Kit drew in a quick breath, and her heart pounded. Hawk was coming. She turned to Mark. "When he gets here, would you . . . could you . . . ?" Her face flooded with color.

He squeezed her arm gently. "Of course." He laughed. "At least you asked. Hawk told me—more like ordered me—to clear out when he got here."

Joy coursed through her body as she hugged the thought to herself. Hawk wanted to see her alone. Well, as alone as possible here in a hospital room with people coming and going all the time.

Mark smiled to himself. *He was glad she and Hawk had met—glad that he had set it up.* He glanced down at his watch.

"Do you have to leave?"

"Soon. I just popped in to see how you were doing. I still have a few things to do before we leave, and I promised Matt I'd check in with him this morning." A look of concern crossed his face as he continued. "How are you doing, Kit? Really? I talked to the doc this morning, and he said medically you're doing well. I'm relieved to hear that, but his statement leaves unsaid how you're doing emotionally. You look as if you didn't sleep at all last night. Didn't they give you anything for the pain?"

"I told them I didn't need it."

"Why on earth not?! You don't have to be strong all

155

the time, Kit."

She looked away from the concern on his face, choosing instead to look out the window behind him.

"Kit?"

"It wasn't that. I needed to think, and the medicine muddles my mind."

She saw the worry in Mark's eyes as he spoke softly. "What did you have to think about, Kit?"

When she didn't answer or look at him, he grasped her chin, turning her head so he could look into her eyes. "Kit, tell me you're all right."

Her mouth crumpled, and tears slipped out of her eyes as she saw the care and concern in her brother's brown eyes. *She couldn't tell him her plans, couldn't let any of them know, hard as it was to keep her secret. If Mark found out, he'd stop her, she knew that.* She sniffled and took a deep breath. *Mark was already worried enough without her falling apart in front of him.* "I'm not all right, Mark. It's . . . hard."

"I know, Kit, I know. I wish I could . . . I just feel so helpless."

Watching him struggle with his grief for her gave her the courage she needed. Reaching out for his hand, she squeezed it in her own and gave her brother a tremulous smile. "Stop worrying, Mark. I may not be okay yet— I'm still getting used to the idea—but I <u>will</u> <u>be</u>. After all . . ." She grinned up at him.

Before she could continue, Mark finished the family maxim for her.

"We Vails never give up." He leaned over and touched his forehead to hers. "I'm glad to see you remember that, Kit." His eyes were still troubled when he straightened up. "I really do have to go now, Kit, but

I'll be back this afternoon. Hawk should be here before too long, and I've been ordered to make myself scarce." He grinned down at her and headed for the door.

"See you later, Kit."

"Bye, Mark—I'm glad you're my brother."

Surprised, he stopped and looked at her fondly. "Me too, Little Bit, me too."

As he left the room, Kit bit her lip, thoughts crowding her mind. *Hawk was coming, and she couldn't stop the tremor of excitement she felt as she anticipated his visit. Until reality set in—she was still* one-legged, *and that would never change. She had to be careful not to let Hawk see too much. His eyes, always hiding his own emotions, had a way of seeing more in hers than she wished. He was coming. She'd learned to recognize his footsteps in the hall.*

He strode into her room, bringing with him the smell of the warm, muggy outside, and she let herself really look at him. *He was so tall, and standing there so strong and straight, the epitome of a recruiting poster—reflecting glamour, excitement, and romance—he took her breath away. But it was his eyes that held her. Dark, almost black, they bore into hers as he spoke.*

"Good morning, Kitten."

No one called her that but him, and she loved it, loved the way he said it. Still unable to speak, she simply stared at him.

He closed in on her, his eyes filled with an emotion she couldn't recognize . . . almost, almost—no, it couldn't be. She shook her head and smiled up at him. "Hi," she whispered.

He leaned over, braced his hands on either side of her body, and touched his lips to hers softly. The kiss began

157

gently, but then his control seemed to slip, and he put his hand behind her head, pulling her to him as he deepened the kiss. When he finally pulled away, they were both breathing rapidly, and Kit's eyes were startled as she looked up at him.

"Did that surprise you Kit? Because it surprised the hell out of me."

Surprise wasn't the word for it, she thought, as he grinned down at her. The kiss had blown her away, but why now—when everything had changed, and she wasn't . . . couldn't be—? She couldn't let him see how much he meant to her, that was all. She'd have to make sure he didn't see.

Still looking at her, he raised a questioning eyebrow, and she realized he expected an answer to his question.

Dredging up an answering grin, she said, "Wow! To what do I owe that greeting?"

Suddenly his grin was gone, and he was looking at her seriously. He pulled up the chair and sat beside her bed. Reaching for her hand, he enfolded it in his, and spoke quietly, slowly rubbing the palm of her hand with his thumb. "I've changed, Kit. You've changed me."

The continued movement of his thumb was doing crazy things to her. A shiver of anticipation, mingled with dread, flowed through her body. *What was Hawk planning? Please don't let him be heroic and ask me to marry him, she thought. She knew in her heart that her courage, no matter how she steeled herself, didn't extend to refusing him face-to-face—not when she'd just realized he was what she wanted more than anything in the world.*

Hawk watched her, saw the expressions flitting across her face, and he was suddenly afraid. He jumped out of his chair, knelt down beside her bed, and grasped both of her hands. "What's wrong, Kit?" he said softly. "I know you're worried about the future—but you're <u>not</u> afraid of me—you can't be, except that's what it looked like just now."

She didn't—couldn't—immediately answer, and he leaned closer. *He was going to kiss her again.* She turned her head. *She couldn't let him, she turned her head quickly. If he kissed her, she'd be lost.*

Hawk sighed in frustration. *Kit was already trying to distance herself from him, just like he and Mark had feared. He frowned fiercely. She wouldn't succeed, no matter how hard she tried. He couldn't let her.* He touched her face gently. "Come back, Kit—don't go away from me." With one finger, he turned her face toward him. "Tell me what's wrong, Kitten."

She lowered her eyes, studying the white sheets on the bed. "You say you've changed, but I'm the one who's changed, Hawk—I'm not the same woman I was. Now I'm a one-legged cripple . . . and I'll never be the same again."

She grimaced as she said the words, and he was stunned to hear her categorize herself in this way. He leaned close to her and spoke slowly, emphasizing each word. "Now you listen to me, Kit." He put one hand on either side of her face. "Listen to me, Kit. You are one special lady. I've known that since the first day I walked into your office back at Taji and saw the most beautiful woman I had ever seen."

She remembered that day. She had been broadsided when she looked up and saw the handsome Air Force Captain standing in her doorway. She frowned. "But then I had two legs, not one leg and one <u>stump</u>."

Hawk put his finger on her trembling lips, rubbing it back and forth gently. "Kit, don't. You're not measured by how many legs you have. You're just as beautiful to me today as you were then."

Could he possibly believe that? Or was he just saying it? Trying to smile, she spoke lightly. "And you truly have a gift for exaggeration—or else you're blind. You've told me I was beautiful in baggy camouflage ACUs, when I'd just come out of a dust storm, and now you think I'm beautiful missing one leg. You have really weird ideas of beauty!"

Her smile was teary, but it was a smile, and he thanked God for it. "You're my idea of beauty, Kit—remember that." He rose, and his thumb brushed away a lingering tear. Then his lips skimmed lightly over hers, as their eyes met. "I can't stay, Kitten. The bad weather was a lucky break, but it won't last." He leaned down and kissed her once more, started for the door, then turned back to face her again as he said fiercely, "Don't forget me, Kit."

"Forget you, Hawk?! How can I forget you, when I lo—" She broke off, biting her lips to stifle the words she had come so close to uttering, words she knew she could never say.

Hawk watched her, waiting for her to go on. When she didn't, he said, "What did you start to say? And why didn't you finish it?"

After a moment, she completed the sentence. "Just that . . . I like you too much to forget you, Hawk." She saw disappointment in his eyes and knew that wasn't the way he had wanted her to finish the sentence. She felt an emptiness that was just the beginning of a loss she wasn't sure she was strong enough to survive.

"Kit, I wish we had more time. We need to talk. I need to tell you—" She froze, her panic evident. He let out a long breath. "All right, Kit. I know this is the wrong time, that you're not ready to hear what I want to say." After another sigh, he returned and squeezed her fingers tightly. "I'll lay off . . . for now."

The 'for now' was said under his breath, but Kit heard. "Hawk, I'm sorry. I can't—"

He placed a finger against her lips. "Shh, it's all right."

When she lowered her chin, Hawk clamped her chin in a firm grip, refusing to let her look away. "Just know this, Kit Vail. This is <u>not</u> over. We <u>will</u> talk later."

She nodded. *If only it could be so . . . but it couldn't. She wouldn't let it. She stiffened her backbone and straightened her shoulders.* "Hawk . . . I'm so glad you could get here. Thank you for coming, for being such a wonderful, caring person. Thank you, for being you."

It sounded as if she was saying goodbye permanently. But their time had run out. He'd done all he could—for now. Mark was coming, and their private time was over. He leaned over, and before Kit realized what he planned, he clasped her in a tight embrace and kissed her deeply, trying to let his kiss tell her everything she wouldn't let him say aloud. At the sound of Mark's voice, he raised up, his hands still gripping her shoulders.

"Ahem! Am I interrupting something?"

"What do you think, man?"

Kit blushed fiercely, but Mark just laughed.

161

Chapter 9

Kit sat in her wheelchair and looked out the window of her sparsely furnished room at the Walter Reed Army Medical Center. *Two weeks ago she had been a company commander in Iraq, with a blossoming romance—and two good legs. Now, she had none of those things.*

Mark had accompanied her home from Landstuhl, and her brothers had been to see her. After visiting her in in Iraq, Jon had gone—returned to whatever secret mission he had been on. It had been good to see all of them, but she was relieved that they were gone. It was too hard to keep up a cheerful front all the time. She hadn't even tried to fool Jon—it would have been useless. Hopefully, she had been successful with Matt and Luke. At least she thought so.

Mark she wasn't sure about. He wasn't so easy to fool. He was still here—but leaving shortly. She couldn't have coped without his help, but now she needed him to be gone too. She had to learn to do things for herself, and the sooner she started, the better. Her leg was most certainly gone, and she might as well get used to it. They would be fitting her for an artificial leg—prosthesis, they called it—soon. She squeezed her eyes tight shut and forced herself not to cry. *She had shed more tears in the last two weeks than in her whole life, and she was determined not to cry any more. What good did it do?*

And then there was Hawk. Was he as gone as her leg? He had been great at the hospital in Balad right after they brought her in, holding her hand all night, telling her she was beautiful, comforting her. But reality would set in—if it hadn't already—and he'd realize he didn't want to be tied to a one-legged lieutenant—would she even be that anymore? That might be another thing that was gone. Even if he wouldn't admit that he didn't feel the same about her, she couldn't let him ruin his life because he pitied her. She had to let him go. But how could she . . . when she needed him so much.

Suddenly, it was if her father were standing right in front of her bed. She could hear his voice saying, "Kit Vail, quit feeling sorry for yourself. Vails don't give up." They had heard that so often when they were growing up. She jumped when the phone on her night stand rang. *No one but her brothers ever called, and always in the evenings.* She rolled her wheelchair over to the table and picked up the phone. "Hello?"

"Hi, how are things going, Kitten?"

She swallowed. *It was so wonderful to hear his deep voice, sounding as close as if he were in the room with her.* "Hawk! I—I didn't expect—"

"What do you mean you didn't expect?"

He sounded angry.

"I told you I wasn't letting you go out of my life. You didn't believe me?"

"Yes. . . no . . . that is, I hoped."

He seemed to relent, and his voice softened. "How are you, Kit, really? And don't tell me 'fine.' I know all about that, remember—that's how we met."

163

She smiled at the memory. "I remember, Hawk."

"So tell me, how <u>are</u> you?"

"I'm doing all right. I am! It's hard, but everyone here is really kind. The other patients are great. Their humor and encouragement help so much. It's just—"

"Aw, Kit. You don't know how much I wish I could be there with you."

"Hawk. Don't. I have to do this on my own."

"Matt and Luke still there?"

"No, they left yesterday. They were here a week, but they had to get back, and it's okay. I'm fine now. Mark leaves today."

"There's that word again. You know what happened the last time you used it."

There was laughter in his voice, and she laughed too. "This time it's true, Hawk. My stump is healing. They're fitting me soon for my first prosthesis, a temporary one. I've already been doing therapy to strengthen my muscles, and as soon as I get the new leg I'll start learning to use it."

"Do you know how long you'll be there?"

"It depends on how quickly I can adjust to the prosthesis . . . a while, I think. How are you doing, Hawk? I've missed you." She bit her lip. *Darn, she hadn't meant to say that.*

"Not half as much as I miss you, Kit. I've been so worried. I wanted to call sooner, but I've been . . . away."

"I know you're busy, Hawk, don't worry about me, please."

"Kit! It wasn't that kind of 'away.' I was . . . of course I'll worry, you know I will."

She heard someone talking to him in the background

and his voice was frustrated when he continued.

"Hell, Kit. I've got to go. Take care, Kitten. I'll be in touch. I . . . goodbye, Kit."

The phone clicked, and he was gone before she could even say goodbye. She sat there with the telephone in her hand, trying not to be disappointed. *He had called her; he was worried about her. But the brief phone call made her miss him even more. She wondered what he was doing, where he had been when he was "away." She had told him she missed him—a fine way to put distance between them. It was time to put her plan into action.*

She had been thinking about it. The necessity for making a plan and working out the details had sometimes been all that kept her from giving in to the pain and discouragement of her situation. Now she had to make it happen.

After coming up with several places to go on her departure from Walter Reed, she had rejected all of them as being too obvious and too easy for either Mark—or Hawk—to locate her. She couldn't ask any of her friends from North Carolina, or anyone from West Point—Mark could too easily check them out. Eventually, she'd decided on Jane Brewer, her best friend all through grade school and high school. When she went to the Point, Jane went to the local community college to fulfill her long-held dream of becoming an RN. They'd exchanged the occasional card or note, but hadn't seen each other recently, and she was pretty sure she'd never mentioned her to Hawk. Even if she had, it would've been such a casual reference he wouldn't recall it. Mark, on the other hand, might be a problem.

She chewed on her thumbnail as she tried to decide whether he would think of Jane. They'd been next-door neighbors, so he knew her. But it had been a long time ago—almost seven years now—and he didn't know that they still kept in touch. Jane didn't know about her leg, yet, but it was a given that once she did, she would help.

A niggling doubt crossed her mind. She had always suspected, but never been able to confirm, that there had been something between Jane and her brother. Jane had a crush on Mark when she and Kit were high school freshmen and he was in college, but Mark had barely noticed her. He'd been a college senior when Jane enrolled as a freshman at the same college. When she came home after her plebe year at West Point, Jane had changed—she never mentioned Mark. Once when she had teasingly asked if she still had a crush on him, Jane had said "No!" so forcefully and finally that she had known better than to ask anything else.

Worrying her bottom lip between her teeth, she tried to work things out. None of them had returned to their hometown in years—not since their family home had been sold—so it was unlikely that Mark would think of Jane. It was her best option—really the only option—and she'd take it—she'd call Jane tonight.

She looked up as Mark entered her room. "You're early, aren't you? I'm waiting for the therapist."

"My flight's been moved up—I leave in three hours. I just stopped by the Therapy Section. They're really busy this morning, and said it would help them if they could reschedule you for the afternoon, so I told them to do it. This way we can visit." He hesitated, "Little Bit, I'm worried about you."

She'd known this was coming, and she tried to ward off his words. "I'm <u>fine</u>, Mark. Stop worrying about me. I'm all grown up now. I <u>will</u> work my way through this

166

. . . by myself," she added determinedly.

Mark smiled thinly. "Right. You put up a good front; I'll give you that. You might have fooled Matt and Luke. Me? I'm not so easy."

She cringed inwardly. *She had to make Mark believe. He was the one who could sabotage her whole plan.*

Before she could say anything, Mark reached out and gripped her arm. "Don't do it, Kit."

His expression was stern, and her heart stopped. How could he know? He couldn't—and yet . . . she looked down at her lap, avoiding his piercing look. "Don't do what? I don't know what you're talking about, Mark."

He let go of her arm and leaned down until his face was close to hers. "Kit Vail, you're not fooling me. You know you never could. I may not know your exact plan, but I do know what you intend to do." When she didn't answer, he continued. "Hawk doesn't deserve this . . . and neither do you."

"Deserve what, Mark? Just what do you think I'm going to do?"

Mark ignored her outburst. "You and Hawk are perfect for each other . . . and you both know it. I'm not saying you should rush into things. Let things develop naturally. Don't shut every door and window—and somehow I know that's exactly what you're planning to do—because of some misguided idea that—"

She couldn't take any more. "Stop it, Mark! Don't say another word. It's hard enough, and you are not helping. I know Hawk is a good man; he's the best, and I— I have to do this. He doesn't deserve to be saddled with a cripple the rest of his life."

He leaned over. "Kit—"

"No!" She raised her hand in the classic 'stop' sign.

"Not another word."

Her face closed, and her expression was so forbidding he knew there was no point in arguing further—Kit's mind was made up. He gritted his teeth, determined not to let her succeed in this wrong idea. As if she could read his mind, she turned in her chair until she could look him straight in the face.

"You'd rather I ruin Hawk's life! Well, I won't. So there! Just stay out of it, Mark . . . please."

Her voice was hard, and Mark recognized the steely strength he and his brothers had been partly responsible for instilling in the little girl she had been. She wouldn't falter or stumble now that she had made her decision, wrong as it was. She *was looking at him with a familiar mutinous expression, and he struggled to find a way to answer that wouldn't prevent his doing something to keep her from making this mistake.*

"Mark, I want your word."

"Maybe you'd better clarify, Kit, just <u>what</u> I'm giving my word about. Tell me what, exactly, you plan to do."

"No—not yet. You've got to promise me you won't tell Hawk <u>anything</u>, that you won't help him at <u>all</u>."

"Kit! Help him what? For God's sake, what <u>are</u> you going to do?" *He definitely did not like the sound of this. When Kit got the bit between her teeth, she was all but unstoppable. He and his brothers had learned that to their cost during their growing up years. Her irrepressible grin surfaced for a minute, and he had to admire her pure guts.*

"This is 'need-to-know' info, and I'm afraid you don't need to know. Now, promise!"

Disgruntled, he answered. "Okay, I promise, but this is the first time in my life I made a promise without

168

knowing what in the hell I was promising."

"Just that you won't do <u>anything</u> to help Hawk find me."

Mark pounced on the words, "Find you? Kit, what are you going to do?"

Uh oh, she had said too much—that was panic in his voice. "I'm not saying any more. Do you swear you won't tell Hawk?" He didn't answer, and she reached out and grabbed his arm, glaring at him fiercely. "I'm waiting, Mark."

"Okay, okay, I swear. I don't like it, but you have my word. I have to tell you, however, you don't know Hawk Hawkins as well as you think you do. He won't give up. When he wants something, he's like a dog with a bone. If you think the Vails are tenacious, you should see Hawk when he's on the trail of something he wants. And let me tell you, sister dear, he wants <u>you</u>!"

Kit could feel her face getting warm, and a quiver of joy mixed with fear shot through her body as she saw Mark's leering grin.

She called Jane Brewer that night. She had gotten the number from Information since all she had was Jane's address. Her fingers were shaking as she dialed the number. She was ready to hang up when someone picked up, and she heard Jane's breathless voice.

"Hello?"

"Jane?"

"Who is this? Kit? Kit Vail, is that you? Where are you? It's been ages since I've heard anything from you. Are you still in Iraq? How come you didn't answer my last letter?"

Kit smiled. *Yep, same Jane.* "Slow down, Jane. I'll tell you everything, but you have to let me get a word in edgewise."

"Yeah, okay. As you can see, I haven't changed—not in that way at least. Where are you?"

Kit took a deep breath and dove in. "I'm at Walter Reed Army Medical Center here in D.C."

"Walter Reed!"

Jane stopped suddenly, and silence hung between them on the phone.

"Kit, what happened?"

She spoke softly, and Kit knew that Jane had immediately realized the significance of her being at Walter Reed.

"My convoy ran into an ambush, Jane."

"Oh no, Kit. What . . . happened?"

There was compassion in Jane's voice, and she hurried to reassure her friend. "It's okay, Jane. They tell me I'm lucky—and I know I am—it's taken a while, but I have accepted it . . . mostly."

"Accepted . . . what, Kit?"

"I lost my leg."

"The whole leg?"

"I still have my knee . . ."

"I'm glad of that, Kit."

"Yeah, me too . . . it could have been a lot worse. Anyway, to get to why I'm calling. I need your help."

"Anything, Kit. You know that. What can I do, just tell me—"

Kit laughed. "I'm <u>trying</u> to, Jane."

"Oh . . . right. Okay, I'll shut up. Talk!"

"I'm getting out of here soon, and I need a place to go for my convalescent leave."

"Of course, you've got to come here and let me take care of you."

"I don't need anyone to take care of me. I can do that myself. I need a place to get away on my own for a while, an opportunity to prove to myself I <u>can</u> survive on my own."

"O-kay . . . I guess. Tell me how I can help."

Jane sounded puzzled, but at least she seemed willing. "Jane, here's what I was thinking. Does your family still have that cabin up on the border?"

"Yes, we do. But you can't be thinking of going all the way up there—not by yourself, Kit."

"That's what I want—what I need, Jane. Will you help me?"

"Kit, you should know—you don't have to ask. Of course I will."

The next morning Kit rolled her wheelchair up to the same small window and looked out at the familiar scene, absently fingering the small medallion in her fingers. *After her call to Jane she should be feeling great. Everything was working out—her plans were set.* She looked down at her leg with its prosthetic foot. *Encased in the running shoe no one would know it wasn't real, and she was learning to get around with it. She could stand and even walk without her crutches for short distances.* She shook her head and blinked away the tears that would come. *She was fortunate, she really was—in previous wars she probably wouldn't have survived at all. She knew all that, but—* The phone beside her bed rang, and she wheeled over and picked it up.

"Hi Kitten."

"Hawk!"

"I just got back from a mission and decided to try to get through to you."

"I'm glad. How was it?" When he didn't answer, she was afraid. "What happened, Hawk? Are you all right? You sound funny."

"I'm all right."

"Hawk, I can tell <u>something</u> happened. If you don't tell me <u>what</u>, I'll imagine the worst."

"Women!"

He laughed when he said it, and she knew he wasn't angry. "So?"

"All right. We ran into terrible weather, and . . . an Iraqi missile." He heard her indrawn breath. "We'd just taken out several missile sites when we received new intelligence and were asked to hit some mobile Soviet-made surface-to-air missile launchers. The storm limited our visibility, and we couldn't get above it or below it. We were dipping down to bomb the site and got nailed with a missile. I expelled the external fuel tanks to increase maneuverability and was able to dodge more strikes. Stuck in bad weather and getting shot at ain't great. After dropping the tanks, I was low on fuel, so with all our weapons dropped, we returned to Base.

"Oh, Hawk."

"I'm <u>fine,</u> Kit."

"But . . ."

"No buts. You were only going to worry if I <u>didn't</u> tell you, right? Well I told you, so stop worrying. That's not why I called anyway. I want to know how <u>you're </u>doing, Kit? Did you get my emails?"

"You mean the one telling me about the double

amputee who was a member of the Army Golden Knights Parachute Team . . . or the one about the guy who lost his leg and still rides his motorcycle . . . or the one who is a helicopter pilot instructor, the marathon runner, or the one reminding me that 17-20% of amputees actually return to active duty?[1] That email?"

After her outburst, there was complete silence on the line. "Hawk, I'm sorry, I didn't mean that the way it sounded."

"No, I'm sorry Kit. I was just trying to help. You sounded discouraged when I called last time, and there just doesn't seem to be much I can do from here."

"You do help, Hawk." She sighed deeply. "I do get discouraged. I try not to—your emails really help . . . a lot. It's just . . . today has been a bad day."

"What happened, Kit? Tell me about it."

"I'm not sure I can, Hawk. It's not anything specific. Just . . . sometimes I want to give up. I've reminded myself of the family motto so many times I'm sick of it, but—"

Damn! She was going to cry, and he was stuck here. "Kit, I'd give anything if I could be there for you. I hate that you have to go through this by yourself."

Kit sucked in a deep breath. *For Hawk's sake she couldn't break down. She had to be strong.* "I know Hawk—and knowing helps. And—I'm not by myself. The men and woman here are incredible. Whenever I get down, like today, I just have to take a look around me and see all those here who are worse off than I am. And

---

[1] Army Rehabilitates Some Amputees Back to Performing Actual Duties, by Sandra Basu

there are lots of them. Hawk, they are so determined, and they try so hard. There is a guy here who has lost both legs, one above the knee, and you should see him—he's a real inspiration. And there's another one who lost one leg, and he keeps assuring me he's still going to be able to ride his motorcycle. I wish you could see them—I wish everyone in the country could see them—they just make me so proud to be a member of the military."

"Kitten, I'm proud of <u>you</u>—so proud."

Her heart swelled under his praise, even if she didn't deserve it. *There were so many times she would have given up except she didn't want to disappoint him.*

"Uh oh! Time's up—gotta go. Hang in there, Kitten. I <u>know</u> you can do it. I'll try to call tomorrow, if I can. Bye, honey."

She hugged the phone to her breast, savoring his caring words—he'd called her "honey." Despite her intention not to see him again, she could tuck the memory of his words away in her heart to take out and dream over in the future—when her life would be empty without him.

Hawk replaced the phone. *Something was wrong. Kit sounded as if . . . he couldn't put his finger on it, but . . . there'd been something in her voice.*

"Come on, Hawk. We're going to be late. How's she doing anyway?"

He'd totally forgotten Rafer was waiting for him. He shook his head slowly. "I don't know. The last few times I've called . . . she seems down."

"Well, isn't that normal? Hell, Hawk, she lost a leg!"

"I know . . . but it's more than that. There's something

174

else going on. Something worrying her that I just can't put my finger on."

"Well, you'll be back there soon."

"Not for another month."

That night, back in his room, his mind still on Kit, he went to his locker and removed a small box he'd put there shortly after Kit had left for the States. *He'd been in Baghdad and noticed a local silversmith displaying his wares. His eye had been caught by a beautiful heart-shaped locket, intricately carved with flowers and vines, and he'd asked the vendor if it opened. Trying to make a sale, the man opened it and showed him there were slots for two photos.*

It made him think of Kit, and he'd bought the lovely trinket and slipped it into his pocket. On the way back to the base, he was surprised at what he'd done, and even more amazed when he found himself several evenings later going through an envelope of photographs taken on his visit to Kit's shortly after they'd met. He'd ended up carefully cutting out one of the pictures of Kit and fitting it in one side of the locket. The next day he'd asked one of his friends to take a picture of him standing beside his F-16. He'd felt silly cutting it out that evening and affixing it in the other side of the locket, but he finished the job.

He'd planned to give it to her the next time he saw her, but now might be a better time. Maybe it would raise her spirits. He wrapped it for mailing, wishing he could see her when she opened it. When it was wrapped, he laid it beside his flight cap—*he'd drop it off at the postal facility on his way to the squadron in the morning.*

Chapter 10

Kit struggled to reach the opposite end of the parallel bars. Her goal seemed unreachable, and she gripped the bars tightly in sweaty hands, trying to navigate on the temporary prosthesis. The thing was heavier than she had expected. At first her thigh muscles hadn't been strong enough, but the exercises had helped. She continued the struggle to make her "leg" take the right action. She bit her lip; beads of sweat appeared on her forehead. *This prosthesis had to be swung forward with each step, using her body weight. The new "permanent" one would incorporate the latest technology and allow a more effortless stride.*

"Great work, Lieutenant. You're doing it. Just keep going—you're almost there."

Her physical therapist, Major Hacker, had worked with her since the beginning, and the major's patience was seemingly inexhaustible. She had been unfailingly firm, patient, and encouraging over the past few months. In only two more weeks, they should let her go— released to 'convalescent leave'.

"You've made it—congratulations!"

Kit rested her arms on the parallel bars and wiped her face. *She'd done it!* "Thank you, Major." She grinned. *Hawk would be so pleased. Hawk! Darn, the man was*

177

always in her thoughts. Despite her determination to oust him, he remained an ever-constant presence in her heart and mind.

"Lieutenant!"

Kit jumped at the Major's touch on her shoulder. "Sorry. Guess I was daydreaming. When do you think I'll be able to get out of here? Not that I don't enjoy your company; however . . ."

The woman's mouth curved up in a smile. "Everyone always wants to leave us, but since that's what we're aiming for, I guess I shouldn't get a complex. You've worked hard Kit, and you've come a long way. They'll be in tomorrow to discuss your release. You need a few more weeks of exercises to get used to your new leg, but at the rate you're going, you'll soon be ready to leave. You'll still require regular checkups—so we'll need to know where you are in order to transfer your records and follow-up instructions."

Kit nodded.

"Where do you plan to go for your convalescent leave, Kit? Will you be going home?"

"No! Not home. I'm not sure yet where I'll go. I'm still working on it." *And I've got to get busy, she thought. Two weeks! I'll call Jane again tonight.*

"We won't be able to release you until we have a place of destination to forward your records," the Major reiterated.

Kit looked down at her hands and took a deep breath before replying. "You'll have it." *If the Major thought it strange that she didn't know where she was going, it didn't show on her face. She turned and called out to the young medic busy stowing equipment.*

"Airman Myers, can you come help Lieutenant Vail

back to her room?"

"Yes, Ma'am. I'll get her chair and be right there."

"Well, Kit, that's it for today. It was a good session. Airman Myers will take you back, and I'll see you tomorrow. I have to leave—my next patient is due any minute."

"I'll see you tomorrow, Major."

The Major left the room, and while Kit waited for Airman Myers to return with her chair, she thought about her upcoming release. *She had talked to Jane a number of times since that first call, but there were still some problems to be worked out. Would she be able to drive? How would she get to her periodic checkups? Would the hospital require her to have someone stay with her? All complicated by the need for speed. Hawk would return to the States soon. By the time she left here, he would have only a couple of weeks left in Iraq.* She brushed her hand over her face and let out a deep breath.

Hawk had continued to call several times a week, not easy to do from Iraq—and it must be costing him a fortune. She smiled, remembering. His calls had made her days, always light-hearted, telling her the funny things that happened in his days, rarely mentioning the downside of the war he was in the midst of. She would miss those calls . . . so much.

Myers rolled the chair up in front of her, and she put her thoughts on hold.

"Ready, Ma'am? The Major said you had a good workout—you must be tired."

"Hi, Myers. I guess I am."

He locked the wheelchair in place and watched as Kit carefully turned her body until she was parallel to the

179

bars. She then transferred her hands, one at a time, to the arms of the chair, before sinking carefully into it with a deep sigh. *She would be so glad to get rid of this chair.*

"Good job—you've really got the hang of it now," Myers encouraged her.

"Thanks. See you tomorrow?"

"Right, Lieutenant. You don't want me to take you back to your room?"

"I can do it, thank you." She turned the chair and wheeled herself out of the huge therapy room, watching all the other amputees hard at work. She felt a surge of pride as she watched them struggling to reclaim their independence. *Most of them, like her, were determined to get their lives back. Loss of limbs occurred twice as often in Iraq as in previous conflicts, except for Vietnam.[2] and most of them came here, or to Brooks Army Medical Center in Texas.*

Acknowledging the greetings from her fellow patients, she rolled her way out of the room.

Fifteen minutes later she entered her room. *There was a pile of mail in the middle of her bed—and it included a package. Hawk had said he was sending one.* She snatched it up and turned it over and over in her hand, examining it carefully. *The bold printing was so like the man who had sent it.* She struggled to free the small parcel from all the tape used to secure it, smiling. *Hawk was nothing if not thorough.* Once she had the outer wrapping removed, she let the small box lay in her lap, as she continued to think about the man who had sent it. Finally, she lifted the lid and stared. *A locket! It was*

---

[2] Michael Weisskopf, "A Grim Milestone: 5000 Amputees"

beautiful, but no one sent such a gift unless he really cared. Hawk didn't seem the sentimental type . . . and he didn't. . .he couldn't care for her like that, so why . . .

She let out a long "ohhhh," as she lifted the lovely piece from its nest of cotton. A long, sparkling chain trailed from it. Lifting it to her lips, she imagined Hawk choosing it, and wondered again what he had been thinking. She studied the engraving decorating the front of the heart-shaped locket. Noticing what appeared to be a tiny catch, she studied the edge of the piece, and then used her fingernail to snap it open. *There, looking back at her was the photo Hawk had taken at their first meeting. At the time he had said it was for her brother, Mark, to assure him that she was all right. The other picture was of him. He was unsmiling, but his flight cap was canted at a jaunty angle. Who had taken it?*

She touched his face with her index finger, and then carefully snapped the locket closed and sat back in her wheelchair. *What was she going to do? She had told Hawk to forget her. Was this his way of telling her he had no intention of doing so?*

Two Weeks Later—

It had been a long, hard struggle, but she was finally standing on two legs, albeit one artificial. She sucked in a deep breath of the crisp, fall air and looked back at the Walter Reed Army Medical Center she was leaving behind.

She had called Mark last night but hadn't told him she was leaving the hospital today. When he had asked about her plans, she had been vague. She hated being so secretive, especially when he had been wonderful through everything. He had been suspicious, and it had been difficult to get off the phone without telling him anything. She'd call him once she arrived safely at her destination. Her intention wasn't to worry him, or any of her family . . . and she knew they would . . . but there wasn't any other way. She had considered every possible angle. She'd just have to make them understand later . . . and hope she could make it up to them. She took a deep breath and raised her chin. *Jane would meet her at the airport in Great Falls. She had no luggage to worry about. All her possessions from Iraq had been shipped to Mark. She didn't need anything—she and Jane could go shopping.*

And then . . . she would be on her way to the camp. The prospect was scary, but she had something to prove. She felt regret when she let herself think of Hawk. Would he panic when he called and she wasn't here? Or would he be determined to find her? Mark had said, "When Hawk wants something, he's like a dog with a bone—he won't drop it . . ." She smiled at the rest of his comment, ". . . and believe me, he wants you." If only . . . if only things weren't so complicated.

Her cab pulled up, and the driver got out and loaded her single bag. She carefully stowed the single crutch she still needed and climbed in the back by herself, proud that she could do it without help. She had once doubted she would ever walk again. She gave the driver instructions for the airport and settled back in the seat. Everything was settled to her satisfaction—except for Hawk. She hadn't wanted to hurt him, but it <u>was</u> for his own good—she hoped. It was certainly painful for her . . ."

He wouldn't have a clue. When they talked last night, she hadn't told him she was leaving today, although he knew her training was going well. He still had several weeks in Iraq, after which he would be going back to Luke AFB with his unit. Then he planned to take thirty days leave . . . and spend it with her.

She couldn't have made it this far without his phone calls, cards, and most of all, his unfailing encouragement. He had teased her, bullied her, even taunted her, angering her into making that extra effort she thought was beyond her. He had sent a constant barrage of emails, quoting success stories of amputees who had run marathons, participated in Special Olympics, even run for political office, until she felt like saying "Enough already." If she were honest, she had to admit his efforts had been successful. His determination had given her reason to go on, even excel—she'd wanted him to be proud of her—not think she was a quitter. He had even had all of his buddies send her cards, and some of them had been a riot. She smiled, recalling.

And then, there was the locket. She reached up and felt it on its long chain under her uniform blouse. It had arrived when she'd been at one of her lowest points. Somehow, he had known. If only . . . no, she wouldn't go there. She looked out the cab windows, and forced herself to admire the brightness of the foliage on the trees lining the road.

Elation flowed through her as the plane taxied down the runway. She had successfully checked her bag at the curb-side station, reported to the gate, checked in, and boarded the airplane—with no help. Yes! She could do this! Hawk would be so proud of her . . .

Hawk again. She kept promising herself she wouldn't look back—but her mind didn't seem to be listening. She was leaving—without saying thank you, without saying goodbye, and without telling him where she was going. She was ashamed of her cowardice. The only thing that kept her going was the knowledge that she was doing it for Hawk's own good. She hadn't shed a tear since swearing off of crying all those weeks ago, but now it was all she could do to keep the tears at bay. She succeeded only by constantly blinking.

Well, in the words of Scarlet O'Hara, she'd "think about that tomorrow." She looked through the window of the plane, taking in the gorgeous October foliage. *Fall had always been her favorite time of year, and today was perfect. The leaves hadn't started to come down here in D.C., but they would be in Montana. I'll take the advice of that surgeon in Iraq who seemed like a chaplain—from here on, I'll only look forward; I won't ever look back.*

When Hawk called and she wasn't there, his next call would be to Mark. But Mark wouldn't be able to tell him anything—because Mark didn't know anything. She'd been so careful about that. And, she had thirty days of convalescent leave to make up her mind whether she wanted to try and remain on active duty or get out and find a new career. At least she still had a choice. In the past, the Army would have immediately released her to the VA for follow-up. But now, if she decided she wanted to stay in, the Army would evaluate her, and—if she could pass the physical—they'd find her a job within the Army. Some individuals had even returned to Iraq, according to one of Hawk's million-and-one pieces of uplifting information. This pep talk she was giving herself was only partially succeeding. She still had a lot of decisions to make, but the camp would be the perfect place to make them.

She felt a twinge of unease that Hawk would be home so soon after she left the hospital—her trail would not have gotten cold yet. It couldn't be helped so, hopefully, her precautions were sufficient. Thanks to Jane, whom she would owe a big debt, it would work out. It would. It would.

It was late afternoon when the plane landed at Great Falls International Airport, and she picked up the single crutch she still needed for balance. Jane was waiting when she came out of the exit tunnel, her face lit with a welcoming smile.

"Kit, I can't believe you're here. You look great! How do you feel? Does your leg hurt? I snagged a wheelchair, just in case. But we don't have to use it, if you don't want to. I—"

"Jane! Slow down." Kit laughed.

Jane looked chagrined and grinned sheepishly.

"I'm fine. My leg is fine. I am tired. I don't need the chair unless we have a long way to go—I'm still a bit slow navigating, and my balance isn't perfect yet, hence the crutch."

"Okay. Well, it is quite a distance, so you may want to let me push you." Jane looked Kit up and down. You look so great, Kit. I've never seen you in your uniform before."

"Thanks. I didn't have a lot of choice in what to wear, coming from the hospital. I'm counting on you to take me shopping before we leave for the camp. Can you?"

185

"Of course. Come on, let's get your luggage and get out of here."

"Actually, I don't have much—only one small bag. I could have put it in the overhead space onboard, but I was afraid I couldn't quite manage it with my crutch, so I checked it."

Twenty minutes later they had collected Kit's bag, and she waited for Jane to bring the car up. She sniffed the air. *I'm really, truly back in Montana.* She looked up at the wall clock—*1800 hours—6 p.m. local time. It would be 9:00 p.m. in D.C. . . . Hawk could be calling the hospital any time now, if he wasn't flying. He could already know she was gone. What would he do?*

At that moment, Jane pulled up in her SUV, and Kit put her thoughts on hold. Jane hopped out and grabbed the bag, then stowed it efficiently in back. She got back in the vehicle, leaving Kit to get in by herself. Appreciating Jane's insight, she gave a prayer of thanks for her friend.

Jane quickly pulled into traffic and headed for the exit.

"How far do you live from here?"

"Just half an hour. We won't have to fight traffic at this time of day, so we should be home by 7:00. Are you hungry—do you want to stop for something? If you can wait, I thought we could stay in and order pizza."

"That's fine. I only had a snack on the plane, but I'm so excited to be here I'm not hungry."

Jane glanced over at her. "I haven't said anything Kit, but I really am sorry about what happened to you. And I admire you for how you're coping."

Kit shook her head. "I'm not special; there are hundreds of us—over 750 amputees from Iraq and Afghanistan.[3] I learned that while I was at Walter Reed. Their courage is unbelievable. I knew if they could do it, I could too. And, the staff there is truly amazing."

Jane skillfully avoided a broken-down truck before continuing. "What about your family? Are your brothers all right with you coming out here instead of going home?"

Kit bit her lip. "Well, actually, they don't know I'm here."

"Where do they think you are?"

"They don't know I've left the hospital."

Jane looked surprised but said nothing.

Kit continued. "Jane, I . . . maybe I should have told you before. I just . . . No one knows where I am, and I'm hoping you'll help me keep it that way."

"Of course, if you wish . . . but . . . why?"

"Well, partly because I need to prove to myself that I can get my life back on track, without depending on them. You have, incidentally, been wonderful."

"And Mark is cool with this?"

Jane apparently knew Mark better than she thought. "Well, actually, no, he's not. But I made him swear not to help Hawk."

"Ah ha! Now we're getting somewhere. Who's Hawk?"

Kit knew she was blushing, and she rubbed her hands on her uniform trousers. "Hawk and Mark are friends.

---

[3] "The News Journal," 6-15-2008, "Artificial limbs keep amputees on the go"

Hawk's in Iraq, and Mark asked him to check on me." She glanced at her friend. "You know Mark."

"I do. That's why I can't believe he's okay with this. So . . . you and this Hawk hit it off?"

"Not at first, but then—we sorta did."

"And he abandoned you after your accident?" Jane's face clouded with anger at the thought.

"No! No, he was wonderful. He . . . I . . ."

When she didn't finish, Jane looked over and saw her friend struggling to maintain her composure. "It's okay Kit; you don't have to tell me."

"No, I want to. After all you've done for me, you deserve to know the whole story. Hawk is in the Air Force. He's an F-16 pilot, and we were at different installations. I was at Camp Taji, and he was at Balad Airbase."

Jane interrupted. "So, did you ever see each other?"

"Some. Not often, but . . . some."

"So, what happened? Why are you hiding out—if that's what you're doing?"

"I guess I am—hiding out, I mean. Hawk's tour in Iraq is up in a couple of weeks, and he'll be coming back to the States."

"That's great, Kit!" At the fierce look on Kit's face, she hesitated. "Isn't it?"

"No! It's not!"

"But why? It's pretty obvious you love him."

Kit froze. *Jane was the second person who had told her she was in love—was it that obvious? She hadn't even admitted it to herself, for Pete's sake.* "What do you mean?"

"Oh, come on Kit. Why else would you defend him so fiercely, and why are you going to so much trouble?"

Kit was quiet for a few seconds before answering. "Maybe I do—love him, I mean—but he doesn't know it."

"You're sure about that?"

Kit nodded. "We've never discussed it."

"Kit Vail! I don't believe you're being so obtuse. 'You haven't 'discussed it.' Good grief! You haven't <u>discussed</u> it! Since when does love happen because one <u>plans</u> it . . . or discusses it?" Jane shook her head in disbelief.

Kit knew she was doing a poor job of explaining. "It's not like that . . . exactly."

"Oh? Then exactly what <u>is</u> it like?"

Kit threw up her hands. "Why is it no one can see? What if I do love him—and I'm not admitting I do—but what if? Look at me! I'm never going to be what I was— I'm a cripple, for heaven's sake! Hawk is a hiker, a mountain biker, a rock climber—everything I'm not."

"So that's what this is all about." Jane exhaled softly. "No wonder Mark was so angry with you."

"What's that supposed to mean? How do you know what Mark thinks?"

"Kit, for an intelligent woman, you are remarkably dense. In the first place, no one looking at you would even know you only have one leg. And, if they did know, so what?"

"I'll know. Know that I can't keep up with—"

"Hah! Don't give me that. You're so competitive and stubborn you'll never let anyone get away with giving you any quarter. I'm willing to bet that within a year you'll be running marathons."

"I never ran marathons!"

"My point exactly. Kit Vail always has to go the extra mile—do more than anyone expects—just to prove she

189

can. Remember that time Moose Crenshaw bet a bunch of us that no girl would ever climb Big Baldy? You immediately took him on, and you did it!"

Kit laughed at the memory—"I almost killed myself."

"I remember. I was the one who had to patch you up."

Jane pulled up into a driveway in front of a neat little house. "We're here."

"What an adorable house."

"I love it. It was Gram's, and she left it to me. Come on, let's get your stuff inside and order that pizza. I'm starved."

Kit looked around curiously as they went inside. *Jane seemed so settled and content. Even though their lives were completely different, they had remained friends all these years.* "Do you have anyone special in your life?" she asked her friend.

Jane busied herself turning on lights, mumbling something Kit couldn't hear.

"What did you say?"

"No! I don't."

Kit stopped abruptly in the doorway, and her mouth fell open. "I don't believe it. You're still carrying the torch for that dumb brother of mine—and Mark still doesn't know it, does he?"

Jane didn't answer, but a blush covered her face.

"No, of course he doesn't, or he'd do something about it."

"Don't go there, Kit, please. We were talking about your life—not mine. Mark and I . . . I'm not his type, and I know it. I just . . . well, we're not going to discuss it."

"Hmmm. Very interesting." *She'd definitely have some questions for her brother one of these days.* "Okay, fine, we won't discuss it. Not now, anyway."

190

Jane spoke quickly, anxious to change the subject. "This is your room. The bath adjoins. Why don't you wash up and make yourself comfortable? I'll go order the pizza . . . and then we can finish our discussion."

Thirty minutes later they sat at the table in Jane's little kitchen, munching on pizza. Kit had exchanged her uniform for sweat pants and an Army t-shirt.

Jane looked up at Kit. "So, were you and Hawk sleeping together?"

Kit choked on her pizza. She reached out and gulped a mouthful of her beer as Jane continued to look at her archly.

"Is that a yes, or a no?" Jane asked, her eyes twinkling.

Kit coughed again. "How can you ask such a thing?"

"Silly girl—because I want to know. Now, give!"

Kit didn't look at her friend as she answered. "Actually—no. Not because I didn't want to, because I did . . . but Hawk . . . "

"Now that's gotta be a first—the man doesn't want to! What kind of man is this guy? Doesn't sound like any Air Force pilot I ever heard of."

Kit was forced to giggle at Jane's sarcasm. "Stop it, Jane. It wasn't . . ." *She knew her face was getting red again.* "Hawk doesn't—he doesn't think he's good enough for me."

Jane's mouth dropped open. She leaned forward and propped her elbow on the table, chin in her hand. "Kit Vail, this is one story I've <u>got</u> to hear."

Several days later they were on their way to Ash Lake

191

and Jane's family cabin.

"I'm never going to be able to repay you, Jane. I could never have done this without you."

Jane turned her attention from driving long enough to give her friend a worried look. "Yes, well I'm still not sure whether I'm doing the right thing, or helping you to ruin your life."

"Jane! I thought we agreed—"

"I know, I know, I promised not to say any more . . . and I won't. It's obviously not doing any good anyway. You owe me nothing. What are friends for?"

"But you've done so much, Jane. Taking me shopping for clothes—and supplies. And now you're driving me. I could have driven myself."

"I don't think so. And anyway, I wouldn't have had a moment's peace—this way at least I'll know that you're safely settled." *Plus, Mark would have killed me,* she thought to herself.

"It's taken longer than I thought. I had hoped to be able to leave a colder trail. Hawk will be back in the States in less than a month now, and it's only been a week since I left Walter Reed. By now he knows that I'm not there. I wish I could know what he thought when they told him I'd been discharged."

"Not having second thoughts already, are we?" Jane taunted.

"No—no! I still think I did the right thing, the only thing I could have done. Besides, it's done now."

"Well, you're lucky Malmstrom Air Force Base is in Great Falls since you still have to check in with a doctor twice a month."

"I know. When I went by to drop off my records, they gave me an appointment for two weeks from now. I was

192

half afraid they might tell me I couldn't go to the lake."

"Did you tell them where you were going?" After several minutes of silence, Jane sputtered, "You didn't tell them!"

"Well, they didn't ask—they probably assumed I was staying in Great Falls."

"And, of course, you just let them think that!"

"Jane, stop being a mother hen! I know my limitations. I won't overdo, and I will check my stump for infection daily, and I'll stay close to a phone . . . so stop worrying. How far would you say we are from the cabin?"

Kit was trying to distract her. She wouldn't stop worrying, but there wasn't anything she could do about it. Kit always had been stubborn. "It's not that far now, maybe thirty minutes. The lake's about 150 miles from my house."

"I hate the fact that you're going to have to come up and drive me to my checkups. If there were only some other way. As soon as they clear me to drive—which will be soon I hope—I'll need to get a car."

"Kit, stop it. We've already gone all over this. I'm fine with driving you. At least that way I can reassure myself that you're all right."

Chapter 11

Hawk hung up the telephone in a daze. *Kit had been released! And she hadn't told him! They had talked just last night . . . and she hadn't said a word. Sudden anger flowed through him, for the moment replacing worry.* He snatched the phone back up. *Mark would know where she had gone. Just wait until he caught up with her— and he would! If she thought— Then he smiled. The woman was going to be the death of him . . . but life with her would never be dull.*

He punched in the numbers and waited. *He should have listened when Mark tried to tell him he was afraid that Kit was planning to do something . . . he'd just never thought it would be this. Come on, Mark. Pick up. He glanced at his watch—2300—about noon in the States.*

"Vail here."

"Mark. Thank goodness! Where the hell is Kit?"

"And hello to you too."

"Where is she?"

"What do you mean, 'where is she?'"

"Don't mess with me, Mark. I am <u>not</u> in the mood. I just called Walter Reed, and they told me Kit was discharged—today! Discharged! They refused to tell me where she went. We talked last night, and she didn't mention a single word about being released."

Mark winced and held the phone away from his ear. In his exasperation, Hawk was practically screaming into the telephone.

"I can't tell you where she is, Hawk. I don't know."

"What do you mean you don't know where she is? You must know where she is. She wouldn't just disappear without telling anyone."

"Well, apparently she did. I might have some idea, but she refused to tell me where she was going."

"Why, for God's sake? What's wrong with her? Didn't she know everyone would be worried?"

"I'm sure she did. This is your fault, you know."

"My fault! How the hell is it my fault?"

Mark knew Hawk would be running his hands through his short hair in frustration, and he could sympathize with his friend. "You know how she's been since the accident."

"But, I told her it didn't matter."

Mark scoffed. "Hawk, telling Kit something has never made a difference once she made up her mind."

"Yeah, I know." Forcing himself to calm down, he said, in a softer voice. "But, where could she have gone, Mark? Is she all right? How am I going to find her? I have to find her. I really do."

"Listen, Hawk, I've got to go, or I'm going to be late for my briefing. Think! You'll come up with some ideas. Then call me when you get back to the States. Take care, buddy."

"Mark, wait!"

His friend had hung up. *Some friend!* He punched the doorframe, and then cursed at the pain, anger and frustration tearing at him. *Think! Right. Mark had to*

195

know something—he didn't sound all that worried—and he would have unless he had some inkling of her whereabouts. Then it hit him—Kit had forbidden him to say anything. That had to be it. Damn!

Pacing back and forth across the room, he tried to recall anything Kit had said in the past that might give him some idea of where she could have gone. *She would have needed help—she couldn't have done this totally on her own—not fresh out of the hospital, for Pete's sake. If Mark really didn't know—and he still wasn't sure he didn't, but if he didn't—then none of the family had helped her to disappear—so who? No one came to his mind immediately. She had a lot of friends here, but they wouldn't be of any help there. Who would she have turned to? She had been stationed in North Carolina, but her unit had deployed with her when she came to Iraq—and was still here. She'd grown up somewhere out west.* He pounded his head. *Think, man, think! Mark grew up there too. Yes! Montana. Mark used to ride in rodeos in* Montana.

Okay, he could do this. Kit grew up in Montana. Who did she know there? Mark could tell him that. Unless . . . that's why Mark had hung up so precipitously. Kit had gotten to him. Damn, damn, damn! All right, Kit. If that's the way you're going to play this, we'll just see who's got the more devious moves. Mark may be your brother, but he's my buddy—and I know more about his skeletons than you do—and I'm not above blackmail if it comes to it. "Love and war," and all that. A half smile crossed his face. *Oh yes, Kitten; you've met your match this time.*

He stopped his rapid crossing and re-crossing of the small room, ending up in front of the window. As he

196

gazed out, he saw nothing of the scene before him. Instead his thoughts were on the woman who had so changed his ideas of what he wanted out of life. *He had taken one look at her and suddenly everything was different. Oh yeah—he had fought it—like a tiger trying to escape the snare of the hunter—but he had been a goner from the first sight of those amazing blue eyes. And no way was he losing her—he'd do whatever it took, but he would find her.* He nodded his head decisively. *So think, man. Who did she talk about? What did she say about West Point, about growing up in Montana?*

Unable to stand still, he began to pace again. He walked to one side of the room, reversed his course, and retraced his steps to the other end, repeating the trip over and over. As he walked, he searched his mind for everything Kit had said during the brief time he had known her. Every name that had ever come up and might help him now. Eventually, a name did come to him—*Jane, her childhood friend. Kit had talked about some of their escapades. He didn't think they had seen each other for a while, but maybe they kept in contact. She'd said Jane was a nurse. And, dare he hope she still lived in Montana?*

Then it hit him. He didn't have a last name. He didn't think Kit had ever mentioned it, and if she had, he couldn't recall it. Nor could he remember the name of the town—if she had ever told him. He didn't even think Mark had mentioned the name of the town where he grew up, just Montana. Still, the name was something. Mark would give him that information. He owed him that much at least. He prayed he was right on this, because he didn't have any other ideas.

He might as well get some sleep; he couldn't call

Mark until tomorrow evening—the time difference made things difficult. He had an early mission in the morning—he'd try Mark when he landed . . . and keep trying until he got him.

He headed for the shower, still angry at Kit for doing this, his mind still busy trying to figure out Kit's action and where she could have gone to ground . . . and how he could find her.

Chapter 12

The small lake-edge community didn't appear to have changed much since the last time she had seen it, the day after she and Jane graduated from high school.

"Well, what do you think?" Jane interrupted her thoughts. Hasn't changed much, has it?"

"No, even though it's been six years since I last saw it! Remember how we thought we were such women of the world at eighteen?"

"I also remember what a job we had convincing my parents and your brother to let us come here by ourselves."

"It's just as beautiful as I remember," Kit said, turning her head to look out over the lake.

"It's getting late in the season. Before long, it'll be getting cold," Jane said. "You aren't planning to be here during the dead of winter, are you?"

"I'm not sure. At least at this time of year there won't be many people here."

"Kit, I thought you were avoiding Hawk, not 'people.'"

"I am—it's just . . ."

"I know, Kit; you're still not used to your leg being gone, but look at it this way, you have to be around people sometime, and this is a good place to start. There really aren't that many. And you'll find you know most of them."

"I guess." *They rounded the last curve in the road, and there was the Brewer cottage.* "Oh Jane, it's just as I remember. I always loved it here."

"We had some good times, didn't we?"

"Wonderful." Kit hugged herself, remembering. *The cottage wasn't fancy. Its rough gray shingles blended into the landscape, nestled in among the pines surrounding the lake. Its single story had a sprawling look, due to additions built on by various generations of the Brewer family over the years. A veranda-type porch ran all the way across the front, and a stone path in the back curved down to a dock with a small boathouse. And tied to the dock was a blue skiff bouncing up and down on the water.* "Jane, the boat is out!"

"I called Hank and asked him to put it in the water for you. His wife, Barbara, offered to open the cottage and air it out. Dad always left a key with them."

Hank and Barbara were the nearest neighbors to the cottage, and two of the few year-round residents of the lakeside community. They must be in their eighties now. "Yes, I remember them. You used to call them Uncle Hank and Aunt Barbara."

"Still do."

"Did you tell them about me?"

"I told them, Kit. They would know soon enough anyway."

"I know. Actually, I'm glad you told them. Now they won't be shocked."

Jane stopped the car in the driveway, and immediately jumped out and went around the car. Kit opened her door and just sat there, looking around and breathing deeply of the pine-scented air. Jane reached into the back seat, removed Kit's crutches, and leaned them against the side of the car. "You better use both of them here. The path isn't all that smooth."

Kit turned in her seat, carefully positioned her feet on the ground and then, gripping the doorframe, pulled herself erect and grabbed the crutches. Concentrating on what she was doing, she started carefully navigating the narrow path to the cottage.

Jane watched, her arms tensed to help if Kit stumbled. "Kit, are you—"

"I can do this, Jane. Stop worrying. I'm tough. Just ask my brothers." An irrepressible grin lit her face at the thought of Mark, Matt, Luke, and Jon. *She missed them, a lot. They had all been so supportive when she was in the hospital.* Her face clouded. *And now they would be so worried . . .*

At the step, she stopped and looked at Jane. "This railing is new!"

Jane shrugged and smiled. "I had Hank do it. I figured it would make it easier for you."

Kit took a deep breath. "Thank you, but I didn't want you to go to any more trouble on my account. What else have you done?"

"Wait 'til you see." As she talked, Jane produced a key from the pocket of her slacks and proceeded to open the heavy oak door. Swinging it wide, she stepped inside, threw out her arms, and said, "Voila!"

Kit looked around hesitantly. *A soft breeze blew through the open windows. In the center of the kitchen table, a bouquet of wild flowers in an old yellow pitcher sat beside a loaf of homemade bread. All the floors were bare.*

Jane saw that Kit had noticed the absence of rugs and

201

said softly, "I asked Hank to take up the rugs so it would be easier for you to navigate without tripping."

As the depth of her friend's thoughtfulness and compassion sunk in, Kit felt a rush of tears, which she brushed away with her shoulder.

"You remember where the fishing gear is?" Jane asked, pointing to a cabinet on one end of the porch. Hank got a fishing license for you, just in case you decide you want to try your hand."

"I can't believe they did all this—I'll have to thank them."

"I'm sure you'll have an opportunity. I told them you came up here to be alone, but you know Aunt Barbara. She'll be bringing you casseroles 'to fatten you up,' and Hank will have to make sure you don't need anything repaired. I did ask them not to tell anyone else. Of course, they're pretty much the only ones here this late in the season."

"Thank you, Jane. I just don't know what to say."

"The telephone is connected—cell phones aren't too reliable up here—and the electricity is on."

Jane opened the back door, and they both stood in the doorway. The porch was screened, and a table and chairs filled one end, with a rustic swing on the other.

"The swing is compliments of my Dad. He thought you would enjoy sitting here in the evenings looking out over the lake."

Kit's eyes widened. "You told your parents?"

"Kit, I had to. This is their cottage. I told them your family doesn't know where you are. They understand, and they won't tell, but they wanted to help."

Fighting tears, Kit looked toward the lake. *A stiff breeze blew, and the water was topped with whitecaps.*

The air was cool, with the tang of fall. "I'm glad I brought long pants and flannel shirts."

"You'll be glad that I insisted you get shorts—it still gets hot in the afternoons."

Kit frowned and shook her head. *No way would she be wearing shorts. She continued to soak in the wonderful view. Beyond the sparkling water of the lake, the dark green of the pine forest came almost to the water's edge, and towering over the tree line, the tops of the distant mountains were already frosted with snow. Above everything was the startling, cloudless blue of the Montana sky. She felt herself relaxing—she could heal here. It would be perfect if only Hawk could be here too. But he's not, and he's not going to be, you've made sure of that.* She turned away from the view abruptly. "Let's get our stuff unloaded; I can't wait to try out the boat."

Jane looked at her thoughtfully. "Kit, I'm sorry—"

"Don't say it, Jane. I'm fine, I will be fine. You don't have to worry."

"Right! I'll haul in the gear. Why don't you make a pot of coffee? I could use a cup."

Kit started to object, and then realized her friend was only being practical. She couldn't be much help so long as she needed the crutches. "Okay. Get the food box first. The coffee's in it. I'll find the coffee pot."

Jane left to get their supplies, and Kit took one last look at the gorgeous view before heading for the kitchen. Her head filled with doubts as she thought about Jane's departure the next morning. *I can do this . . . I know I can—but it is going to be a challenge. This will be my first time totally on my own since I lost my leg. At least here I can learn to make the necessary accommodations without anyone around to see my*

203

failures. When I'm sure I can do it, <u>then</u> I'll be ready to see my family . . . and maybe Hawk . . . if he still wants to see me after what I've done.

"Hey, how about opening the door. My arms are full."

"Coming!" *Plenty of time to worry later.* Jane was laden down with a suitcase and a bag of groceries. Leaving her crutches against the wall, Kit planted both feet firmly, and reached out to take one suitcase. She gripped the doorframe for balance.

Jane opened her mouth to tell Kit to be careful, but immediately clamped it shut again as Kit staggered a bit but managed to regain her balance and carry the suitcase down the hall, keeping one hand against the wall. "I love it here, too. Every time I come, I wonder why I stayed away so long. I wish I didn't have to go to work Monday."

Kit laughed. "Don't sound so pitiful. You know you love being a nurse, and you adore the challenge of the ER."

"I do. It's . . ." She shrugged and set the groceries on the counter, but continued to stand there, without looking around.

"Jane. What is it?"

"Nothing. I really do like my job, but sometimes I have the feeling that life—real life—is passing me by. I'm twenty-four years old for heaven's sake, and I'm still living in my hometown. I've never been out of the state of Montana! You've traveled clear across the world."

"I never realized you felt this way. At one time I hoped you and Mark would . . . whatever happened between you two, anyway? I know something did—that first Christmas after Mark sold the house, and we all went to Matt's for Christmas. It was like Mark finally noticed you, but then . . . something happened, didn't it? I've always wondered, but Mark is like a clam when it comes to his personal life."

Jane turned around slowly, her eyes sad as she shrugged and shook her head. "Nothing happened."

"If you don't want to tell me, that's fine, but I know there was something."

Jane shook her head. "It was a long time ago." She turned and headed back out the door. "I'll bring in the rest of the stuff. How about that coffee?"

Kit looked after her thoughtfully. *It might be a long time ago, but it was very strange that neither one of them had ever had a serious attachment to anyone else. Another thing to think about later.*

Chapter 13

His plane landed at Great Falls Airport, and Hawk gathered his briefcase and the loose flotsam of a long trip. *He had returned to the States five days ago, and his 30-day leave was now down to 25 days. Twenty-five days to find Kit and convince her that he loved h*er.

He had used up three of his days in Washington, D.C., talking to the amputees and doctors at Walter Reed Army Medical Center, satisfying his need to understand what Kit was going through, how she felt, and how he could help her. Everyone there had been exceedingly helpful, and he knew his decision to stop there first had been the right one. Still, he was feeling pressured by the shrinking time. He could only hope he was on the right track.

Mark had given him Jane's last name—Brewer—but nothing else. With the help of the Internet and the long-distance operators, he had pinned her down to this town in Montana. He had a telephone number, but at the last minute had decided not to call her—afraid that she, too, might refuse to help him. Face-to-face was harder to turn down—he hoped. So here he was, getting off the plane in a place he had never been, knew nothing about, on what he hoped was not a fool's mission. He stopped at Baggage Claim and then headed for the car rental counter.

★　★　★

Hawk left the airport in a rented pickup truck and headed for Jane Brewer's house. According to his map, the address was about thirty minutes away. It was nearing 1700 or 5:00 p.m., so he decided to find the house first, and then get something to eat. *By then, Jane should be home from work.* He didn't know what she did or what her hours were, except for a half memory of Kit saying she was a nurse. *If he couldn't locate her at home, he'd check out the local hospital.*

Since talking with the amputees at Walter Reed, he had a better understanding of Kit and her need to be alone—*but she was not going to close him out. No way!*

According to the street signs, he was close to the area he was looking for. *Jane's house should be on the next street.* He turned the corner and slowed down. *There it was—139 Carter Lane.* The house was small and neat, and the front yard was a riot of flowers. *Unless her car was in the attached garage, she wasn't home yet, but he hadn't expected to be that lucky.* It was just 5:00 p.m., so he would follow his backup plan—return to the restaurant he had passed a few blocks back and get something to eat. *He'd missed lunch; the plane had served only pretzels and beverages, and he was starving.*

He circled the block and headed in the opposite direction until he located the restaurant. *Must be a popular place, judging by the number of cars parked in front.*

He pushed the door open, and was surprised to find he had apparently picked the local kids' hangout. The place was full of teenagers, but the waitress had already noticed him and nodded to a booth in the back.

"You're in luck, Mister—there's one booth left. I'll be with you in just a second."

Deciding the atmosphere of the place didn't matter, he ambled toward the booth, looking around as he went. *The place gave him a feeling of nostalgia; it didn't look all that different from the place he and his buddies—and their girlfriends—used to hang out in when he was growing up.* He'd barely sat down when the waitress approached. She was middle-aged and motherly-looking, and she gave him a friendly smile.

"Howdy Mister. You're obviously not from around here."

He grinned back at her. "What was your first clue?"

"Well, it might be your shock when you opened the door and saw all those kids. And then again, it might be that 'high and tight' haircut. My husband's a retired Marine, and I can still pick 'em out."

She seemed nice, and she might know something that would help him. "You're right—I'm Air Force. I'm on leave right now."

"Just back from Iraq, right?"

He was surprised, but just nodded.

"What are you doing in this little town? The only military base in the area is Malmstrom, across town. Are you based there?"

"No, I'm stationed at Luke."

"Arizona?"

Again he nodded. "Actually, I'm looking for someone."

"Someone from here?"

"Her name is Jane Brewer. She used to live here."

"Still does." She looked at him suspiciously.

"Actually, you're pretty close to where she lives for someone who isn't sure if she lives here."

His cheeks reddened. *That was a dumb move. Good thing he didn't have to make a living working for the CIA.* "You're right. I had her address, but I just came from her house, and there was no one home, so—"

"So you thought you would check it out?"

He grinned again. "You've caught me, Ma'am."

"Margo. Margo Schwartz." She stuck out her hand, and he gripped it.

"I'm Hawk Hawkins. I'm a friend of a friend of Jane's. *He was omitting enough to give the wrong impression; hopefully it wouldn't matter.*

She seemed reassured. "Jane is a nurse at the local hospital. She works the 7 to 3 shift, usually, but they're shorthanded, and she's been working twelve-hour shifts. She won't get off until 7:00 tonight."

"You know her?"

She laughed. "Mister, this is a small town. Everyone knows everyone here. Jane comes in here on occasion to get a meal when she gets off late. Speaking of which, what can I get you?"

"The biggest burger you've got, and fries—and a chocolate shake."

"You got it. I'll be back shortly."

As she turned to leave, Hawk stopped her. "Would there be any possibility I could catch her at the hospital?"

Margo looked at him thoughtfully. Then, apparently satisfied with what she saw, she answered. "She's an ER nurse. The hospital's a couple of blocks from here, that long, low building you passed when you turned off the Interstate."

209

"I remember it."

"Just ask for her at the desk. You might have to wait if she's with a patient, but I'm sure they'll let you see her."

"Thank you very much."

"Sure. I'll be back with your food in a minute."

After she left, Hawk smiled, a feeling of hope going through him. *Maybe his luck was turning at last. He just had to hope that his hunch was right, and this Jane would know where Kit was . . . and would tell him. If Kit had sworn her to secrecy too, he was afraid he might lose it—he was nearing the end of his rope.*

Margo returned less than ten minutes later, with his food, and he dove in. *The food was good, and he was starved.* As he ate, he observed the action around him. *The place was nearly empty now, and those coming in were older. The after-school crowd was mostly gone, and the customers now seemed to be people stopping in for dinner on their way home from work.*

Margo seemed to know everyone, and most called her by name. Stopping here had been a lucky choice.

He finished his hamburger and stopped at the counter to pay. Margo took his money, and as she handed him his change, said "Good luck."

He smiled and thanked her.

As he got in his pickup, he took a deep breath and let it out. *It was now or never. He started the truck and moved out of the parking lot onto the street, heading back toward the Interstate and the hospital where he would find Jane.*

The hospital parking lot was emptying as Hawk

approached it a few minutes later. He parked in a vacant slot and opened the door of the truck, then sat a few minutes looking around. It wasn't a big building, only one story and sort of sprawling, with an arched portico in the front and an ambulance delivery area at the rear. He stared at the blue and white sign, then put his feet out of the vehicle and forced himself to stand. Now that he was so close, fear gripped him—it was so long since he had seen Kit—held her in his arms. What if he were wrong about everything? He slammed the door and squared his shoulders.

Inside the building, he headed for the reception desk. A young woman looked up from the pile of papers she was sorting and smiled at him. "I'm looking for Jane Brewer. I think she works in the ER."

Curiosity and speculation glinted in her eyes as she looked at her watch. "She works in the ER, down the hall to your left. " As he thanked her and turned to go, she spoke again. "She's probably on break right now. Check the break room—first hall to your right. It's the second room. You'll see the sign."

Hawk thanked her again and walked off, unaware of the interested look she gave his back. "Staff Break Room"—the sign drew him up sharply. *Should he knock . . . or just go in?* Compromising, he rapped briskly on the door, and then opened it, sticking his head in first. Three heads swiveled to look at him. *He hoped one of them was Jane.*

They studied him curiously, and he realized they were waiting for him to state what he wanted. "I'm looking for Jane Brewer. They told me she might be in here. I'm sorry to intrude, but I really need to see her."

Two heads swerved to look at the third woman, an

211

attractive blond. She stood up and smiled faintly. Coming toward him, she put her hand out. "I'm Jane. You must be Hawk."

Hawk expelled a breath he hadn't realized he had been holding. "Thank God!" he said. *Then it dawned on him—she wasn't surprised to see him—and she knew his name!* "You were expecting me?"

"Mark expected you to find me."

"That son of a gun—he could have told me."

She laughed and looked at her watch as she put her hand on his arm and motioned him toward the door. "Come, let's walk. I have fifteen minutes of my break left. Could you use a cup of coffee?"

He nodded dumbly, his mind still working through the fact that Mark had told her to expect him. Suddenly he could wait no longer. He burst out, "Do you know where she is? Or did she swear you to secrecy too?"

Jane smiled. She found herself liking this young man of Kit's—and there was no doubt he was hers. His eyes revealed worry and caring.

"Hold on two minutes and I'll explain everything I can." She pushed open a door marked 'Dining Room', and headed toward a coffee bar. Nodding toward a seating area, she said, "You get us a table—I'll grab two coffees. How do you take yours?"

Still recovering from shock, Hawk mumbled, "Black. I take it black." He stopped at the first table and sat down heavily, rising again in a few minutes to pull out Jane's chair for her.

She grinned at him as she slid one cup toward him. "You're right on schedule."

"What?"

"Mark told me to expect you in five or six days."

212

Hawk shook his head. *He didn't know whether to be angry—or what.* "I didn't know—didn't realize that Mark knew you. I thought you were Kit's friend."

"I am, but we all grew up together. We lived next door to each other here in Great Falls, until their parents died. Kit and Jon lived with my family during our last year of high school. The other boys were already in college."

He'd had enough of this. It was time to get to the point. "So, do you know where she is?"

Jane's reply was soft, and compassion filled her. "I know, and to answer your previous question—no, she didn't swear me to secrecy . . . except to make me promise not to tell Mark where she was. Mark and I both think she didn't say anything about me not telling you because she never expected you to find me."

"Then she doesn't know me as well as she should."

Jane smiled at his fierceness. "I tried to talk her out of this. Mark and I both did, but you obviously know her."

"Do I ever!" Hawk said with feeling. "So, where is she?"

"She's staying in my family's cabin at Ash Lake. It's about 150 miles from here, near the Canadian border."

"She's there by herself?!" Hawk exploded, unable to believe what he was hearing, worry tearing him apart.

Jane reached out and grasped his forearm, sympathizing with this man who obviously cared deeply for her friend. "She's okay, Hawk. I couldn't convince her not to go, and she wouldn't let me stay with her—but I did have the telephone connected. I had to promise not to call her, but I made her promise to call me every couple of days so I would know she was all right. She finally agreed to that. I talked to her yesterday, and she

213

said she was <u>fine</u>."

There was that word again. It did not reassure him.
"So, she'll call again tomorrow?"

"She should, yes."

"Promise me." He gritted his teeth and gripped both of her arms. "P<u>romise</u> me you won't tell her about me."

She nodded. "You want to surprise her?" He didn't answer immediately, and when he did, his eyes were filled with pain.

"That too. But, I'm afraid if she knew . . ."

He hesitated, and she could see what the admission was costing him.

"I'm afraid she might take off again."

Jane didn't think so but decided not to interfere—although she ached to relieve some of Hawk's worry. "You'll be leaving tomorrow, I trust."

"I guess it's too late to leave tonight?" he asked.

"Not wise."

"I know you're right. I just hate to waste any more time."

"You can be there before lunch tomorrow if you get an early start in the morning." She glanced at her watch again. "I'm sorry; my break is over. I have to go back to work. I just live a short distance from here—"

"I know where your house is," Hawk said sheepishly.

Jane laughed. "I should have known. Mark said you were good. Well, come by the house at 7:30 tonight, and we'll talk some more. It's pretty deserted up there, and you'll need clothes you probably don't have with you. You'll need to get some things. While you're waiting for me to get off work, go by Otto's Outfitters—it's on the main street, and tell him where you're going and he'll fix you up. When you come by the house tonight, I'll give

214

you a map and directions to the cabin."

Hawk agreed, unable to hide his excitement. *He finally knew where Kit was. And this time tomorrow they would be together.* A shadow flitted across his face. *He still had to convince Kit, but he'd gotten this far—he wouldn't fail now.*

"I'll see you tonight," Jane said. "I've got to get back."

"Thank you—for helping Kit as well as me. I really appreciate it."

Jane shrugged. "That's what friends are for. See you tonight."

Hawk followed her out of the dining room and headed down the hall toward the hospital exit. Once outside the building, it was all he could do to keep from yelling out his exultation. *He knew where Kit was! He finally knew where she was! And the first thing he was going to do was call his friend Mark—who had not been any help at all. He hadn't asked Jane for Kit's telephone number, afraid he wouldn't be able to keep from calling her in his anxiety to talk to her. He didn't want her to know he was anywhere in the area until he was face-to-face with her. Mark he could call. This time tomorrow he would see Kit. His heart sang. He had two hours until he was due to meet Jane. After his call to Mark, he'd head downtown to Otto's, and then out to Malmstrom and see about a room in the VOQ.*

The phone rang several times, and just when Hawk was about to hang up, Mark answered.

"Captain Vail here."

"I ought to kill you, buddy."

"Hawk! I trust you found Jane?" Mark said dryly.

"No thanks to you, you son of a—"

"Now, now—did I give you her last name or didn't I?"

215

"Well, yeah, you did that much," Hawk said grudgingly.

"Where are you?"

"I'm here in Great Falls. I just had coffee with Jane, and I'm meeting her at her house after she gets home from work tonight. You never told me you knew her."

"It never came up."

"Well, it might have been helpful."

"I had confidence you'd work it out."

"I appreciate your confidence all to hell."

Mark laughed, happy that Hawk had solved the mystery. "I take it you found Kit. Where is she, and when are you going to see her?"

"I know where she is, but I'm not sure I should tell you. I think I'll wait until I see her first. Jane's going to give me a map and directions tonight. I plan to leave early in the morning. It's about a three-and-a-half-hour drive, according to her. I can't believe you all let her go to such a remote place all by herself."

"Let her? Let her?! This is Kit we're talking about. I notice you weren't able to stop her. And in the second place, I didn't have a clue until you came up with the idea about Jane. After you called, I talked to Jane, but Kit was already gone, and Jane wouldn't even tell me where she was. I did think about their family cabin and the possibility of checking it out, but—"

"Right! And, you'd have given her another chance to take off. I would have killed you then, Mark—best friend, or not."

"That thought did cross my mind—so I didn't bother trying to get the number." Turning serious, he continued, "I have been worried, Hawk. You'll call after you get there?"

216

"Maybe not <u>right</u> after I get there."

"Hawk, I'm not kidding."

Hawk laughed, and it felt good. "I promise, I promise." Then, in a serious tone, "I know you love her too. I'll call."

Mark didn't miss that little word, "too," and he smiled to himself. Hawk and Kit would be good for each other. They should have an interesting life together.

"I gotta go now, buddy. It's already 1600. I'm meeting Jane in a couple of hours and I gotta get to the outfitters and get some clothes, and I also have to get a room at the base."

"Good luck, Hawk. I'll be waiting for your call."

"Thanks, Mark."

It was barely light the next morning when Hawk pulled onto the highway and headed north. Jane's map was beside him on the seat, and he had water bottles and snack bars. *He didn't intend to stop except for gas. Otto's had taken care of all his needs clothes-wise—he now had boots, sweatshirts, and jeans. Together with the stuff he'd brought with him, he should be set for his remaining leave time—time he planned to make good use of.*

Traffic was light at this hour, and he relaxed for the first time in several months as he watched the sun rise over the mountains. *It had been over three months since he'd seen Kit, and he hungered for her. It was bad enough when she was in Walter Reed, but at least then he could call her, could hear her voice.*

He had such hopes for the next couple of weeks. If only he could convince Kit that they belonged together.

Any doubts he might have had disappeared when she'd been hurt. He never wanted to live through another trauma like Bones' call in the middle of the night. He ran a hand through his short hair. *Just thinking about it still made his gut tighten.* He inhaled a deep breath and let it out slowly. *The sun was poking up above the mountains, and it was going to be a beautiful day. He pushed doubts and fears out of his mind and let himself think of his reunion with Kit.*

Traffic began to pick up as the sun rose higher, and after three hours on the road he decided to stop for gas. Back on the road again, he figured he had maybe a half hour of driving left, according to Jane and the map. That would put him at the cabin before lunch.

Chapter 14

Unable to sleep, Kit rose early and reached for the crutches instead of her leg. *She'd take a shower before strapping it on.* Heading into the kitchen to make coffee first, she found herself mesmerized by the sight of the sun coming up over the lake. *It was so beautiful here.*

Once the coffee was perking, she headed for the little bathroom and her shower. She had already learned she couldn't do much while trying to balance on one leg with two crutches, so she didn't try to fix breakfast until after her shower. In the bathroom, she propped her crutches against the wall and held onto the towel bar as she divested herself of the t-shirt she wore to sleep in. She then grabbed the crutches to get herself into the shower, after which she set them back against the wall. She had finally figured out a way to balance herself in the shower, holding onto the spigot with one hand while using the washcloth with the other. She had no mishaps this morning. After the first morning—when she had dropped the soap and been unable to retrieve it—she had realized the wisdom of the soap-on-a-rope one of her friends at the hospital had suggested. Since then she had made sure that was what she used. Finishing, she used the crutches again to get out of the shower and sit on the toilet to dry off. She shimmied into her panties and donned her bra which she had left on the edge of the sink where she could easily reach them. Then she "crutched" herself back to her bedroom to sit on the edge of the bed. She reached for her leg and, before strapping it on, examined her stump as the doctors had told her to do to ensure it was not irritated. She pulled on the "sock" that protected her stump and strapped on her "leg." Pulling herself erect, she donned a faded West Point sweatshirt against the early morning chill, and sat back on the bed to pull on the matching gray sweat pants. White socks and an old pair of jogging shoes came next, and she was dressed. A pang of regret shot through her as she tied her shoelaces. *She missed running—it had always been her solution when she needed to think, when life got too hard, when she needed a lift. It had gotten her through the Point when at times she was afraid she would never make it. Even in Iraq, it had been a way to release tensions and get rid of fears.*

Well, as her mother always told her and her brothers whenever they had a piece of misfortune, "Get up and get on with it." She stood and found she was getting the hang of it without overbalancing as she had in the beginning. Taking the crutches with her, she went into the kitchen and propped them against the wall beside the back door. After setting up the coffee pot, she headed for the back porch to wait until it was ready. The sun was still coming up over the lake, and she sat down in the swing to watch. A lone loon called to his absent mate, then flew off with a splash of water. Their tremolo calls brought back pleasant memories of other summers here. *It hardly seemed possible she had already been here a week. She had talked to Jane three days ago, and was due to call her again today. She better not forget to* make the call, or Jane would panic and be sure something dire had befallen her.

She leaned back in the swing. *Coming here had been a good idea. The fear and discouragement she felt when Jane drove off were gone. I coped. I did it. I've still got a long way to go, but I'll get there. It might take a while, but I know I can do it.* She could still see Hawk's face that last time, when they'd said goodbye. *Would she ever reach the point where he didn't fill her every thought during the day and her dreams at night? What was he doing now? It had been two weeks since she had talked with him, and Lord she missed him. His calls and his encouragement had been the high point of her days when she was at Walter Reed. Looking back, she could see how much they had helped her get through that difficult time.*

Using the porch support post to steady herself, she stood and went inside. *She had to stop looking back—and she was hungry. Time to get some breakfast.* She switched on the little radio on the shelf beside the door, wondering what kind of reception she would get this far North. When it came on, the sound startled her and she realized how used to the stillness she had become. And to the lack of human voices. The station was obviously Canadian, and came in clearly. She left the radio on as she moved around the kitchen, getting eggs and bacon from the fridge and a skillet from the cupboard. The radio was simply background noise, until she caught the phrase, " . . . an American F-16 crashed in Iraq . . ."

She stopped still, and then moved until she was right in front of the radio. The announcer had already given most of the details. "I repeat, an American F-16 went down near Baghdad yesterday. And now, closer

221

to home . . ." Dazed, she reached up and turned the radio off. She pulled a chair out from the table and sat down heavily, all thought of eating gone from her mind. *Oh God—what if it were Hawk? He should be back in the States, shouldn't he? But he hadn't said the exact date of his departure. It would be close, but knowing Hawk, he would fly right up to his last day if they needed him. She propped both elbows on the table and leaned her head on her hands. She had to find out, but how? Mark! Mark would know—or he could find out. She had to know.* She stood and yanked the receiver from the telephone on the wall, punching in Mark's number with no thought to the time difference, or what she was going to say, knowing only that she had to reach her brother. She heard the phone ringing, and then her brother's voice.

"Captain Vail."

"Mark! Thank God I got you."

"Kit? Where are you? What's going on? Are you crying? Kit, what the hell is wrong?!"

She had scared Mark to death. Trying to get control, she hiccupped and took a deep breath. "Oh, Mark, I just heard it on the radio."

"What? You heard what? Where are you?"

"The F-16 that went down in Iraq, who was it? Didn't you hear the news?"

He understood immediately—Kit didn't know that Hawk was already in the States—and well on his way to reaching her. He didn't reply immediately, thinking.

"Mark, can't you find out who it was? I have to know.

He made his decision. "Kit, what if . . . what if it was Hawk . . . what if he wasn't killed, but was badly hurt, maybe disfigured . . . or missing an arm . . . or a leg?"

"Mark! Have you heard something? Where is he? I've

got to get there. You have to help me. Where is he?"

He had gone too far! No matter how good his intentions, he couldn't do this to Kit. He'd already known her feelings for Hawk and had just been trying to get her to admit them, but he couldn't do this. It was too cruel. He let out a long sigh. "Kit, settle down. I didn't say it <u>was</u> Hawk. I don't know who the pilot was—but Hawk's already left Iraq—"

"Thank God! Oh, Mark, I don't know what I would do if something happened to him."

"So you've <u>finally</u> come to your senses."

"What do you mean?"

"Kit, think about what you just said. When I let you think it could be Hawk, and he could be maimed or disfigured, what did you say?"

There was only silence on the phone.

"Kit?"

"That I had to get to him?"

"Right." He heard her swift intake of breath before she continued.

"You think Hawk might . . . feel the same way . . ."

"He might. Mark, I'm sorry I scared you. I have to think. Maybe . . . maybe I was wrong . . ."

"You think?"

"I don't know—maybe . . ."

"Kit, are you all right? Where are you?"

"I'm doing all right. You don't have to worry. I needed this time. I'm not ready to tell you, yet, but I'm going to be okay. I know that now. I just have to think . . ."

Mark smiled to himself. "All right, Kit. But you think about what you just learned."

"I will Mark . . . and thank you. Mark—when did Hawk get back? Where is he?"

"I don't know where he is." *Well, he didn't know exactly where he was.* "He called a couple of weeks ago and wanted to know if I knew where you were."

"What did you tell him?"

"What do you think? You made me swear not to tell him anything . . . and made sure I didn't know anything I could tell him."

"Okay. I just wondered—"

"Take care, Little Bit. Don't stay in hiding too long."

"I won't, Mark. I'll call you soon."

"Bye, Kit."

"Goodbye, Mark." She replaced the receiver and poured herself a cup of the now-ready coffee. *Thank God, Hawk was all right. Still, he probably knew the pilot who was killed, and that was sad. But what really had her reeling was her reaction when she thought Hawk might be severely injured. Why had the possibility never occurred to her that he might feel the same way? Should she let him know where she was? A frisson of fear went through her—it might be too late. Hawk might not want to hear from her after what she had done. But, he had asked Mark about her. That had to be good.*

Of course, he'd be angry—he had a right to be. Could she make him understand? He was assigned to Luke AFB. Would he be there yet? Or already on leave? She reached for the telephone, then pulled her hand back and let it drop. *What if he didn't want to talk to her?*

Unable to sit still, her thoughts in turmoil, she stood suddenly and almost lost her balance. She grabbed the edge of the table, then turned and went out on the porch, forgetting all about the cup of coffee she had just poured. She sat down in the old swing and began idly pushing it back and forth, staring unseeingly at the lake.

For the first time since it had happened, her thoughts weren't on her leg. Her whole attention was on Hawk and how she had treated him. *She had been so positive she was doing the right thing—and now she wasn't sure. In fact, she wasn't certain about anything, had never been so confused in her life. She thought of her next call to Jane. Should she tell Jane of her confusion? No! This was her problem, and hers alone, and she had to solve it—alone. She couldn't rely on her brother or on Jane.* The swing moved back and forth in a slow rhythm, and she thought back over the short time she had known Hawk Hawkins. *Only four months ago he had come into her life. Determined not to like him when Mark had told her he was coming, her first sight of him had told her that wasn't going to happen.*

They were so different. She smiled, remembering. *She was quick to anger and determined to be independent. Hawk was slow to get mad and never tried to change her mind—he just waited her out.* As that thought sunk in, she stopped the swing and sat bolt upright. *What if . . . what if he was doing that now . . . waiting her out? Did she dare to hope? If she was wrong . . .* She settled back in the swing and set it in motion again as she went over her options, evaluating and discarding them one by one.

I could just wait and see what happens—except I can't stand not knowing. I could write a letter and send it to Luke AFB and wait for him to check in and pick up his mail. No! What if he misunderstands the letter . . . and how long will it be before he gets it? No! The telephone was looking more and more like the best solution, provided she could find him. She had a feeling Mark probably did know where he was, despite what he had

225

said. But she didn't want to call him again. It was important that she do this by herself. Making her decision, she stopped the swing again and stood up. *She'd call the fighter squadron at Luke and ask for him.*

It was 10:15 a.m., and Arizona was in the same time zone, so she should be able to reach someone. It was amazing that it was so late already. She hadn't realized how long she had been sitting there thinking. Back in the kitchen, she picked up the phone, dialed information, and asked for the number of the Luke AFB switchboard. While waiting for the call to go through, she tried to get her thoughts in order. *At least she was doing <u>something</u>. If only it's the right something.*

"Luke Air Force Base Operator."

"I need the number for the 421st Fighter Squadron.

"Operations or the orderly room?"

For a minute, she was undecided. "Could you give me both numbers, please? I'm not sure, and I'm calling long distance."

The operator gave her the numbers and then asked if she wanted to be connected to one.

"Try the number for Operations, please." She was gripping the telephone receiver so hard her knuckles were white. *She had so much riding on this call.*

"Operations, Major Detrick here."

She knew that name! They had met at least once while she was in Iraq—he was a friend of Hawk's. She hesitated for just a minute, then took a deep breath and plunged in. "Major Detrick, this is Lieutenant Vail. I'm calling for Captain Hawkins. Has he checked in yet? I know he's back from Iraq, but—"

"Kit? Is this Kit?"

"Yes, yes Sir." Panic filled her. *How much did he*

know? Would Hawk have told him not to give her his number?

"I'm surprised you haven't heard from Hawk. I thought you two were—" He seemed to realize he might have put his foot in it and stopped. When he continued, there was no expression in his voice. "Um, Hawk's not here yet."

"But, he is back from Iraq?"

"Yes, but he's on leave—he doesn't have to report in for several weeks yet."

"Several weeks!" Kit's heart sank. "Thank you, Major."

"No problem. You doing all right, Kit?" he said gruffly.

"Yes, yes sir Sir, I'm fine."

"Do you want to leave a message for him when he checks in?"

"No, no message. Thanks again, Major. Goodbye." She slowly hung up the telephone and turned around, almost sick with disappointment. *Now what? Would Hawk be in Boston? His aunt was dead, and he'd said he didn't have any other family.*

What to do, what to do. She definitely couldn't eat, even though she hadn't had breakfast. She grabbed her crutches, let herself out the screen door, and carefully followed the rough path. At the water's edge, she dropped the crutches beside a big rock adjacent to the wooden pier. Using her hands to catch herself, she eased down onto the rock. It was warm from the sun, now almost overhead.

She drew her legs up, and leaned her head on her knees, trying to keep the misery from overwhelming her. *She had made a mess of everything. There was no one to blame but herself; everyone had told her she was wrong.* Slow tears trickled down her cheeks, leaving shiny tracks on her face. The tears finally stopped. The sun was warm on her back, and her eyes drifted closed.

Chapter 15

He had to be close to his destination. It was mid-morning, and he'd been in the Glacier National Forest for a while now. *The last sign for the lake had indicated only five miles to go. He trembled with a mix of emotions: excitement, anxiety, fear. This was the most important mission of his life, and if he failed . . . His stomach clenched.* Then, calm determination settled over him. *He wouldn't fail—that wasn't an option.*

According to Jane's instructions, he should be nearing the dirt road where he was supposed to turn off for the cabin. *There it was, Bear Track Lane.* Pine trees hugged the sides of the road, their scent coming in through the open windows of the truck and surrounding him. He slowed down, sensing he was close to the cabin. *He didn't want Kit to see him before he saw her. He wanted to see the look in her eyes the first minute she saw him.* Anticipation flooded through him and he forced himself to calm down. The cabin was just ahead, well back from the road. He slowed down, pulling off to the side of the road as soon as he reached the clearing. *The spot was beautiful—serene. He began to understand why Kit had wanted to come here.* He got out of the truck and stood with the door open, carefully searching for any sign of her. Seeing nothing, he eased the door shut soundlessly and began slowly walking toward the cabin, glancing from side to side, listening. Except for the sound of a bird, he heard nothing. *The stones on the path were rough and uneven and must be hard for Kit to navigate. She hadn't had her prosthesis long, although Jane had assured him that she was doing very well with it.*

At the foot of the steps he hesitated. There was no sign of life in the cabin, so he veered off to the left and headed around to the back, pausing every few steps to listen. At the corner of the building, he stopped, awed by the beauty of the scene in front of him. Then he saw Kit, and excitement slammed through him. His first inclination was to race forward and grab her up in his arms, but he didn't want to scare her, so he forced himself to go slowly. *She was asleep. Her arms hugged her legs, and her head was pillowed on her knees. At last.* A tenderness he hadn't realized himself capable of flooded through him. Bending down, he noticed tracks of dried tears on her face, and felt tears well in his own eyes. He knelt in front of her. "Kit." He spoke softly, not wanting to startle her. Her eyelids flew up, and she frowned. Still not fully awake, she reached out to touch him.

"I dreamed about you, and you came."

No longer able to restrain himself, Hawk gathered her into his arms and stood up, gently rocking her back and forth. Burying his face in her hair, he whispered, "Didn't you know I would come? Ah, Kit, I didn't know it was possible to miss anyone so much. I told myself while I was searching for you that if I ever found you, I would never let you go."

"Hawk. It was so hard for me to give you up—the hardest thing I have ever done in my life. It almost killed me. I don't know if I can do it again." Tears eased their way out of her eyes and rolled down her face. "I don't think I could—"

"But, Kitten . . ." He leaned forward and used his calloused thumbs to gently wipe away her tears. "Kitten, you don't have to do it again. In fact, I won't <u>let</u> you do it again. I can't give you up either, so please don't think of running away again."

Her blue eyes looked directly back at him, glistening with unshed tears. "Hawk, you don't know what you're saying. I will never be the way I was—and you didn't want me then —"

"What?! What in the hell do you mean, I didn't want you?!" *She was looking at him with a world of hurt in her eyes.*

"I could see you fighting. You didn't want to give up your freedom, you didn't want me to get inside your head, to know your feelings. You kept backing off every time I tried to get closer—"

Hawk burst out laughing. "Ah, Kitten. Don't you know <u>all</u> men do that when they know they're falling for a woman? We're scared—scared of losing our independence; scared of being hurt; scared of losing control. You might as well know, I was a goner from the first time I saw you across that desk at Taji. I took one look at those sky-blue eyes and that cloud of soft blond hair . . . and when you just about took my head off, a tiny little thing like you . . . that did it. I started scrambling to get out of the net, but I knew it was already too late." As his arms tightened around her, a look of awe and hope came into her eyes, and he felt the stiffness leave her body. She started to melt against him, and he breathed a sigh of relief. *Finally! He must have found the right*

231

words. She believed him!

Kit snuggled her head into Hawk's neck. *She was home at last. Maybe she was dreaming, but if so, she didn't want to wake up.*

Hawk let out a long breath. "Kit." When she lifted her head to look up at him, he kissed her gently and squeezed her as if he would never let her go.

"Oh, Hawk. I've missed you so much. I was so wrong."

"On that point, I'll agree with you—but what changed your mind? I was half afraid you would slam the door in my face when I got here."

Without looking at him, she snuggled further into the warmth of his body. "I called your outfit at Luke."

Hawk looked up at her, astounded. "You called my squadron?! When? How did you know—?"

"This morning. I got the number from Information. Major Detrick answered." She raised up and looked at him. "The Major seemed surprised that I didn't know where you were."

She ducked her head in embarrassment, and he used his finger to raise her chin and smiled into her eyes. "That's because he knew how I felt about you. I'm afraid everyone in the outfit in Iraq knew. You're all I talked about."

Kit couldn't believe it. Joy flooded her heart. "I was afraid you might have told him not to give me your number."

Hawk's face registered his astonishment. "Why would I do something like that?!"

"Well, I thought you might be so angry at what I had done you might not ever want to speak to me again."

"Kit, sweetheart, I <u>was</u> angry . . . at first. I couldn't

232

believe you'd disappear without telling me—especially when we had just talked the night before. If I could have gotten my hands on that pretty neck of yours after Mark refused to give me any information because you had 'sworn him to secrecy'—if I could have gotten my hands on you <u>then</u>, I might have wrung your sweet little neck."

Kit's eyes widened, and she bit her lip.

Hawk squeezed her shoulder and kissed her again. "But after I had a chance to cool down, I understood—sort of. I know you're fiercely independent, and I realized you would want to see if you could learn to walk again without anyone watching you."

Kit took a deep breath. *How did this man know her so well?*

"But I have to say, Kit, I was deeply disappointed that you didn't feel you could tell me."

She reached up and put one finger on his lips, silencing him. "I know now—it was wrong. But, you have to know, it wasn't because I didn't trust you—it was because I didn't trust <u>me</u>."

Hawk frowned. "What do you mean?"

"Hawk, I love you so much. I thought—wrongly, I know now—that it wouldn't be right to tie you down to someone like me."

Hawk's face showed his anger. "Kit Vail—"

She silenced him with a kiss. "Just let me finish. I was upset and confused. I knew that if I saw you again, I wouldn't be able to put you away from me, so—"

"Well, when did you change your mind about that noble, but stupid, idea," he muttered gruffly.

Kit's eyes clouded. "Hawk, whose F-16 went down?"

Surprised at the turn in the conversation, he was quiet

for a minute before answering, and when he did a shadow of pain crossed his face. "It was Blue. You didn't know him. He was in the unit that replaced us. They'd only been in country about two weeks. How did you know?"

"I turned the radio on this morning for the first time since I've been here. I just caught the tail end of a Canadian news program, and the announcer said an American F-16 had gone down in Iraq. The bottom dropped out of my world. I was so afraid it was you."

"But I had already left Iraq."

"I didn't know that. I panicked. I didn't know what to do, except that I had to find out."

"Is that when you called the Squadron?"

"No—I called Mark and asked him. I was crying so hard he couldn't figure out why I was calling. He thought something terrible had happened to me. I finally made him understand why I was calling. He—he told me he didn't know who it was, but then he asked me a question that shocked me."

"What?"

"He asked me what I would do if it <u>were</u> you . . . and you weren't killed but were disfigured . . . or lost an arm . . . or a leg . . ."

He saw where this was going and silently thanked God for Mark's perception. "And . . . "

"At first I didn't realize he had said 'What if?' I just knew I had to get to you. I screamed at Mark that he had to get me to you right away. He told me to calm down and realize what I had just said. He told me it couldn't be you because you were already back in the States, and that I needed to do some serious thinking. I was stunned. I don't even remember saying goodbye to him. I tried to call you. It took a lot of courage for me to make that call to your unit, to admit to myself that I could have been really wrong—and that you might have felt the same way I did."

"_Might_ have?" Hawk yelled. "Woman, what do I have to do?"

Kit shushed him and continued. "All right. It only took me a minute to get from 'might have' to knowing you would have felt the same way I did when I thought it had happened to you. That's when I sat down on the rock where you found me. I knew I had ruined everything. I was afraid you might never forgive me."

"Is that why you were crying?"

Kit's head flew up. "How did you know I was crying?"

"I saw the tear tracks on your face, and it nearly undid me."

Kit became silent, a thoughtful look on her face, and Hawk wondered what was in her mind now. When she spoke, she surprised him again.

"Hawk—you know my biggest regret?"

"What's that, Kit?"

"That we never got to make love before I lost my leg."

"Kit, don't waste time regretting something like that."

She drew back as if hit. "What do you mean?! That I, that you . . ."

Damn! He'd said the wrong thing and hurt her again. "Kit, let me finish. I mean, don't regret it until I've had a chance to show you how good I . . . _we_ can be—with or without a leg." She leaned back and studied him, and he saw the glint of laughter in her blue, blue eyes.

"Kind of sure of yourself, aren't you, big guy?" _It felt_

235

good to laugh and tease again, she thought as she saw his cocky grin.

"Just reserve your judgment, Ma'am," Hawk said, waggling his eyebrows. "Shall we move inside, and I'll begin the demonstration?"

"Okay. Unless you want to eat first. I didn't have breakfast, and I bet you haven't had anything to eat, either."

He sensed she was nervous and, understanding it, decided to let her get away with the delay . . . for now. "All right. We'll have breakfast, but I'm warning you right now woman. After that we've got some serious business to take care of." He pulled her back against him, and nuzzled her hair aside to kiss the soft skin of her neck.

Kit shivered and turned into his embrace, raising her face to kiss him. When his mouth came down over hers, she could feel his uneven breathing. She reached up and put her arms around his neck. *She needed to be close to this man she had missed so much.* His kiss deepened as his tongue explored her mouth, and she whimpered with wanting.

Hawk groaned and pulled away. *She was looking at him with confusion in her eye, and it was all he could do not to pull her back against him.* "You better get away from me and get that food on the table if we're going to eat. A man only has so much control."

She wanted to forget the food, but she slowly turned away and headed toward the house.

He reached down and picked up her crutches. "Here, don't forget these—that path is rough, unless you want me to carry you."

Hmph! You just told me to get away from you.

236

Anyway, I'm used to the path. I'll just hold your hand—will that be all right?"

He dropped the crutches and swept her up in his arms. "To hell with it, come on woman. Let's get in there and get breakfast over." Once inside the house, he set her on her feet, but when she began to move away, he grabbed her back in his arms and kissed her passionately. "Kit, I need you so much."

She read the question in his eyes and nodded. "My bedroom is over there. The food can wait."

He swept her back up in his arms and strode down the hall, kicking the door to her room shut behind them. He sat her carefully on the bed and knelt in front of her. "Let me take your leg off, Kit."

"Hawk, I'm not sure I can do this."

"Sure you can. Don't you want to, Kit?"

"More than anything, but . . . " She bit her lip, trying to form the words to tell him how she felt. "But, Hawk . . . my leg isn't . . . pretty any more. The stump is ugly. You won't—"

He pulled her into his arms and comforted her. "Kit, nothing about you will ever be ugly to me. You are totally beautiful."

"But you haven't seen it."

"I've seen others . . ."

She looked up, surprised, but he didn't explain, only repeated his question.

"Let me do this, Kit?"

Seeing the love shining in his eyes, she nodded and stuck her leg out toward him.

He stood her up and slowly eased her sweat suit down her legs. Then he sat her back on the bed, and gently lifted her leg and propped it on his knee. Carefully, he

237

undid the fastenings and removed the prosthesis, laying it down beside him. Then he leaned over and kissed her leg, above the protective sock. Looking at her tenderly, he began to slowly remove the sock.

"No, Hawk! Don't. You don't have to—"

He pulled her into his arms again, his lips covering hers in a soft kiss. He pulled back and stared into her eyes. "No more hiding, Kit." At the panic on her face, he smiled reassuringly. "I promise you, Kit. I'm not going to be shocked."

There it was again—that reference to knowledge she couldn't understand him having. He carefully pulled down the sock. She held her breath, knowing what his reaction was going to be. *After all, she saw it every day, and she still wasn't used to it.*

The sock in his hand, Hawk studied the stump where her leg used to be. *He didn't seem repelled at all, or even surprised.* He moved her leg from side to side and examined it from all angles. Then, as if satisfied with what he saw, he leaned down and placed a soft kiss on the healing scar.

"Hawk!"

He looked up into her wonder-filled eyes, noting the sheen of tears. Very slowly, he eased the sock onto her leg. Then he stood, leaned over, and picked her up before sitting carefully on the bed and pulling her onto his lap. She squirmed, settling in, and the bulge in his jeans got even bigger. He forced his mind away from the fit of his pants and concentrated on reassuring the woman in his arms. When she squirmed again, he almost came off the bed.

Kit reached up, put her arms around his neck, and pulled his head down until she was looking directly into

238

his eyes. "Hawk, how come you weren't shocked? How come you knew what you were going to see when you looked at my leg?"

"Do I have to explain now?" he asked with a pained expression.

"I think you do."

"I actually got back in the States almost a week ago. I spent three days at Walter Reed."

"But . . . you must have known I wasn't there—"

"No thanks to you, but I did know. I called the night after we talked, and they told me you had been discharged. I couldn't believe it. It hurt, Kit, that you didn't tell me."

Kit's face warmed. *If only she could go back and do things differently, but wishing couldn't change what had happened.* Curious, she asked a soft question. "But why did you go there?

"I needed to find out more about your amputation: how people reacted, what to expect, how I could help. I talked to the patients there. They were very helpful. They showed me their stumps, told me how they put their arms and legs on, and how they take care of the stump. I talked to the doctors about the difficulties amputees face."

Tears filled her eyes, and she let them fall, unable to stop them. She kissed him softly, the tears wetting his face. "Hawk Hawkins . . . You are the most amazing person. I love you . . . so much I can't think of a way to tell you how much . . . except this way. She began to slowly unbutton his blue shirt, her eyes locked with his as she did so. She pulled the shirt loose from his jeans and pushed it off his broad shoulders. Then, smoothing her hands across the furred expanse of his chest, she

239

leaned forward and kissed each of his nipples.

A tremor shook him, and he gripped Kit more tightly. "Kit, are you sure? If you're not, we better stop now, or I'm afraid I can't be responsible. You're doing things to my control no woman has ever been able to do."

She smiled. *He made her feel all woman, leg or no leg, and her heart filled with love for him.* "I'm sure, Hawk." She grinned and reached for his belt buckle. "Do I have to do all the work here, or are you going to help?"

A shout of laughter bubbled out of Hawk as he hugged her to his chest. "Kit, I've been so afraid I'd never get you back."

She looked up, not understanding.

"It wasn't just your body I wanted, Kit—I wanted your soul too, and for a while I was afraid it was gone. I missed that laughing, loving, full-of-mischief sprite— but now she's back, and I thank God for that." He gripped the bottom of her sweatshirt and yanked it over her head.

Laughter rippled out of her mouth, and her eyes sparkled. "You may just rue the day you wished for that." She loosed his belt and undid the snap of his jeans. When his engorged manhood popped free, she reached out and gripped it lovingly, all shyness gone.

He stilled her hand, and she looked up, frowning. "Did I do something wrong?"

"You did something too right, sweetheart. But if you don't stop, I'm going to lose it right now. And we need to get rid of some of these clothes first."

Her face colored, and he thought again how lucky he was to have found the woman of his dreams—when he'd been so sure no such woman existed. He leaned forward and kissed the rosy-tipped breast visible through the sheer lace of her bra. A sigh escaped him, and he murmured, "Beautiful. You're so beautiful, Kit." He reached around behind her and easily released the catch on her bra, and then gulped as the bounty of her breasts fell loose.

Indulging a past dream, she leaned forward, letting her breasts rub against the soft mat of dark hair on his chest. Instantly, she felt heat through her entire body, settling in the spot between her legs. "Hawk, you don't know how I've dreamed of this . . . and I never thought it would happen."

He moved her off his lap and leaned over to unlace his hiking boots. When he stood to push his jeans down over his legs, Kit groaned. "You know, Hawk, this is the first time I've ever seen you out of uniform."

"And?"

"And I'm loving it. Those jeans do something for your butt . . . although your flight suit wasn't bad either, but what's underneath—that's just plain gorgeous!"

Hawk waggled his eyebrows. "Why Kit Vail, you shock me."

"Yeah. Well hurry up. Get down here, and I'll shock you some more."

He toed off his boots and kicked his jeans free; his briefs followed. He tossed his shirt on the floor beside them and pulled off his socks. Leaning over the bed, he pushed Kit down and gently pulled her lacy panties down her legs. He drew in a deep breath as he took in her loveliness.

Kit looked pointedly at his manhood. "Are you planning to do anything with that, or not?"

He flopped down on the bed beside her and pulled her

into his arms. "I'll show you what I'm going to do with it, you shameless minx." As he laid Kit back on the bed, he could see the trace of panic in her eyes and knew she was still not completely sure of herself. *Apparently, his assurances about her leg hadn't been sufficient.* Bracing himself on his elbows, he clasped her face in both hands, forcing her to look at him."

"Stop worrying about your leg, sweetheart. It's going to be fine. Trust me, Kit."

"I do trust you, Hawk—with my life . . ."

Hawk exhaled. *At last. He had her trust! She was looking at him worriedly, and his heart dropped, as he heard a "but" attached to the previous statement.* "What is it, Kit? You just told me you trusted me—so do it— trust me enough to tell me what's worrying you." She looked back at him, biting her lip. *What the hell was wrong?* "Kit, you're scaring me here. Please tell me what's wrong. Don't you want to do this—I thought you were sure?"

"Oh Hawk, I am sure, and I do want to do this—more than anything. It's just—just . . ."

Lowering her head, she spoke so softly that he couldn't hear her last words.

"Kit, what? What is it? Look at me and just tell me."

She abruptly lifted her head, her chin raised defiantly, and eyes daring him.

"Well?"

"Well—I've never done this before."

He reached out and pulled her to him. "Kit, I know you haven't made love without a leg before. I thought I made you understand it won't be a problem. We'll—"

She reached up and closed his lips with one finger. "Not that, Hawk. I—I . . ."

242

Suddenly, he knew. Unbelievable as it was for a woman her age in today's world—Kit Vail was a virgin! He couldn't believe it. A wave of exultation coursed through him, and he laughed with utter delight. He could feel her begin to pull away, and he squeezed her against his body so tightly she squirmed in an effort to get her breath.

"Hawk?"

"Oh, Kitten, you never stop surprising me—"

"Are you upset, Hawk?"

"Upset?! Kit, you've given me the greatest gift a woman can give a man. I feel nine feet tall, as if I could move mountains. I can't believe that you never wanted to give yourself to anyone . . . until me. I'm humbled . . . and grateful, and . . .."

His voice trembled, and when she looked up, Kit was amazed to see tears in his eyes.

"Hawk, I'm so glad—glad that you're the first."

"It's an amazing present Kit, and I treasure it, but I'm glad you told me. Knowing it's your first time, I'll be very careful so it won't hurt, much—but I'm afraid it will hurt some."

"I don't care, Hawk. I want you so much, and I trust you." *It was true—all her fears were gone. She did trust Hawk—completely.*

He felt her relax. *She had finally given him her complete trust. He was overwhelmed to think he had found this woman—and that she loved him enough to give him everything. He vowed he'd never give her reason to regret it.* His lips covered hers, and their tongues danced together in a kiss that shook them both. When he broke away, his breath was coming in gasps. Then he began an assault on Kit's body that had her

243

writing. His kisses began at the soft skin behind her ear, and followed to the delectable hollow of her neck. When he covered one breast with his mouth and began suckling it, Kit gripped his shoulders, her nails digging in.

"Hawk, now, please now. I can't—"

"Not yet, Kitten, not . . . just yet."

He continued his line of kisses down across her flat tummy. When the fingers of one hand tangled in the soft curls between her legs, he heard her sharp intake of breath, and when his fingers dipped inside the warm wetness of her core, she shivered in ecstasy, calling out his name in a long sigh.

"Hawwwk."

"Yes, Kit."

"Hawk, it's too much. I can't—"

"Yes, you can."

He continued with the exquisite actions of his fingers, and she felt herself reaching, reaching for something not quite within her grasp. Suddenly, she felt the explosion and her body tremored with delightful waves of sensation, which seemed to go on and on. When she began to settle back to earth, Hawk was smiling down at her.

"Was it good?"

"Sooo good, but Hawk, I wanted both of us to—"

"We will, Kit, we will." He leaned down and kissed her lips, then her breast, as he put one knee between her legs, and moved his body on top of hers.

She reached up to place her hand on his cheek, softly stroking it. He could see the love in her eyes and knew that whatever happened in their lives, he would never forget this moment. He reached down and retrieved the condom from the pocket of his pants and quickly sheathed himself. Then, positioning himself carefully, he slowly entered her. When he felt the slight obstruction, he hesitated. "This is going to hurt Kit, but just for a second." He kissed her deeply in order to distract her from the pain, and then pushed his shaft home.

She let out a sharp, "Oh."

"Are you all right, Kit. I'm sorry about the hurt. It'll be okay now."

"It's fine. Don't stop, Hawk. Please don't stop!"

He laughed. "You don't need to worry about that. I'm just getting started." *He had intended to make this long and slow, but once he felt himself sheathed in her tight warmness, he lost all control and began driving deeply into her body.*

Kit raised her legs and gripped his hips tightly, urging him on, reaching and searching for something she knew was there if she could only find it. And then it was there, and she heard herself call out Hawk's name. Minutes later she felt him shudder, and then he fell, exhausted, on top of her, using his arms to keep from crushing her. She lay back, letting the waves of feeling gradually subside. When Hawk started to roll off her, she held on.

"Not yet, please."

"I'm too heavy for you."

"No."

He held her tightly and rolled over, bringing her on top, leaving them still connected. "All I can say, Kit, is 'wow.' You don't know how long I've dreamed of this."

She smiled dreamily. "And did it measure up to your dreams?"

"Ah Kit, you have to be kidding." He pulled her head down and kissed her. "Are you all right, Kitten? Did I hurt you?"

Her head snapped up, and she frowned at him. "No, of course not. It was absolutely wonderful."

Hawk kissed her lingeringly. "I was referring to your leg. I noticed you managed pretty well." He grinned down at her. "I felt your legs—both of them— gripping my body like bands of steel."

Kit's face warmed, and she tucked her head into his neck.

"Don't Kit. It's nothing to be embarrassed about. I love your passion. I just wanted you to realize what I already knew—not having a leg didn't hamper you a bit, did it?"

Her mouth flew open, and a flash of wonder crossed her face. "Hawk! I never . . . I didn't even think about it."

"Did I tell you there'd be nothing to regret? Did I tell you—"

"Yes, you did. And you were right. No regrets."

A strong finger lifted her chin, and Hawk's eyes were warm as they met hers. This time she could see his love reflected in the depths of his incredible black eyes.

"Never think you're lacking <u>anything</u> Kit—you're all woman . . . and you're all mine." When she remained quiet, he said, forcefully, "Aren't you?"

She was surprised that this man who exuded so much confidence, and performed so surely, still needed reassurance, reassurance which she was happy to give. "Hawk Hawkins! How can you ask after what we just did? Surely you don't—"

As he laughed joyously, and squeezed her lightly against his hard body, she realized she had never heard him laugh so often. She grinned to herself.

"What are you grinning about?"

"Mark was right."

"About what?"

"He told me you would find me—that I didn't know you as well as I thought if I doubted it. He said you never give up when you want something . . . and he said you wanted me."

"He said that, hmm?"

He did."

"Then I guess he won't be upset that I found you."

"You don't think you have to worry about his threat?" she teased, laughing as she said it.

Hawk grinned too. "Nope."

She reached for him. *She would never get enough of this man.* She put her arms around his neck and pulled his head up for her kiss, at the same time sliding her body up, smiling as the action created another action in his body.

"Whoa, Kit! That did it. I can't believe what you do to me. We just made wonderful, passionate love, and I already want you again." Although a blush of pink covered her cheeks, Kit's answer thrilled him.

"I'm ready whenever you are."

"Oh, Kit, you're everything this man could ever want."

She laughed as he rolled her under him, putting himself on top. This time their lovemaking was as slow and tender as Hawk had intended the first time.

Afterward, they lay back on the bed, and he whispered softly, "Happy, Kit?"

She nodded. "Incredibly."

He believed her, as she nestled her head in the space between his chin and his chest and released a sigh of pure contentment.

★   ★   ★

Several hours later, Hawk woke with Kit nestled against him, his arms around her. He took the opportunity to watch her sleep. Her breath puffed softly in and out. Her silver curls were tousled, one lying on her forehead; he reached out and lifted it, letting it twine around his finger. He marveled at the thick lashes now fanned across her cheek. *Lord, she was so beautiful. And he loved her so much.* He drew his finger across her lips, then leaned down to brush his own lips across hers.

She slowly opened her eyes and smiled up at him, and he grinned broadly. "I guess we'll have to call Mark and Jane, and tell them to get ready for a wedding."

"Hawk! You never said—"

"Didn't think I needed to," he said without looking at her.

She hesitated before saying softly, "A woman likes to hear the words."

"Kit, a long time ago I swore that I would never say 'I love you' to anyone again. I told myself I didn't believe in it, figured I was unworthy of love even if it did exist, and I—"

She didn't let him finish, but threw her arms around his neck, hugging him with all her might. "Oh, Hawk. You are—you so truly are. You're my reason for living—the reason I'm here. I would have given up in that hospital room in Iraq without you. It was your voice telling me not to be afraid, reassuring me that it would be all right. All those days in Walter Reed when I knew I couldn't do it, couldn't face the outside world, it was you that kept me going. Your emails making me laugh,

248

your phone calls telling me I could do it, acting as my own personal cheering section. Even the times you made me so mad, so angry that I was determined to prove to you I could. Hawk . . . you saved my life. How can you say you're not worthy?"

He laughed. "Well, although I'm certainly glad to hear you feel that I am worthy of love, what I started to say was, I realized quite a while ago that I no longer felt that way, that I did believe in love—and that I love you with all my heart and soul. I also realized that while I might not have <u>been</u> worthy, I would become worthy—or die trying. That's how much I love you, Kit Vail . . . and I don't mind saying it at all. Marry me, Kit—make my life complete."

She felt him shudder as she put her arms around his neck. She pulled back to stare into his depthless dark eyes. "Are you sure, Hawk? You know, I'll never—"

"Don't say it, Kit." Never, <u>never</u> say it again. Maybe you don't have two complete legs, but you listen to me, and you listen good." He stopped and framed her face with both of his big, strong hands, and looked directly into her eyes. "Kit Vail, I love what's left—to me you're absolutely perfect, and I will always love you, <u>all</u> <u>of</u> <u>you</u>. Do you understand?" She nodded slowly, and the look in her sky-blue eyes told him that she did understand, at last. He leaned forward and kissed her, a deep feeling of relief flowing through him.

Much later, hunger forced them to consider leaving the bed. *She wanted a shower, but even after all they had just done, she hesitated to let Hawk see her struggle—and it was a struggle—to take a shower. He was ahead of her again.*

"Come on, woman. We're taking a shower—

249

together—and then I'll show you what a great cook I am." He stood and drew her up beside him. "Can you get your stump wet yet?"

"Yesss, but . . . I need my crutches."

"No, you don't. Not with me here." He swept her up against his hard chest and carried her into the bathroom, where he set her on the toilet while he turned on the water and adjusted the temperature. Then he picked her up, set her down in the shower, and got in beside her.

Hawk proved to be as good a cook as he had promised. Kit stopped eating her scrambled eggs and bacon. "Hawk, are we really getting married?"

"You better believe it—I told you, you're mine, and I'm not taking a chance on losing you again."

"You won't lose me, Hawk. My running days are over—" She grinned. "Well, maybe not, but I promise—my days of running <u>away</u> <u>from</u> <u>you</u> are over. I just might try running again."

"Hallelujah! She's back. Now, I know you're truly all right."

The light in his eyes as he said it warmed her all over. *She was home at last.* "How soon can we get married? Let's not wait, Hawk."

"Those are my sentiments exactly—but . . ."

"But?"

"But, don't you want the wedding every girl dreams of? I thought you would probably want your brothers to give you away, the white dress, and all those things."

The dreams he could see in her eyes told him how much she really did want that wedding. The fact that she

250

had been willing to sacrifice it for him told him how much she loved him. "I want you to have it, Kit. We'll get married a month from now. Will that be enough time to get everything done?

"More than enough—Jane will help. Oh, Hawk! I was supposed to call her."

"I'm sure she'll understand that you might have been a little busy."

She felt the heat rush to her face. "I forgot she knew you were coming."

Hawk rose and pulled her chair out, then leaned down and gave her a light kiss before helping her to rise. Since she wasn't wearing her prosthesis, and her crutches were still in the bedroom, he sat her on the counter in front of the telephone. "Call her. I'll call Mark as soon as you're through talking to Jane. I've probably made him suffer long enough."

Kit lifted the receiver and then turned back to face him. "Where will we get married?"

"Your choice, Kit. We can get married here in Montana, or back at your old post, or at Luke."

"Let's do it at Luke. All your friends are there. My outfit is still deployed."

"Which of your brothers will you ask to give you away? Excluding Mark, of course."

"Why 'excluding Mark'?"

"I'm asking him to be my best man."

"Oh, right. I guess whichever of them can get there for the wedding. It would be wonderful if Jon could get back, but that's probably wishful thinking."

Chapter 16

One Month Later—

Hawk stood beside Mark at the front of the Luke Base Chapel. The brilliant autumn sun shone through the tall windows and drew glints of light from the row of medals on his dress uniform. The large chapel was filled with their Air Force and Army friends who had flown in from around the world to help them celebrate this moment, and he smiled, realizing they were his family.

The music changed, and Jane stepped out from the chapel's entry. She was lovely in her yellow dress, and he heard an indrawn breath from Mark, standing beside him. For a brief moment, Hawk speculated on what past those two had between them—*until the Wedding March began, and Kit appeared in the entry on the arm of Jon.* He'd finally gotten home from his secret assignment— just in time to give her away. Hawk smiled. *Who would give her away had been solved when Matt had gotten special permission to perform the ceremony, and Jon had insisted he, being her twin, had the right to walk her down the aisle. Luke finally agreed to serve as an usher. Jon and Kit might not be identical, but the resemblance was definitely there*, he thought, as the sun glinted off two heads of almost white-blond hair, and two identical sets of sky-blue eyes looked back at him. Kit's loveliness

252

in the long, white dress and filmy veil brought a lump to his throat. His hands fisted nervously as he waited for her. Mark's voice rumbled in his ear.

"Hang on, Hawk. Don't get nervous now. She'll do fine. She's almost yours."

Almost his. He glanced quickly at his friend. *He would never be able to repay Mark for insuring that he and Kit had met. He would, however, spend the rest of his life trying.*

His attention returned to the rear of the church where Kit stood waiting, her arm through Jon's. At her glance, Jon winked at her, as if as if to say, "Let's get this show on the road." She nodded and turned her attention forward, and he watched her step out, firmly and confidently, a beautiful smile on her face, and her eyes shining with love.

He watched her sure-footed progress down the aisle. As he thought of all she had conquered to get here, he felt a dampness in his eyes. He blinked, determined to keep the tears from falling. *Hell, Mark would never let him forget it if he saw him crying at his own wedding. Neither would the rest of his friends.*

Kit reached the altar and stopped in front of him. *She had tears in her eyes too.* Jon placed her hand firmly on Hawk's arm, and the fierce gleam in his blue eyes said he'd better take good care of his sister. *No worries there. He intended to spend the rest of his life doing just that.*

Read on for a preview of the exciting new
sequel in the Vail Family Series

To Forgive the Past

Chapter 1

Mark Vail came awake slowly, reluctant to let go of
the dream, a dream starring Jane Brewer, whom he
hadn't seen in five years—until two days ago. *And with
whom he was having dinner tonight! This was better
than the dream—this was real life.* He sat up and swung
his long legs off the bed, planting his bare feet on the
smooth wooden floor.

He thoughtfully rubbed his hand over his whiskery
face and shook his head. *He couldn't believe she had
actually agreed to go out with him. She didn't trust him,
he'd been able to see that in her hesitation . . . why
would she? Still, she had said yes—so maybe she didn't
hate him. Maybe, just maybe, Fate was giving him a
second chance . . . and if so, he knew for damn sure, this
time he wouldn't throw it away.*

His conscience reproached him, and he ran his hands
through his short hair and flopped back on the bed,
overwhelmed with memories. He'd known Jane Brewer
all his life. His sister Kit's best friend, she'd been like
another kid sister—*until Christmas 2004.* He'd been able
to get leave, and the whole family had gathered at Matt's
home in Alabama. Kit had begged Jane to join them. Kit
had been at West Point and Jane at Montana State, and

Kit had pleaded they wouldn't see each other otherwise. *It was the first time he'd seen Jane since joining the Air Force two years earlier. In that time she'd grown up, metamorphosed into a real beauty—a fact that had hit him like a ton of bricks.* During his two-week leave, they had been inseparable, and on his last night, he'd taken her to the lake to say their private goodbye . . . and ended up making love to her. *It had been wonderful, unforgettable—and stupid.* He'd never forgiven himself. Jane deserved better, a whole lot better. *That one night could have changed both of their lives irrevocably—it had definitely changed him.*

She'd thought she was in love with him—and he'd known it. He clenched his fists as the memories came flooding back. *She was Kit's best friend for God's sake. He hadn't meant for anything to happen. He'd just thought they'd do some heavy making out, say their goodbyes, and he'd leave the next morning.*

Instead . . . instead, she had joyously given herself to him, body and soul. *He had been blown away . . . by her love, by her passion, and by the sheer wonder of the experience.*

They'd said goodnight at the door to her room that night in Matt's house. *He knew she expected to see him in the morning, thought he'd call her when he returned to his Base. She'd had every right to think that. Hell, he'd meant to.* But it hadn't happened that way. *He'd stayed up all that night, unable to put her out of his mind, or to figure out what to do.* Looking back now, he realized that the young Mark he was then had been scared out of his mind, filled with emotions he had no idea how to handle.

In the end, he had chickened out. *That was the only*

way to put it. He'd thrown honor and courage out the window and woke Matt at 0500 to say goodbye and tell him he had to get back to duty early. *He hadn't explained, and Matt hadn't questioned him . . . although he'd obviously wanted to.* When Matt asked, "Have you said goodbye to Jane?" he'd only replied, "Yes."

He breathed deeply. *Not his finest hour, not by a long shot.* Since then, whenever he thought of her, and it had been often over the years, he'd always envisioned the same scene—*her rising the next morning expecting to see him and her shock at learning he was gone. He'd planned to call her, write her. But things had happened . . . things always happen . . . not an excuse.* In his case, he'd been deployed to Iraq, and the more time that passed the harder it got for him to call and explain the indefensible; *he'd never been any good at writing.* Eventually he just gave up and tried to put the whole incident—and her—out of his mind.

Angry and frustrated by the memories, he let out a groan and slowly sat up. He'd neither seen nor talked to Jane for almost five years—until Kit had lost her leg in Iraq, and then disappeared from the hospital without a trace. Desperate to find her, Jane was the first person he thought of calling. *He'd expected her to hang up on him, but to his relief, not only had she not hung up, she'd been exactly the same as always . . . his sister's best friend . . . expressing only concern for Kit. He'd wanted to apologize, to say he was sorry for being such a jerk that last time, but the words refused to form. Instead, he had simply thanked her for her help finding Kit . . . and hung up, making no reference to their past.*

Then had come the wedding. He was Hawk's best man, and Jane was Kit's maid-of-honor. *Knowing he'd*

257

see her, he'd still been broadsided when he saw her for the first time at the wedding rehearsal. She was gorgeous, every man's dream.

Unable to get her alone for even a minute until after Hawk and Kit left for their honeymoon, he'd known she was avoiding him. *He'd finally managed to catch her coming out of the ladies' room and blurted out a request for her to have dinner with him tonight. He could tell she didn't want to—she'd almost said no—but the gods had smiled on him, and she had agreed.*

Soooo! Here he was, having dinner with her tonight . . . *and he still didn't know how to explain his unforgivable action—or why it had taken him so long to try.* He picked up his watch and looked at it—*exactly ten hours to figure it out, to plan a campaign that would get Jane Brewer back in his life . . . and keep her there.*

The window of Jane's hotel room looked out over the parking lot three floors below. It was filled with cars and people, but she saw neither, her mind totally absorbed with thoughts of yesterday's wedding.

Four weeks ago Kit had called to tell her she and Hawk were getting married, and to ask her to be maid-of-honor. Their marriage was no surprise. She'd seen them together. She and Kit had been best friends since fifth grade, so being asked to be her maid-of-honor wasn't a surprise either.

There was no way she could have refused to be in the wedding—*not without telling Kit why—and she couldn't do that.* She had agreed, knowing it would be difficult to see Mark again—*and it had been—was. She had gotten*

258

through the rehearsal and wedding—with Mark as Hawk's best man—on sheer nerve and resolve.

Now, Hawk and Kit were married, and on their honeymoon in Cancun. The wedding, in the Luke AFB Chapel, had been beautiful and as romantic, as military weddings usually are, giving no hint of the difficulties the two parties had endured to get there. Only four months ago Kit had called from the Walter Reed Army Medical Center—where the Army sent her when she lost her leg in Iraq —and now she was Mrs. Hawk Hawkins, married to Mark's best friend. *The same Mark she, Jane Brewer, had had a crush on in high school, fallen in love with in college . . . the same Mark Vail who had never even noticed her.* Until his leave five years ago, *when he'd finally seen her as someone other than his kid sister's friend.* They'd had two wonderful weeks—which ended with their making love on the shore of the lake. *She had never been so happy; it was the culmination of all her dreams . . . until she arose the next morning and found Mark gone. He'd just walked away with nothing— no goodbye, no 'I'll call you,' just—nothing.* She'd told herself it would be all right, that he would call, or write . . . but he hadn't. Mortified, she'd never let anyone know, although his family might have suspected something since she and Mark had spent every minute of the time together. *She'd cursed herself for a fool and forced herself to get on with her life. When, six weeks later, she'd found herself pregnant with his baby, the hurt was so deep she never even tried to contact him. She <u>knew</u> he would have assumed responsibility, but if he didn't care enough about her to keep in contact with her, she definitely didn't want him to come because he thought he <u>had</u> to.*

Now, her worst fears were realized—Mark was here—*and she wasn't over him, couldn't hate him, still wanted him. Hearing his voice on the telephone when he had called about Kit, had been bad enough, but seeing him—ah, seeing him.* The memories had come back—loosed from the locked box in her mind, and she couldn't cram them back in. She'd been so sure she'd put it all behind her—*but she hadn't. Oh God, she hadn't . . .* Squeezing her eyes tightly shut, she tried to turn off the scenes playing out in her head, but the images continued to play, and she stumbled to the bedside chair and slowly folded herself into it.

She'd barely gotten through the rehearsal and wedding. *When she had put her hand on Mark's arm as they prepared to exit the chapel, she'd felt the shock through her entire body—while he seemed unaffected.*

In the car on the way from the chapel to the officers' club for the reception, he had been driving, with her beside him, and Hawk and Kit in the back seat. *Afraid to look at him, she'd stared out the window. Thankfully, Kit and Hawk only had eyes for each other.*

They had almost reached the Club when Mark leaned toward her and whispered, "Do you still hate me, Jane?"

Startled speechless, she'd just stared at him. *He thought she hated him! My God!* Thankfully, she was saved from having to answer by their arrival at the reception site.

As Hawk helped Kit out of the car, her own head was spinning. *All these years, he'd thought she hated him . . . and she'd thought the same thing about him.* As Mark had come around to help her out of the car, she'd lowered her eyes to prevent him from seeing the panic in them.

He'd opened the door and reached for her hand, then leaned down until his head was close to her ear, and whispered, "We need to talk Jane." His voice was rough with emotion, and she could only nod.

It was all happening again. *He'd been gone, now he was back and noticing her again.* She should have blown him off, told him to get lost when he'd asked to take her to dinner tonight. *But she hadn't . . . couldn't. How stupid was that, giving him another chance to break her heart?*

She dashed angry tears from her eyes with the back of her hand. *At least he didn't know how bad it had been for her—and she would never tell him.* Inhaling a deep breath, she huffed it out in anger and frustration. *Why in the world had she agreed to have dinner with him tonight? She was flying back to Montana in the morning, and she'd never see him again—just like before. Lord, she could see this train wreck coming . . . why couldn't she stop it?*

She shrugged her shoulders. *What was done was done. In the words of her sainted mother, it was time to "get up and get on with it." He'd be here shortly.* She stood and walked over to the closet. *What to wear? It had to be something that would knock his socks off, that's for sure. Whatever happened, she wanted to be able to walk away with her pride intact.*

Thank goodness, she'd thrown "the dress" in her bag at the last minute. It was one she'd seen in a store window over a year ago and bought because everyone should have at least one "little black dress." It wasn't really her—more what she wished she were—and it wasn't exactly appropriate for Sunday night at the Club . . . but it was that or slacks. She raised her chin. *The dress it was.*

Already showered, she brushed her short blond hair until it stood out in a golden halo around her head, donned the dress, looked in the mirror—and swallowed. *The dress did everything she had hoped. It looked perfectly plain on the hangar, but the way it was cut made it look oh so different once she put it on. It showed off every line and curve of her body. She almost looked glamorous, but . . . could she carry it off? The trick was to make Mark see what he had lost—want what he couldn't have.* She felt a slight twinge of trepidation. *Was she sure he couldn't have her? No!* She tossed her head. *She was not going there. Once was enough. This was about getting her pride back. Proving she wasn't just Kit's little friend, available for the taking. Right!*

She was still dithering when the knock came. Taking a deep breath, she smoothed out the dress's clinging lines, and opened the door. He wore tan slacks, a dark brown sport jacket, and a cream-colored shirt, open at the neck. *The man was even better looking than he'd been five years ago, no trace of the unsure youth he'd been.* This Mark was all man—hard-muscled, lean hipped, broad-shouldered, and confident. His dark eyes, however, were the same deep, velvety brown, with long, dark lashes that any girl would die for. For just a second, there was a flare of some emotion in them, but it was gone before she could read it. Then his gaze swept her from head to toe, and his eyes popped.

"Jane?" He swallowed as if he couldn't believe what he was seeing.

She refused to look away, and when his eyes returned to hers, her chin was up, and she was looking right back at him. *Yes! she thought. Exactly the reaction she had hoped for.*

Mark just stood there, looking at her and shaking his head.

What was the matter with him? The dress was perfectly respectable—if it wasn't what she usually wore. She grinned, pleased with his reaction. "I'm ready, just let me get my wrap." As she spoke, she slowly turned around, peeping over her shoulder at him as she did so. The dress while high in the front dipped into a sweeping curve in the back, its built-in bra permitting the low swoop

Mark swallowed again.

"What's the matter Mark? Don't you like my dress?" she teased.

"Is that what you call it, a dress? More like a stealth weapon," he muttered under his breath.

"What did you say, Mark? I couldn't hear you."

"I said it's . . . you're beautiful. Actually, you take my breath away." *He was so in trouble. His little sister's friend had turned into a bombshell.* "I was planning to take you to the Club for dinner, but we can forget that."

"Why?" she said innocently. "What's wrong?"

"No way am I taking you to the Club looking like that." *She was enjoying this.*

"Why not? I don't want to shame you. Should I change into something more . . . casual, slacks maybe?"

He gritted his teeth. *The little minx was enjoying this —and he had to admit she probably had the right.* "I am not ashamed of you. Don't change a thing. But I'm not about to let those wolves get their eyes on you." *Not*

263

when I intend for you to be mine, he thought.

"Oh. I was looking forward to meeting your friends."

Instead of answering, he took the dark cape she held in her hand and carefully wrapped it around her shoulders, gulping again as he took in the creamy white expanse of her bare skin. He wanted to lean down and touch his lips to the vulnerable neck and the soft curls lying close to her head . . . but he knew he couldn't. Gritting his teeth, he placed his hand lightly on her waist, and felt a warmth in his groin.

He opened the door and let her precede him into the hall. When they reached his car, a black Jaguar, she raised her eyes to his and mouthed the word, "Wow!"

He had a sheepish grin when he answered. "My one luxury! I always promised myself one."

"I'm glad you let yourself get it. You deserve it, Mark."

He started to ask what she meant but changed his mind and helped her into the luxurious car. He handed her the seat belt and watched her fasten it before shutting the door.

Once he was in the driver's seat, she took a deep breath and exhaled slowly before speaking. "So, where are we going then?"

Deep in thought, he looked at her in confusion.

"You said, 'No way am I taking you to the Club.'"

"Oh. Do you really want to go there?"

"It would be nice to meet your friends . . . but if you don't want—"

"I was kidding." *In a pig's eye*, he thought, and realized *he really didn't want to share this woman.*

She turned toward him and smiled, and he knew he couldn't, absolutely couldn't, let her go again. Several minutes later he realized she had apparently asked him another question and was waiting for his answer. "What did you say?"

"I asked about your job. Is flying everything you dreamed it would be?"

"More! I love the feeling I get when I'm soaring up there, surrounded by nothing but blue sky. It's peaceful . . . most of the time."

"You mean, except when you're in combat?"

"Yeah."

"Were you in Iraq?"

"Yes."

"I'm glad I didn't know."

"Why?"

"Uh, no reason." *That was close. She was going to have to learn to guard her words more carefully if she didn't want him to know how much she still cared about him.*

"So, tell me about you."

"Well, I got my nursing degree, and I work in the emergency room at the local hospital."

"Do you like it?"

"I do, except . . ."

"Except what?"

"Sometimes I feel as if I'm the only one who never went anywhere or did anything. When Kit came to stay with me after she lost her leg, I realized how boring my life is. She's—you've all—been so many places, while I'm still living in the same town where I was born."

"I wouldn't call working in the ER a boring job."

"It isn't, exactly. It's just . . . oh, I don't know. I'm fine."

"There's that word again."

She laughed. "Kit told me what happened when she kept telling you she was fine—that she and Hawk met when you asked him to check on her while they were both in Iraq."

It was his turn to laugh, "Yeah. She was really ticked at me for sending him to check on her . . . but she got over it."

"I'd say so! They make a perfect couple. Do you think she'll stay in the Army?"

"I don't know. I don't think she knows. She's going to meet the board and see what they have to say. If they agree she can remain on active duty, then she and Hawk will have to make some decisions. It would be easier if they were both in the same service. Then the government would try to keep them at the same installation. It's not so easy with him in the Air Force and her in the Army."

She was surprised when he stopped, and she realized they were at the officers' club. She had worried about finding something to talk about, but the conversation had flowed as if they had never been apart.

About the Author

D. K. Taylor worked at Dover Air Force Base, Delaware, for seven years before she transferred to Chateauroux Air Station in France, where she met and married her husband, an Air Force Staff Sergeant. In the next ten years, they had two children over the course of eight assignments during which she set up homes in six different quarters. With her husband retiring from the United States Air Force, her son from the U.S. Army, and her son-in-law from the U.S. Navy, she has an unending source of inspiration for the military romances she loves to write. She currently resides in Pennsylvania.

Made in the USA
Columbia, SC
29 August 2018